THE

BLACK CAT

BOOKSHOP

E.M. McConnell

To my children, who love books almost as much as I do.

OTHER WORKS

CONTENTS

THE BOOKSHOP ARRIVES

It was a rainy day in Oxford. The streets were slick and grimy. Passers-by did not look out from under their umbrellas. They looked down at their feet, avoiding puddles and buses. Nobody noticed a shop on Walton Street, or 23 Walton Street, to be precise, transform itself from a boarded empty building into a rather smart-looking bookshop.

It had a black door with a brass door knocker on it. The windows were both double-fronted and sparkling, and the inside looked appealing with brand-new oak bookshelves laden with books. The sign in the window and over the door said, "The Black Cat Bookshop."

Curious. And curiously enough, there were black cats in the bookshop. Some were young, some were old, some with long hair, some short. But they were all black, they were all sleek and healthy, and they were all very handsome.

But nobody noticed this curiosity. Not one nose pressed itself up against the window, not even when the cats paraded themselves in front of it, their tails high. The bookshop was ready to open but not yet ready to be seen. So, nobody did see it. Not yet.

"Do not act as if you had ten thousand years to throw away. Death stands at your elbow. Be good for something while you live and it is in your power."

Marcus Aurelius

GHOSTED

Frank had stood her up. Again. Embarrassment burned Rachel's cheeks as she held her coffee cup up to her face. Just act normally. Don't look at your phone too much. You're just out for a coffee by yourself. Nobody will know.

And nobody seemed to, talking to each other loudly over the hum and roar of the coffee machines, spitting and burping out steam and hot roasted drinks. Customers were barking out orders of drinks to go, and baristas were calling out names in a tired fashion.

Two 'o'clock, he had said. Her eyes flicked to the wall clock opposite. 2.20. He wasn't coming. Or he was late, what if he could be late? But he could have messaged. He could have let her know instead of leaving her on read. Again.

Rachel sighed and looked into her mug for guidance. She saw a tepid circle of coffee, with leftover foam climbing the sides. There were no tea leaves to consult from here. It was time to go. She picked up her phone, stowing it straight away in the deepest recesses of her bag so she would not be tempted to check it.

Standing up, she looked out of the window, wondering if she should go straight home or do some shopping. She still had presents for her family to buy but she was putting it off. That was something she did not want to face today. She would bury her head in the sand, as usual, and ignore it.

A shop caught her eye, with brand-new paint and spotless windows. It was a bookshop. Since when had that been there? But it was Oxford; there was probably a bookshop popping up on every corner.

Leaving the coffee shop behind, Rachel crossed the street at a brisk pace, keeping an eye out for the inevitable feral cyclist to hurtle towards her.

As she got closer, she read the sign. The Black Cat Bookshop. Cute name.

Rachel had a start of fright as she stepped towards the door – up a black cat jumped, eyeing her with piercing green eyes. It looked at her as if to say, well, come on, what are you waiting for? That was it, she decided. She would go in, buy a book, and pet a cat or two. Present buying could come later. She pushed her way inside, hearing the bell jangle cheerfully.

It was warm. The place smelled nice; of new books and polished floors. Rachel breathed in, enjoying the warmth and smell. A cat came over, tail high, purring, as it brushed against her. She leaned down, giving it a slight pet before straightening again to look around. The bookshop was more spacious than she had expected from the outside, with stairs going up to another floor on the left and another section through a passageway behind the till that stood empty before her. The walls above the bookshelves were white and bare. From the corner of her eye, she saw another cat uncurl itself from above a stack of books, shake and make its way slowly towards her. So, this was just what she needed today!

"Look at you, you pretty thing," she cooed. "Aren't you just lovely!"

The cat purred, pushing against her hand in a pet me more, gesture. Rachel obliged; enthusiastically. A low laugh broke the silence, and Rachel straightened up, feeling distinctly self-conscious.

"He is a flirtatious one, isn't he? Hello dear," a woman said, as she emerged from the back holding two books in her hand. She was tall with long wavy hair, green eyes and wearing a blue vintage dress. She had glasses on; black frames that sat almost on the edge of her nose. Rachel blushed, feeling dishevelled and decidedly inelegant in her jacket and jeans.

"Don't mind me," the woman said. "If they need petting, then you just go ahead. They love it. And we are the servants of the felines, are we not?" She laughed again and Rachel smiled. "I love cats," Rachel said. "I can't have any where I stay as I am in rented accommodation, and the landlords are really strict."

The woman frowned. "That is not good. We all need cats in our lives!" She nodded to the cat, still circling Rachel's legs, sniffing her boots daintily. "That one is called Christophe. He is a terrible flirt, but he is quite a good mouser. So we'll keep him." She smiled as she moved behind the counter and leaned on it casually.

"I'm Meredith Smart, the owner of this bookshop. It is nice to meet you! We have only just opened."

"I had wondered about that!" Rachel burst out.

"I'm Rachel, by the way. Rachel Phillips. I'm studying here, at the University." She paused, for just a moment. "Philosophy," she tagged on at the end. She did not usually tell people that, but as this was a bookish lady, perhaps she would want to know.

The woman, or Meredith, Rachel corrected, raised her eyebrows. "Oh, very nice."

"And are you here to get books for your assignments today? We do have some, but we tend to leave that for the University bookshops and the like. As they always have your reading lists, you know."

Rachel shook her head. "No, I just saw the shop, and I wanted to visit. I don't have any specific books to buy. I mean, I love books; I love reading books. I don't have all that much time to read them. Books that are not on my reading list, anyway."

She sounded wistful, she realised. She should make time for more proper reading, instead of swiping right on dating apps because her brain was just fried of late. She opened her mouth and closed it again. The bookshop owner watched her with a half-smile playing on her lips as if she understood exactly what she had been thinking.

"It sounds like we need to find you a book. What do you like to read? And have you thought of buying books as Christmas presents? I am very good at choosing for people, and I must say, I am rather good at gift wrapping, too. Just in case you're not prepared yet!"

Rachel felt a rush of something, relief, maybe? She even sagged a little.

"No, I am not prepared in the least. I've got to see my parents, well, my father and stepmother, in a week, and I am very behind. It's impossible to find them anything. But you know, I would love a book to read. I have a train to take up to Durham to visit them and I always get bored. A book would be just the ticket. And gift wrapping, you say?"

Meredith winked. "I am sure we can handle this between us! Let's start with you. What do you like to read?"

Rachel thought hard for a moment. The cat, Christophe, came back, purring as he stretched, arching his back against her legs. His warm body was a comfort.

"Romance," she said, a little shamefacedly. "I do read other things too, but when I am studying –"

"There is no need to explain anything. Books are books, and they come in all flavours. Alright. Is there a particular kind of romance that you like, or shall I pick something good?"

Rachel shook her head. "Just pick something. I really don't know much about the genre."

The shop owner smiled a half smile, her eyes narrowing slightly.

"And tell me about your father and step-mother. What do they like to read?"

"That's a difficult one. Hmm. My father likes clever things, mostly. He only reads The Times or The Independent, and he reads a lot of non-fiction. My stepmother is very smart; I haven't ever seen her read anything low-brow. She doesn't approve of the things that I read."

Meredith narrowed her eyes slightly as she thought, her finger stroking her lip.

"Does your step mother read self-help or spiritual books or poetry?"

"No she would never read anything related to self-help. She thinks it's rather crass."

Meredith laughed, a small motion that made her eyes crinkle with amusement.

"I understand entirely. I think I have just the thing for both of them. This year, you will hit the spot for Christmas, Rachel Phillips, Philosophy Student. Now, I want to narrow down your romantic preference. If you were to meet the perfect man, what would he be?"

Rachel paused. "You know, I don't know. Clever, certainly. Interesting, a little handsome, tall, and honest about what he wants. I get tired of men just being wishy-washy all the time. I thought men were supposed to be big go-getters, knowing what they wanted. I never seem to find that type!"

She hesitated, laughing self-consciously.

"That was more information than you needed, probably. I'm not keen on those books where the female character treats men badly. I like a nice ending."

Meredith nodded. "I know what to pick for you. Now, why don't you pay Christophe some attention while I go and get them for you? I'll be just a jiffy!"

And with that, she was up, sweeping off in the kind of dignified manner that Rachel could never hope to emulate. She turned away, seeing the cat sitting back on his haunches with a decidedly huffy expression. These cats were well-versed in charming customers indeed. Crouching down, she petted him, to his delight, as she thought about the impending visit home. It was only for five days this time, thankfully, as she had exams to prepare for in the New Year.

She just wished that one time, one year, she wouldn't be a disappointment to them and not be compared to the Perfect Cecily. Cecily who had the Degree, the Dress Sense, the Husband Prospects, and the Perfect Job. And here she was, not even able to find a boyfriend for now, let alone a husband.

"If only men could be like you, Christophe," Rachel whispered to the purring cat.

"Dark and handsome, beautiful eyes, lovely name. Someone who likes the same things as me, and isn't afraid to show it."

Christophe stared back, his eyes mesmerising. Purring. For just a moment, Rachel felt strange, a little dizzy.

Shadows collected at the edge of her vision, with rolling black clouds that swept across the floor. And Christophe stared, his gaze locked on hers. She shivered, wondering what he might do. How he could hurt her.

But that was ridiculous. He was a cat, and she was in a bookshop. She shook herself, giving him a final pat and straightening, resolving to look composed when Meredith returned.

The shelves to her right caught her eye and she stepped over, looking at the titles. They seemed to be the kind of self-help books that her stepmother hated, all black covers and smart designs, with cheerful soundbites of reviews. "Guaranteed to change your life!" "This is amazing!"

One stood out as different, a lighter cover among the sea of edgy dark, offering to help her build better habits. She snagged it carefully. This one was for her. "A new Year, a new start," Rachel said out loud, with determination.

As she turned back to the counter, Meredith bustled back, three books under her arm. "This one is for you, dear," she said as she handed it over, putting the other two in front of her on the counter. "Take a look and see if it floats your boat, as they say."

Rachel glanced at it perfunctorily. It was another dark cover, but it looked rather elegant. Nodding, she placed it with the improvement book on the counter, watching Meredith wrap the books with fascination. Her hands flew, folding the edges of the paper as if it were an origami competition, easing the books into paper and ribbon and bows to a level that she could never achieve. Meredith looked up and smiled.

"Your stepmother has a very popular poetry book, which I think will appeal to her high-brow sensibilities. Your father has a biography of an esteemed journalist, which he will enjoy. They will be pleased. I guarantee it."

The bookshop owner leaned down, rummaging under the counter, before emerging with a fancy cotton bag with typing on it. "I do love a good reusable bag, don't you? This one is for free. As you're one of my first customers."

Rachel smiled, resolving to visit again. "I'll tell everyone about the place! I'm so impressed."

Meredith winked. "You just go out there and live life, Rachel. That's all I ask. Life is too short to be wishing our lives away! Oh, and Merry Christmas!"

Rachel left, fancy bag in hand, dazed and beaming. Was this the first day of the rest of her life? She thought it just could be.

A MEET CUTE ON THE 1740 TRAIN FROM PADDINGTON STATION

The train pulled in at last, and Rachel breathed a sigh of relief. She loathed Paddington Station: it was grimy and far too busy. As the doors opened, she made her way over to climb the stairs, hefting her small case, book bag and bag with relative ease. She looked for her reservation, ticket in hand. Hopefully they hadn't cancelled all the reservations this time! She reached her seat, seeing the cheerful red light blinking over her seat, confirming her reservation to Oxford. And in the seat was a man, sprawled, his hair slightly covering his face. He appeared to be asleep.

Rachel sighed inwardly. She hated seat snatchers. She shut her eyes and channelled her inner heroine. Her thoughts landed on Allie Kendrick, the feisty heroine in her latest, most perfect book. What would Allie Kendrick do?

She smiled to herself.

Be more Allie was an excellent byword.

Rachel cleared her throat loudly; twice. The man cracked open one eye and peered at her. She put on her best unimpressed expression and resisted the urge to tap her foot on the carpeted floor. He straightened in his seat, looked up at the reservation and smiled, rather disarmingly.

"Oh, I'm sorry, did I fall asleep in your seat?"

Rachel nodded, determined not to be charmed by this rather attractive stranger. He would have to try a lot harder than that to be impressive! But a tiny smile did tug at the corners of her mouth as she waited, seeing him at least have the good grace to blush slightly. He ambled to his feet, unfolding his lanky frame and putting his hands onto the seat, bending his head slightly as he stepped out from the luggage racks. He smiled again, a little sheepishly.

"I do apologise, miss. I hadn't looked. Do you, er, mind, if I –" he gestured to the empty seats on the other side of the table. "If I sit over here? It just means I don't have to move my cases."

His voice was nice, a little low, cultured, perhaps. Rachel wondered if he was studying here, as he didn't sound local. He was looking at her enquiringly and she mentally kicked herself for gawking.

"Of course," Rachel stammered, resolving again to be more Allie. She put her bags onto the table, putting her suitcase in the overhead compartment and smoothly sitting into the spot he had vacated. She wondered if she should get her book out for the last leg of the journey. It was just an hour, but that could lag a bit if you weren't doing anything. It was a new book, something she had picked up in the train station bookshop in Durham. Sadly the shop was not as well equipped as the bookshop in Oxford, or it did not have an owner with such good book choosing chops. Rachel had to admit that she was decidedly underwhelmed with the book she had chosen and the characters. They paled in comparison with The Perfect Storm, which Meredith had chosen. If she could, she would step right into it and live Allie's life!

The man was eyeing her book bag with interest, his eyes narrowed, and his lips pursed. He glanced at her then, his eyes a flash of blue, humour lurking in their depths.

"Great quote," he said.

Rachel's brow furrowed for just a moment, and he pointed to the bag.

"The bag. The quote is by Marcus Aurelius. It's one of my favourites."

"Oh, you mean the bag! Yes. I got it in a wonderful bookshop in Oxford just before Christmas. I did like the quote, but I wasn't familiar with the author."

He nodded, the smile lurking in the depths of his eyes as he studied her.

"Do not act as if you were going to live ten thousand years. Death hangs over you. While you live, while it is in your power, be good."

The quote had power. It leapt from its mouth and formed itself between them, as if it was advice given by someone sitting right there. Rachel swallowed, nodding.

"It's very good! I take it you're familiar with the writer?"

The man smiled. "A little. Only in texts, as he lived long ago. But I do feel as if he is still applicable today. I teach Classics at the University."

The University. That could only mean one University. He was local then. Rachel nodded.

"I'm reading Philosophy."

His eyebrow arched, his smile rising just a little.

"How lovely! Are you travelling home then?"

"I'm returning from visiting my father. He lives in Durham."

"A long journey, then," the man said with a wince.

"And here you find me asleep in your seat!" He laughed, and then extended his hand. "I'm Jeff."

"Rachel," she returned, smiling, shaking his hand. His hand was warm, his handshake firm. She let go of his hand reluctantly, leaning back in her seat.

She felt just a glimmer of excitement and was reminded again of Allie, who seemed to stumble into the most delicious of romantic escapades.

Was it so awful if she enjoyed this one? She smiled again at this rather attractive fellow who had blundered onto her path. Be more Allie, she resolved again. And she smiled.

"IT'S THE MEREDITH EFFECT"

"It's the Meredith Effect."

The words resounded in Rachel's mind as she inspected herself critically in the department store mirror. Really, the words themselves sparkled, as if they were the headlines of an expensive perfume ad. She had to admit, she looked fantastic. Thanks to her stepmother's advice over Christmas about draping and colour analysis, she had switched colours around, wearing better clothes next to her face. The results were spectacular. And she really did suit red! The dark red beret looked great against her dark hair and that scarf just set it off. Very nice indeed. Perhaps she would wear it for her date this weekend.

Her lipsticked mouth curled up at the corners in a satisfied fashion. The lipstick was a new touch, another detail she had borrowed from her book heroine, Allie Kendrick. YSL lipstick. Even the packaging oozed glamour, all gold gleam and smooth lines.

She had been implementing the 'Be More Allie' rule for a fortnight, and it was certainly working. Instead of repeating the humiliating episode in Starbucks when Frank the Flunk stood her up, she was being pursued by interested, eligible men. Archie, the new one, was already a huge fan, and Mr Train Man, aka Professor Jeff, was becoming a rather fond fixture in her phone.

Rachel was fairly sure that Professor Jeff was, in fact, married, looking at the times that he messaged, but that wasn't her business. She stifled the quick pang of conscience that tried to speak up. It's not like it was her sin, after all. She wasn't cheating on anyone. She was having fun.

Paying for her purchases with the fancy new upgraded card that her father had bestowed on her at Christmas – thank you, Daddy – she smiled again, looking at the smart black card that probably had a very high credit limit.

Perhaps it was useful to be nicer to her stepmother, after all, she mused. And she was useful about the colour theory, which she would never have mentioned if she hadn't been so pleased with her Christmas present. This was indeed "the Meredith effect."

As she considered her bookish saviour, Rachel resolved to drop by and visit. She needed more reading material, and maybe it was time to have a reading upgrade, too. Did a Philosophy student really need to read Romance? Perhaps she could start on something a little more high-brow to complete her look. Rachel strode out of the department store, head high, her beret at a jaunty angle, feeling quite on top of the world. "The Meredith Effect".

Oh, yes. Rachel was going places at last.

The bookshop bell rang as she entered, emitting a tinkling sound. Rachel imagined the sound to be the welcome home sound from the bookshop, recognising its best customers. She looked around for the cats, but no black shapes appeared, much to her disappointment. She waited for a moment for Meredith to appear, then walked over to investigate the bookshelves.

The nearest one to her on the left was a tall one, lining the walls, and a small sign on it said Travel Books. There were rows of gleaming hardbacks tucked in with the odd display copy showing beautiful photographs of far-off lands. One caught her eye; a mountain vista in the snow with a train riding through the middle. The snow was pearl white, and the sky was blue. It was perfect. She picked the book up, imagining herself on the train, drinking white wine, looking out at the scenery. What kind of person could she be on that trip? What would Allie be?

"Are you planning to leave us already, Rachel?" a voice asked, laced with amusement. Meredith stood there in the doorway, a smile playing on her face. She was holding a small notebook this time, which she quickly tucked into her pocket. Rachel admired Meredith's outfit for a moment, noting her burgundy vintage slacks, braces and a black silk shirt. Her hair was loosely plaited and she was wearing black cats-eye spectacles on her face. Rachel sighed inwardly.

"That Meredith Effect" was really quite a lot to live up to. Perhaps she should look into adding some vintage elements into her own style.

Rachel put the book back on its display rack carefully.

"Sadly, no, I have exams to do before I can even contemplate travel, and I really should do some kind of internship this summer. My father will be expecting me to go into business soon. But I would like to travel one day!"

Rachel looked again at the picture longingly. "Maybe not alone. I don't think I could do that."

Meredith nodded, deep in thought. "Solo travel is not for everyone. It usually depends on why you travel – if you are seeking something or running away from something. When you know that, you can know more about the person you are."

Her contemplation was interrupted for a moment as she looked up and to the side. Her features formed a slight frown, almost as if she was listening or straining to hear something. Then her face cleared, and she looked back at Rachel.

"I could have sworn I heard someone calling me for a moment! What a notion. So, Rachel, what can we do for you today? And how did your parents like the books?"

"They did, thank you. Daddy was thrilled with his and has resolved to visit for more recommendations the next time he is in the area. Grisela, that's my stepmother, she loved the poetry book that you recommended. She was very pleased to receive it. I am entirely in your debt, Meredith!"

Meredith laughed, her white teeth showing. "That will be exciting! Don't worry. I don't have any plans for your soul!"

Rachel laughed too, until she heard a slight echo dancing in the rafters of the bookshop. She shivered slightly.

"I have come for more recommendations, if I may. I enjoyed the book you chose so much! I am very much taken with the female main character. I would like to read more fiction, but perhaps more literary fiction, stories about women coming into themselves, that sort of thing?"

"The butterfly emerging from her chrysalis? Oh, that's always a lovely story, isn't it? And perhaps a little less romance this time? I have just the thing. A new shipment arrived with some contributions from local authors who I think you might like. Two are historical novels, one is contemporary. Would that work?"

"You're a treasure, Meredith," Rachel beamed. "What would I ever do without you? And that reminds me, your lovely book bag was admired by a new friend of mine, you could say. He seemed to be rather fond of Marcus Aurelius."

Meredith smiled widely then, her eyes sparkling.

"That's lovely. It is nice to hear of kindred spirits out there. I was always fond of Marcus Aurelius. Such a clever man. Voracious reader, too."

Rachel raised her eyebrows in astonishment. "Did you study Ancient History too? I had never heard of him. Jeff said that he died thousands of years ago."

"Yes, he did indeed. He is fondly remembered still, even now the Roman Empire is at an end. But of course, I read Ancient History. I read everything. I am, of course, a bookshop owner, and what kind of bookshop keeper would I be if I did not read? I am surrounded by books!"

Meredith gave Rachel a keen, assessing glance. "I must say, you are looking very well, dear. Is that a new hat? It looks stylish. You are quite the emerging butterfly yourself, aren't you?"

Rachel blushed, feeling her cheeks grow hot.

"If I am, then it is because of you, Meredith. I feel so much more myself of late; I am brimming with ideas of what I want to do. I am finally being the leading lady in my own life! All these wonderful things are happening. I feel very grateful!"

Meredith smiled, her expression shifting as she pursed her lips slightly and narrowed her eyes.

"You know, I think this is simply wonderful. Long may it continue! I'll just locate those books. They may still be packed!"

She turned, disappearing quickly into the back of the shop. It was hardly a moment before she returned, her hands full of three paperbacks. Meredith placed them on the counter.

"I think you will like these. But please do not neglect your studies, you have exams soon. I do not want Professor Keys to have my head because your grades slip!"

Rachel laughed, eagerly paying and scooping up her purchases. It was only when she was out on the pavement, breathing in the frosty air, that she recalled what Meredith had said. How did she know her

Professor's name? Had she ever told Meredith her Professor's name? Rachel puzzled for a moment and then shook her head. She must have told her; it was as simple as that!

Reaching into her bag, she pulled her phone out, glancing at the notifications and messages. There was one from Daddy, two from Archie, and one from Jeff. Rachel smiled as she put her phone back. Being in demand for a change was just the ticket. She turned her face towards home, her smile growing into a broad grin. "The Meredith Effect," she said out loud to the cold air. "Yes!"

CHOSEN

The quiet fell heavily inside the bookshop as Rachel left, her slight figure pausing for a moment on the pavement outside. One by one, the cats returned, their eyes gleaming, tails waving. Cold swirled slowly in the bookshop and Meredith's breath came out in soft mists. She eyed the door thoughtfully, her eyebrows drawn together, lips slightly pursed.

Something stirred, its presence within the mist growing darker, and she turned to listen.

"What did you say... that she is a suitable candidate? Well, she certainly has the potential. What do the Guardians say?"

Meredith paused again, listening. "Very good. It has been decided. Let the game begin."

Something sighed in the air and the air darkened. Meredith looked back at the door, her head cocked slightly to one side. The cats each stayed frozen in place, one with a foot slightly raised, another a statue poised to wash.

"So, Rachel, the Guardians have chosen. Enjoy your newfound fortune, until you are called to pay the price. Let's hope the price is not too high."

She narrowed her eyes for just a moment and then turned, clicking her fingers in the air. Time unfroze, the cats unfolded, and the sighs died away.

COFFEE AND MIRRORS

Her feet were cold. Rachel could feel the soles of her feet grow numb as the stone cold feeling seeped into her bones. Gasping, she looked around, hoping to see something that she recognised. Where was she? Dust flew slowly in the air, catching the light somehow so they almost glowed. Rachel realised that the air was warm, even if the surface she stood on was not. She put her hand out, reaching, searching. The walls felt like rock under her fingers but it was somehow warm to the touch.

Frantic, she pushed her hands against the rock. She could feel something pulse against her fingers. Almost like a heartbeat. Was there something there? Where was she?

Rachel looked down, seeing not her normal sleep attire but a white nightgown. It reached to her feet, covering her arms all the way to her wrists with lace at the cuffs. She brought her hands up, touching her neck, feeling the fabric was encasing even her throat in lace. Her hair was long, she noticed, reaching nearly to her waist and loosely plaited. She shook her head in confusion. This must be a dream. How very strange!

"It's just a dream," Rachel whispered.

"You must have been working too hard of late. Wake up now!"

She raised her voice for the last words, hearing it echo slightly around the room. The silence continued, punctuated only by that strange throb, the pulse that she had felt earlier. She put her hand back out, drawn to the pulse, the heartbeat.

"Is there anyone there?" Rachel called out. Her words did not echo this time but fell into the silence like stones. "Rachel," she heard faintly, whispered. "Rachel." She spun around wildly, eyes huge, wondering. Who had said that? The corridor just stretched out in front of her, still dim, with no obvious source of light.

"Rachel," the voice said again in a thready whisper, behind her this time. "Rachel."

The walls pulsed harder, the heartbeat stronger. Rachel looked up, terrified. She started to scream as the walls closed around her.

Rachel woke breathless, heart pounding.

She blinked, three times, before registering she was in her own room, seeing the white curtains, her bed, and the books piled up on the desk next to the computer screen. In bed next to her was a figure, fast asleep, a man. Her clouded brain stared at the man-sized shape huddled under her quilt for a moment, wondering who on earth he was and how he had got there.

Archie, she thought, as her brain supplied the name. Jeff never stayed overnight. He had to be having an affair, that one.

She shrugged, sliding from the bed and gathering her clothes up in a smooth action. Absently, she felt for her hair, letting out a sigh of relief when she felt the blunt edges just passing her shoulders. She left her room without looking at the man sprawled on the pillow, her mind on the dream.

Her living room was just across the hall, light and cheerful. Rachel pulled on sweatpants and a vest as she walked, silently resolving to put on something more girlfriend-suitable before Archie woke up. Eyeing the glasses stained with red wine that sat on the coffee table, she guessed that he wouldn't be awake for a while. She shook her head, trying to remember the previous evening and forget the nightmare. Her memories were fuzzy. How did she get back? Weren't they supposed to be out having dinner or something? She put her hand up to her head, closing her eyes.

A whisper of the dream came back, that moment where something whispered her name. "Rachel." She shivered, picking up the wine glasses and moving towards the kitchen. It was fairly tidy, so they clearly hadn't been back that early. Archie was horribly messy. He was certainly not husband material, not unless he earned enough for a housekeeper!

Not that he would be husband material at all, really. She did not think her father would approve of an Art History student. It had to be something sensible, like Maths, Medicine, or Science. She rolled her eyes inwardly as she thought of him. Stuck in his ways. He meant the best for her, of course, but it was alright if she studied Philosophy, because she would get married one day.

Rachel sighed, reaching for her phone, which had been plugged neatly into the charging cable. Saying thank you to Yesterday Rachel for being organised, she scrolled through the notifications, noting idly that her Daddy had messaged only once, that Jeff had sent a good morning message, and she had two from Fatima, who she had neglected in the last few weeks.

She looked at the calendar on the wall. Mid-February. Alright make that a couple of months. How did that happen?

Her fingers found the phone, opening the message and replying quickly, guilt fuelled.

It has been too long! I've been caught up with studying, and you know... When can I see you? Shall we meet up for coffee, next week?

She put the phone back, wrestling with the cable to keep it as neat as how she had found it. How could she forget so much? What had happened?

She eyed the bottles suspiciously. No, Archie was never shy about drinking wine, she certainly wouldn't have hogged those bottles. Her hands found the counter, flexing uncertainly. Rachel stretched, breathing out, holding onto the cold surface, needing the stone under her hands. She breathed in. It was just a dream. She breathed out. She was fine. She breathed in. It was just a strange dream. Her fingers gripped the counter, knuckles pale. She eyed them.

"You're playing too hard, Rach," she said out loud. "Meredith said so. She said keep an eye to your studies. It's all well and good that you've found a nice man - *men,* she amended silently – although that won't be the case forever, they never last – not for me, anyway."

A vision of Allie leapt into her mind, technicolour in miniature, complete with pompoms. Rachel shook her head, laughing quietly.

"Not even you are successful in love, Miss Kendrick. Well, not right away. You are in your book, and your story is finished. I'm just beginning mine."

She glanced into the kitchen mirror, a simple affair tacked onto the kitchen tiles, her housemate's straighteners resting underneath. Her face reflected back, a little tousled, shadows under her eyes. Her eyes looked back at her, challenging.

"It was just a dream. Right?"

Her reflection nodded back at her, face determined, chin set.

"And I am going to take Meredith's advice and get on with my studying. No more entertaining. At least for a while. Agreed?"

Her reflection agreed meekly.

Rachel laughed suddenly, feeling freer. She cast her eyes to the coffee machine, thinking of the time. She could get a little time in now while it was quiet, get some studying in, make headway on the essay due in, perhaps. She moved towards it, unheeding, not noticing the mirror, where her reflection stayed, watching her step out of view. Her reflection remained for a moment, expression changing from amusement to sardonic observation to something altogether more terrifying.

But Rachel did not see it. Her attention was absorbed by the whirring of the coffee machine and the splutter of the spout as it leapt into life. She did not see the reflection step back from the mirror. She did not see the slight mist that curled outwards, reaching towards her.

CHANGES ARE AFOOT

"You're changing, Rach." Fatima eyed her steadily over her coffee cup, her heavily made-up eyes a strong contrast against the white of the china. Fatima had ordered the Venti-sized mocha, a veritable bucket with a handle that came festooned with a tower of cream and chocolate dusted precariously on the top. Rachel wondered idly how Fatima always managed to not put cream on her face, and how she stayed so lean drinking that stuff. Rachel stirred her own more modest grande flat white carefully, waiting for her friend to continue. She always did that.

She would make a statement, pause dramatically, and then continue. It was her signature move.

Fatima did continue, pursing her lips as she blew on the mocha then set it down carefully. The cream mountain wobbled as the cup landed back on the saucer with a clink.

"I'm not saying it's bad, you know? But you've changed a lot since before Christmas. How you look; it's so put together, even your mannerisms are different. I like the look, by the way. Did you get your hair done?"

Rachel put her hand up to her hair self-consciously, having a moment of wanting to swish it about like the models always did in the adverts. "No, I had my colours done, actually. Grisela has been studying it, and she did some draping on me. I was really shocked by it! But it's made such a difference to me. I feel like a whole new woman. With colours that are right for me for a change!"

Fatima looked nonplussed. "That's.... very nice of her," she murmured. "I thought you two didn't get along?"

"Oh, we never did, you're right. But she was quite pleasant over Christmas. Maybe she mellowed!"

Fatima laughed but didn't look entirely convinced. Rachel felt a fleeting moment of annoyance, which surprised her. She quashed it quickly. This was her friend! Fatima was interested, she cared about her. Or maybe she was a little envious. She could understand that. too.

"So, did you get up to much after Christmas?" Fatima asked, her hands holding that ridiculous mocha again. "Did you see Frank again?"

"Frank? Goodness, no. I got tired of him ages ago. I met a lovely new chap at the library, actually, he's studying Art History. His name is Archie. You'll have to meet him. Perhaps we can organise something for the next time we go to the Hatter for drinks!"

Fatima smiled, the proper kind, when the corners of her mouth lifted and her eyes sparkled. "Now maybe that's the change that I saw! You're in love. How nice! I am pleased for you, Rach. You were far too good for Frank. He seemed to be messing you around too much. I'm glad you ditched him. I'm proud of you!"

There was that flash of annoyance again. Rachel stirred her drink, trying not to bash the tiny spoon against the insides. She forced a smile onto her face as she thought. How was it she felt? Vexed. Yes. She felt a little vexed. Fatima just didn't get it at all.

Rachel zoned out, nodding at the appropriate times, exclaiming at the appropriate points, as Fatima waxed lyrical about Rachel's certain romantic future, Fatima's course, all the work she had to do, her dad's garden, and where she was going for Reading Week. It was all so mundane. They were studying at arguably the best university in the British Isles, they had the world at their feet. Is this all they had to talk about?

She sighed inwardly. She needed friends like Allie Kendrick had. Or like Caroline did with her exciting, go-getter friends. That was it. Along with her new look, her life needed an overhaul. Starting here. Starting right now. For just a moment, she shivered, as the door opened to the coffee shop and sent a cold breeze wafting in. But she hugged her flat white and nodded along to her friend's prattle. "Be more Allie," she thought. Starting now.

BOOK BOYFRIEND

The lecturer lectured, voice shifting into a dreary monotone as he flicked pages on a screen behind him. Rachel struggled to keep her eyes open and her pen moving as she took notes mechanically. Two rows in front of her, a student had given up the good fight, dozing precariously with his head resting on his hand. To her left a man was tapping away on his laptop, face a study of concentration.

What was the lecture even about today? Oh, yes, Descartes. She stifled a yawn. Why was she studying Philosophy anyway? It wasn't like she would get a good job out of it. Daddy had already said that she would be starting in the business for the summer and had hinted at a very lucrative salary package. Sure, computers weren't her thing, but for a decent salary, she would do anything.

Rachel...

She jumped at the sound of the whisper coming from just behind her. Turning, she looked at the blank faces behind her, looking past her at the screen on the stage. Nobody leaned towards her to whisper a message. A cold chill ran through her for a moment.

Rachel...

She heard it again. Goosebumps rose on her arms. Who was it? Should she answer them? Shivering, she shut her eyes tightly. *Calm yourself, Rachel. Calm yourself. Go to your happy place.*

She did. She brought up her favourite daydream, that one where she met Quentin quite by accident at the lovely café that Allie Kendrick frequented. It was busy, with small round tables outside, embossed in the middle with the bee symbol set into a hexagon. She pushed the glass door open, stepping inside. The inside was perfect. On one side, there were sofas with low tables, surrounded by bookcases filled with books. On the other, opposite the glass counter showing off the cakes, there were tables, all different sizes, with unmatching chairs around them. She headed for one of the tables, nodding to the waitress who bustled past. She settled into the chair, sighing, opening her new book at page one.

The door opened, letting a fresh breeze flow in. In stepped a man, tall, dark floppy hair and sparkling hazel eyes. He looked around hopefully, then his face fell for a moment. All the tables were taken. He stepped over, smiling politely. "Excuse me," he said, "Would it be alright if I shared your table?"

Rachel smiled back, making a gesture of invitation. "Of course, please do. I'm Rachel, by the way."

He reached out to shake her hand. His handshake was warm and strong. He lingered for a moment, looking at her with an appraising glance. "Quentin," he replied.

A flicker of lights in the lecture theatre brought her back with a jolt. Had she been sleeping? Daydreaming? She looked around, panicked. But everyone continued as normal, not looking her way. She looked at herself. Her hand was moving, taking notes painstakingly, her head bowed. What was happening? Was she still dreaming?

"Rachel," she heard. But this time, it was not a husky whisper. It was Quentin's voice.

"That's such a lovely name. And where are you from?"

She was back in the café, a cup of coffee in front of her, gently steaming. This had never happened before. She could feel the hard chair underneath her, the feel of the table in front of her. Gingerly she picked up the coffee and tasted it. It was richly flavoured and warm. Quentin waited, his face open and interested.

This was... perfect. Perfect.

The door opened again, ushering in a bright-eyed woman wearing a beret with shoulder-length dark red hair. Rachel stared.

Was that... Allie Kendrick? Here? It was. It was Allie Kendrick herself, the character in the most perfect book, right here in front of her. But she did not sit down. There were no tables, and Quentin did not look around at her. No, he was looking at ... her.

At Rachel.

Allie Kendrick ordered a coffee to go, taking one of the reusable cups with the bee logo on and the name, The Tea Hive. She chatted for a moment, then bustled out, coffee cup in one hand, bag in the other. She was gone. Rachel smiled, looking closely at Quentin. Allie Kendrick did not meet with Quentin after all. She did. Rachel did. Oh, the possibilities! She leaned as he talked, his eyes smiling, not taking them off her face. The café continued around them, customers coming in and out, ordering cake, coffee, brunch, a spot of lunch. And they talked and looked and smiled. All the while, her body continued to write, taking notes mechanically.

Rachel... the voice whispered again. But this time, Rachel heard the voice as Quentin's voice, *her* Quentin's voice, and she smiled.

SMOKE AND MIRRORS

Rachel was dreaming again. She was back in the strange place, her hair long, with that strange white gown on. She looked around, finger tips trailing against the walls. She felt a shiver from the walls, the heartbeat echoing in her ears and under her fingers. What was this place? *Rachel,* she heard. *Rachel.*

Was Quentin here? "I'm here," she called, walking down the corridor, heedless of the cold against her bare feet. The passage opened up, widening, and then ahead of her she could see two passageways, going in different directions. She paused, looking at them, wondering which way to go. The one to the right seemed to lead up, towards a light. But her feet turned to the left, the one that was darker, and going downward.

"Let's see how deep the rabbit hole goes," she murmured to herself. "I keep coming here, I wish to understand it better."

Her hands stroked the walls absently, feeling a warmth under her fingers. It was pleasant. *Rachel,* the voice came again. *Can you hear me...* "I can hear you, Quentin," she called. "I'm coming to find you!" *Yes...* returned the whisper. *Yes...*

Rachel stumbled forward, a small white figure in a maze of tunnels. Her hand stayed on the wall, stroking the surface gently. The vibrations lulled her, the heartbeat calmed her, and the voice called her on. She walked and walked, blind in the dark, following the voice. As she disappeared into the dark the walls themselves shook, and the voice spoke again. *Yes.... Rachel... yes...*

Rachel's bedroom was dim, subdued. She was alone, a prone figure under rumpled sheets. She did not stir as a wind blew through her room, carrying with it a quiet sigh. *Rachel.... Rachel....* The sleeping figure smiled, murmuring. Her hand flexed. The two books on her night-stand quivered, pages opening, the wind flying through the pages. They opened, closed, and opened again, like hungry birds waiting for their first meal. The wind slowed, letting the pages meander to a stop. They did, the pages swaying gently as if waiting for their next orders. They did not come. The wind died away slowly. But a figure appeared in the mirror in Rachel's room, looking out. It stood still, long hair arranged in an elaborate do, dressed in a beautiful white gown. The figure stared with hungry shadowed eyes at the sleeping figure in the bed. A smoke billowed out from the frame of the mirror, falling to the floor and moving slowly in fits and starts towards the bed. It crept up, incorporeal fingers gripping the edge of the bedframe and climbing, creeping towards her. She slept on, a dreamy smile on her lips. Slowly, slowly, the smoke seeped into her face, into her body, absorbed into her skin. The figure in the mirror watched, its features absorbed in the event. *Yes....* the voice whispered. *Yes....*

And Rachel slept on.

AN IMMERSIVE BOOK EXPERIENCE

Rachel really needed a cup of coffee. She felt like she was swimming through mud. Her brain was so foggy of late, and she just could not keep track of the days. What day was it today anyway? It had to be a weekday as she was at university... but she did not remember getting there. Did she take the bus? She would surely remember that...

Did Archie drop her off perhaps? No, she hadn't seen him in ages. Had he even texted? She couldn't remember. The crowds washed past her. Was she going to lectures? Had she been to one?

Putting her hand to her head, she shut her eyes for a moment. She really didn't feel good.

"Miss? Miss?" She opened her eyes, blearily trying to focus. A man was squinting at her, either concerned for her wellbeing or thinking she was some kind of exhibit. She quelled a sudden urge to laugh. What was even happening?

"Yes, yes, I'm fine," she replied, automatically conjuring a smile. "It was a difficult morning. I'm just going to get a coffee."

"And sit down for a while, miss, you look as white as a sheet. Go on now," he said, still staring at her in that strange manner. She nodded, stumbling as she left, thinking hard. Which way was it to the cafeteria? It did terrible coffee but perhaps she could manage... just this once...

The corridors all seemed the same for a moment. Pausing, she noticed the lifts in front of her and reoriented herself. The coffee shop was behind Student Services. She could get there. She pushed her way through a group of people in a tight line, all talking at top speed. She saw the doors and pushed them open.

The cheerful waitress in the Tea Hive smiled pleasantly. "It's nice to see you again. Is it the usual?"

Rachel sat down in relief. "Something stronger, please. Lectures have been intense today!"

The woman nodded.

"Coming right up. There was a nice chap looking for you earlier. I think he's in the corner, reading a newspaper."

She winked significantly before turning her ample bulk away to tackle the steaming coffee machine, the sound of coffee beans whirring in a high pitched shriek. She looked towards the corner, noticing that her headache was entirely gone. Or what was it that she had? The man put his newspaper down, folding it neatly. His brown eyes crinkled as he smiled, a wide, genuine smile.

"Rachel! I am glad I caught you. I wasn't sure if you would come today. Please," he said, as he stood, pulling out a chair. "Please, sit. Did you give Wilma your order?"

"I did, she's bringing me something special."

"Something special for a special lady," he quipped, as he eyed her speculatively, lifting his cup to his mouth.

"It is very nice to see you again, Rachel. I have been thinking about you, you know."

She felt a flush of something rush through her, a warmth that started in her toes and rose right up to her face, causing her to blush. A tiny smile played on his lips.

" I appreciate that, Quentin," she murmured. "I think of you too."

Wilma bustled over with a cup on a tray and a piece of cake on a flowered plate.

"You looked a bit peaky when you came in, love. Eat up and tell me how that is, it's a new special!"

Rachel thanked her warmly, taking the cup and plate carefully. She glanced up again at Quentin, her eyes feasting on his handsome face, his thoughtful expression. This was the kind of man she wanted in her life. At last, she knew. But there was something not right, something she could not quite put her finger on. She thought hard, looking down at the table, at the towering confection on china in front of her. What was it about Quentin that wasn't right?

He leaned forwards, his hands reaching for her.

"I would like to come and spend more time with you, Rachel, I mean, not just here in this café. Would you like that too?"

"Yes, of course," Rachel agreed. "Come and visit me anytime you like. I would love that."

He frowned, hesitating for a moment, doubt marring his fine features.

"It isn't quite as simple as that, Rachel dear, I'm afraid. I have to stay here, you see. I cannot find a way to you, not in the current situation. You see, there has to be an exchange, a payment, if you will. And I believe your payment is, er, due."

"My payment?" she asked in confusion, looking over at Wilma behind the counter, as she fumbled for her bag.

"I can pay now, it isn't a problem, I wasn't aware -"

"No," Quentin soothed, gently taking her hand.

"This is a different kind of payment, Rachel. I will be waiting for you; I'll come through as soon as I can. As soon as you've made the payment. Alright?"

The café was fading, the sounds retreating in her head, the colours disappearing as if someone had spilled water over a delicate painting. She was back in the university corridors, standing in front of the rather grimy-looking coffee shop. She took her hand away from the door quickly. She certainly did not want to go in there. Turning away, she mulled on Quentin's words.

Payment was due. Who did she owe a payment to? How was she supposed to pay this?

And pay she would, there was no question of that. She had a chance of being more Allie, with her very own Quentin. Sunlight streamed in through the entrance, the white doors of the Radcliffe Building open to the sun. She went to adjust her bag on her shoulder and paused. There was a scrap of paper in her hand.

Unfolding it, she saw a receipt for The Black Cat Bookshop, not the printed kind but more like a written invoice.

The Perfect Storm; the immersive book experience. Free trial ends soon. Drop in to discuss payment terms!

Meredith had signed it with a jaunty flourish and a butterfly hovering over her name at the end. Rachel stared at the slip, feeling people slip past her.

Well, there was nothing else to be done but to go and see Meredith, she decided. She wasn't quite sure what was happening here, and why she was seeing Quentin in her daydreams, but if there was a possibility that he could become more than a book acquaintance, then she would pay it. Her credit card was healthy; her father never minded her buying books, after all. It would be just fine.

"Tomorrow," she resolved to herself. She would go and stop by the bookshop, have a chat with Meredith, and see what terms were available. She hugged her bag to herself as she imagined what it would be like to introduce Quentin to her father and stepmother. Surely, Grisela would swoon over his bookish air and dark eyes. Her father would approve of his solid career options and, of course, his devotion to Rachel. Her father would be happy, that at last, Rachel was settling down and finding her own roots, her future. And if it cost a little to put together, what did that matter? Quentin wanted to spend time with her here.

Perhaps they could visit the Botanical Gardens, she mused, walking towards the entrance and the sunlight. He could punt on the Thames while she read poetry out loud. What an idea. She resolved to order some poetry for herself when she went tomorrow, and then she would be prepared.

"Oh, this will be just perfect, Quentin," she thought to herself. *"Now, just let me arrange things at my end. We will be together soon. I promise."*

Her slender figure skipped and danced her way out of the building and into the courtyard outside, her long hair swinging against her back.

FIND A CHEAT
OR A THIEF

On Walton Street, the bookshop stirred, drawing out a sigh that made the shelves shiver, and the cats prick up their ears. The air was electric, thrumming with an air of anticipation. One of the cats flinched, tail waving, and ran to the corners of the shop. A whisper emanated from the centre of the bookshop, the quiet, sentient core.

Rachel.

In a modern building on Woodstock Road, a pale smoke circled around Rachel's apartment, gently stroking the windows before sliding in. Rachel sat motionlessly at her table in the living room, surrounded by papers. Her eyes were blank. Her hair was long, tied in a plait. Slowly, the mist slithered, touching the legs of the table, gently pressing itself against the couch and the big floor lamps, then wrapping itself around Rachel's legs. She did not stir.

Yes, sighed the mist. The long mirror that stood in the corner of the room started to ripple as a translucent shape stepped from it. It turned, formless features appearing on its face, hair sprouting from its head. Its movements were jerky, hesitant, but it stepped closer and closer still, standing behind the figure of Rachel. *Rachel.*

Hands that came to rest on Rachel's shoulders solidified, sinking into skin, into her body. Slowly, the shape fell into Rachel, being absorbed.

Yes, the bookshop whispered from its spot not far away. And Rachel smiled.

The tunnels were quiet and dark. Rachel walked along, her fingers gently grazing the sides, listening for the heartbeat. She could not hear it this time, and she wondered at it, feeling disappointed. Somehow, the heartbeat made her feel at home. The floor underneath her was smooth and even. Her feet were bare but she did not mind that, as the ground underneath her was warm. She quickened her pace, knowing that she had to find something, someone, soon. Sounds became amplified in her ears. She heard the echo of her feet padding on the floor, her steady rush of breath, the swish of her white gown as it curled and flowed around her legs.

She was searching for something. She knew that. It was something that she needed, a key, perhaps. Was it a key? A person that was a key? A chime of recognition sounded in her mind, a feeling of rightness. A person. She was searching for a person. That was it. She pushed on. She was searching for something. This was the test, the key to finding it. The answer was in the passageways somewhere. And she would find it. Her eyes felt sharper in the dark as she looked from left to right. She felt the air, cool air, brushing her cheeks. There was an opening ahead of her. A way out. She walked faster, her fingers touching the wall absently so she did not get lost.

"I'm coming," she whispered to the air. The air blew gently, softly, in response. The passageway widened, the light growing slowly. She hurried, her feet flowing faster, the silk of her gown swishing in a whisper, a flurry of material. The light grew and the passage ended abruptly, tipping her out into faded carpet and bookshelves that guarded the way in front of her, looming high.

"Bookshelves?"

That was unexpected. Rachel looked around, her eyes taking it in, unsure. What was this place? She was being watched. She could feel the slight rise of the hair on her neck as she felt the scrutiny first, of eyes observing her. She turned to look, seeing a silhouetted figure standing in an archway, slightly leaning, their arms crossed.

"Hello, Rachel. Nice of you to stop by."

She knew that voice. Her eyes narrowed as she thought, but the voice did not match the figure in front of her, the ominous shadow, the strength lying quiet. But she knew that voice.

"Hello, Meredith."

The figure unfolded itself, flowing sinuously towards her. The hair was the same, the face, perhaps, but she seemed taller. More ominous.

"You have come at my summons, Rachel. You have been chosen for a great fate. I do not bestow my gifts on just anyone. But I need something from you to complete the transformation."

"The transformation," Rachel whispered, her eyes wide.

The figure quirked a humourless smile, her face twitching imperceptibly. "Yes," she said.

"You have found love, I understand. You wish to join Quentin, or rather, that he joins you, here, in this world. Is that correct?"

Quentin. A vision of his face, his heartfelt eyes, his hand reaching towards her, flashed in her mind. "Yes," she breathed.

The figure that looked like Meredith but not quite nodded, briefly.

"Good. We are on the same page, as it were. You can have this, but you will need to make an exchange. For Quentin to join you in this world, you will need to bring me something. Is that acceptable?"

Was that acceptable? Her hand reached for her purse, for her chequebook, but she carried nothing with her. Daunted, her hands fell to her sides, and Meredith smiled.

"Oh, I will not need your money this time, Rachel. I require you to find me a person. Find a cheat or a thief. Either will do, but they must have been caught cheating or thieving. Do not bring me one who has considered it or has mastered the art of it.

I wish to collect one failed rogue, a pathetic specimen, really, one who does not deserve to walk in society. You do not even need to bring them to me. Come tomorrow, to the bookshop, when it is light. You can, if you agree, sign the final paperwork and take with you a book, which you will hand to the person you choose. And then you merely need to wait for the magic to happen. Then you will have Quentin."

Rachel felt dazed. Is that all she needed to do? Find a thief or a cheat, and give them a book? She could do that. Her brain stuttered for a moment. Did she even know a thief or a cheat? Where would she find one?

"Er, may I ask one question?"

Meredith's eyes narrowed. "You may. But do not test my patience, Rachel. I have been clear."

The warning tone was apparent. Rachel gulped. "How long do I have to, er, find the payment?"

"You have one month. One month, that is all. If you do not find one, then Quentin will be gone forever, and you, Rachel, will belong to me. The clock, as they say, is ticking. Tick, tock. Tick, tock. Tick, tock."

PAYMENT DUE

Rachel pushed the door open, hearing the cheerful jangle of the bell as she felt that familiar, comforting brush of a cat tail against her leg. She smiled down at the beauty who walked past her, tail high, and she looked into the bookshop. "Hello," she called. "I've come to pay my invoice!"

"Just a moment!" came a muffled voice from the back. "If that's my favourite customer, Rachel Phillips, I left the books on the counter. Feel free to grab them! But I'll be right with you."

Rachel stepped to the counter, smiling to herself. Her favourite customer. She could live with that! There were indeed two paperbacks lying on the counter, gleaming with shiny covers. She picked them up, intrigued, looking more closely at the covers. The top one was a plain cover with a boy sitting alone in the dark. *Oliver Twist*, by Dickens. She set it down carefully. She had never read it, but she had seen the musical many times with her father, who was a big fan of Dickens. She hadn't ever been able to find the love for it, much to his disappointment.

The other was not as familiar to her. It was a monochrome book, framed in black, with the silhouette of a woman in black on the cover. It was titled *Assuming Names*. She had an urge to flick through it but she put it down, not wanting to break the spine or crease the pages. The books looked back up at her from the counter and held her gaze for just a moment, making her feel dizzy.

"Ah, good morning, Rachel!"

Meredith bustled in, smiling, her black glasses perched on her nose. "It's nice to see you! Thank you for stopping by, and thanks for taking part in my little event!"

"Your event?"

"Oh, yes, did I not explain properly on the phone? I want to bring more people to the bookshop for our bespoke choosing service, and generally introduce myself to the community more. So, I would like my favourite customers, my ambassadors, to spread the word and hand out a couple of books. I was thinking these would be good choices; what do you think?"

She looked closely with an enquiring look and a slight raise of the eyebrow. "Would these work?"

Rachel shook herself out of her reverie. "Of course, yes. Yes. They're perfect. And I give them to..."

"Whoever suits, dear. You'll know. We operate on our instincts here at The Black Cat Bookshop. The right customers find us. Like you, dear."

Her hands hovered over the books, red nail polish gleaming on perfect nails. Rachel blinked, looking at them. She could almost see herself in the shape, a strange silhouette in the reflection. There was something ... different about it... she looked more closely, wondering. Meredith's voice cut through her stupor, bringing her back to the present.

"Shall I wrap these up?"

"Yes, thank you. Thank you. I have... I think I have an invoice to pay?" Her voice was higher than she expected, a little uncertain.

Rachel shook herself. She was certainly not feeling herself of late! What was she thinking?

Meredith smiled in a conspiratorial fashion. "Your invoice for the trial? Don't you worry about that, Rachel. You're helping us out here at the bookshop so much, I think we can extend it for you! If you get one of these books out to a new customer, then I can convert the trial for you. But do not forget that life waits for no man!"

Rachel smiled. "Death hangs over you. Right?"

Meredith smiled back, her eyes gleaming. "Marcus Aurelius was such a wise man. Exactly. Do not act as if you are going to live ten thousand years."

Rachel listened, feeling the resonance in the quote, feeling layers of meaning within it. "Did you say that Marcus Aurelius was a Roman?"

"He was, dear. A great academic and philosopher, in fact. Have you not studied him?"

Rachel shook her head, confused. Had she studied him? Why did that quote resonate? For a moment, she heard a man saying those words and felt her lips smiling of their own accord. And then she was back in the bookshop, in front of Meredith, who was beaming in a knowing fashion.

"So, I'll see you when you have dropped that book off, Rachel? And then we can see about transforming you, butterfly-like. Alright?"

Rachel nodded, feeling the books thrust into her hands, wrapped and bagged in tiny white canvas bags. Before she knew it she was standing in front of her car, wondering what happened. What did she do next? Why did she feel distracted? What was happening here? She pulled the end of her plait absently for a moment before transferring the books into her left hand, looking for her keys. Who would she give the books to? Who would appreciate the bookshop as much as she did?

As she slid into the car seat, she could hear a clock ticking deep inside her mind. Tick, tock. Tick, tock. Tick, tock. Tick.

GIVING TO RECEIVE, WITH LOVE

The train whisked Rachel past green fields and farms, the landscape flying by. She had the carriage almost to herself, which was to be expected this early in the day. She left her ticket out on the table and opened her laptop, wondering if she was up to date with her assignments. She felt disoriented still, as if she had been sleeping too long. She logged in to her account swiftly, her fingers flying over the keys. Hmm. Everything had been submitted, and in fact her scores were looking very good. Why had she not remembered that? Well, it was something else to tell Daddy when she arrived, Rachel mused. He would be pleased to hear that she was doing well at University.

The books were in her bag, but she felt like she could see them. Nervously, she double-checked to make sure they were there. She really wanted to give them to the right person, but she wasn't sure who. Meredith had said that she would know, that she could act on instinct. Who though? She had considered dropping off one with Fatima, but no. No. For some reason, she did not want to do that. It had to be someone else. A stranger. The train conductor, perhaps? A passenger? Sighing, she leaned her head back against the headrest. The train was slowing a little, perhaps reaching another station. She heard the hiss of the glass door as someone entered the carriage, nodding briefly to her as they passed, walking awkwardly with a big pack hanging between their fingers. They moved past, lurching with the movement of the train. Rachel shut her eyes, lulled by the gentle noise.

She woke with a start, not sure how long she had been asleep. The other passenger was talking loudly on the phone, their voice harsh and angry.

"Yeah, I know, I know."

There was a pause.

"Look, I don't know either. It was a moment of madness. I was under a lot of pressure, you know?"

"I've talked to them. They said it's out of their hands, that I plagiarised. Yeah."

Rachel's ears pricked up. Plagiarism. What did he do? Was he at university? She shrugged, unsympathetic. Everyone knew that assignments were checked for plagiarism nowadays: it was almost a foregone conclusion that you would get caught for cheating. The passenger was still talking.

"Yeah, I don't know how long it will take. I'm going to come home for a few days, let the dust settle and then see if I can appeal. Yeah. Alright."

Silence fell in the carriage. Rachel stared out of the window for a moment, thinking. She got up abruptly, her hand fishing in her bag, a book leaping eagerly into her palm, turning towards the passenger who was slumped in the seat, his face sullen.

"Here," she said, placing the package on the table in front of him. "I've got a couple of free books to give away; it's a promotion from my local bookshop. I thought you might like one."

She smiled, and the young man smiled back. "Cheers," he said, pleasantly. "That's kind!"

She nodded, feeling pleased. Meredith was right; it was easy to know who needed a book. That felt good. She started to hum a tune as she returned to her seat, thinking about what she would do when she got to Durham. Perhaps she should take Daddy out for dinner and get tickets for the theatre, maybe. She smiled at her reflection, and her blood-red lips curved up. The Meredith effect. Yes. Life was good. And it was going to get better.

The train arrived on time, for a change. Rachel stepped off the train to crowds thronging the platform, eager to leave the city and head south. She picked her way through them, seeing Daddy and Grisela waiting for her a short distance away. Grisela was waving, her other arm clutching Daddy as if he was going to blow away. Daddy was on the phone, of course, his face distracted.

"Hello, Daddy, Grisela."

She kissed her stepmother on the cheek, smelling her perfume. She was wearing something expensive, something that smelled of iris and old stage lipstick. She resolved to ask her what good perfumes to choose when she was next in London, something she could wear when she next met Quentin. Daddy patted her awkwardly on the shoulder as he took her case, his phone still glued to his ear. He walked on a little, leaving Rachel to walk with her stepmother, who was talking nineteen to the dozen, her mouth full of the small events that littered her day.

Rachel did not understand how her father, driven and intellectual as he was, could have married a woman who enjoyed such trivial things. Perhaps it was the contrast, she mused. After a day of important decisions, her chatter calmed him. She let it calm her, too, nodding and reacting at the appropriate moments, weaving her way out of the station. She was a pleasant sort, Rachel supposed, now she had warmed up to her. And it was nice to be fussed over for a change. She wondered how Grisela would react to meeting Quentin. She wondered when she should bring him to visit and show him off. Perhaps Grisela would plan one of her dinner parties. That would certainly work. She imagined how he would look, there, elegant fingers holding a prosecco glass, talking animatedly, but holding her gaze with those dark eyes of his. It would be perfect. At last, her life was coming together.

She had her degree, almost finished, she had her friends, her apartment, she had a future with Quentin, and Daddy was proud of her. She smiled, enjoying the moment. Everything was really just perfect.

On the train, a young man who was facing an uncertain future unwrapped the book that he had been given so unexpectedly on the train. He looked curiously at the cover, his finger tracing the image of the woman on the cover, and he read the title out loud. "Assuming Names. Hmm. Interesting."

He opened the book, reading the inscription. "From The Black Cat Bookshop, with love."

The book sighed, and a tiny breeze blew through the carriage. The man did not notice.

Yes, whispered the bookshop, and the figure on the book cover smiled. *Yes.*

CATCHING A THIEF

"You know, it is so nice to have a shopping buddy for once, Rachel," Grisela gushed, her lipsticked smile curving. "I am very pleased that you have embraced your colours, darling. That red suits you so beautifully! And I love the long hair. It really suits you."

Rachel stroked the plait, smiling back.

"I am pleased, too; I haven't felt more myself since learning about what colours frame my face. I'm glad we bonded over this!"

Grisela squeezed her arm, pulling her in close.

"Your father is very happy that we get on well. It makes us such a lovely little family! Look, we just have to stop into this new boutique around the corner. It's fairly new; the owner is some kind of fashion person fresh out of University, I believe. I think you will love it!"

Rachel smiled good-naturedly, amused by her stepmother's youthful enthusiasm. While she enjoyed fashion and the effect it had on her success because there was no denying that looking put together did make a difference, she still could not muster such enthusiasm for it. Grisela came across as empty-headed sometimes, despite her education. She did not know how her father tolerated it. She could never imagine falling for someone who was not at least as intelligent as her.

As ever, her thoughts slid to Quentin, with his clever mind, his soulful eyes. Would he appreciate her mind? Or would he prefer someone like Grisela? But then, Allie Kendrick was smart, and he loved that. No, she had chosen correctly. Now she just had to wait for him to arrive in her life. The sooner, the more romantically, the better.

They turned into a rather beautiful-looking parade of shops, with a glass covered roof and ornate old-fashioned style street lamps. The shops were surrounded by wrought iron and greenery that fluttered around the doors, giving it a vintage look. Rachel loved it immediately.

The shop in the middle had an array of elegantly clad mannequins set out in the window, with a rather avant-garde sign over the top simply saying, House of Wears. She followed her stepmother in, noting the space in the shop, the nicely arranged clothes, and the elegant shop owner who was displayed at the front of the shop, with a huge modern art piece behind her. The owner nodded at Rachel and came forward to greet Grisela with great animation.

She was a regular customer then, Rachel noted. As they chattered in shrill tones punctuated by air kisses, Rachel looked at the wares, considering the quality and the fabric. She wondered idly if the boutique stocked any vintage type clothes. She turned to ask, taking advantage of the lull in conversation.

"I was thinking of changing my style somewhat, and would love to incorporate some vintage elements, particularly from the 30s and 40s. Do you have anything like that?"

The woman looked Rachel over with a practised air.

"I may have something, yes, I think I had some wide-legged trousers from last season still that I haven't put out for sale yet. Shall I go and check for them?"

That suited Rachel just fine, as she nodded, resolving to examine the accessories for something suitably chic, something bold, perhaps. Her fingers moved to pick up a handsome bronze bracelet which sported bold amber studs when a movement caught her eye. She turned, just in time to see her stepmother slipping something into her pocket, her face a mixture of guilt, fear, and something else. Was it excitement? Her hand rose back up, her face flushing guiltily. Rachel wondered at it. Why would she need to steal? She had enough money, her father certainly earned enough.

She turned back to the bracelet, her mind awash with ideas. They did say that women who were bored with their lives sometimes stole things to get a thrill of excitement. Perhaps that was what this was. She laughed to herself. Well, as long as she wasn't caught, but it wouldn't be long if she was so obvious about it like that.

The woman returned, her arms draped with dark pants and two of those silky types of shirt that Rachel had seen Meredith wear, one in an off-white, one in a dark red. Grisela rushed to her side, nodding in enthusiasm.

"Yes, she would suit these perfectly, Andrea; you do have excellent taste. Oh, yes. I think Rachel would like all of these, wouldn't she?"

Grisela looked enquiringly at Rachel, her cheeks still flushed with colour. With shame, perhaps.

Rachel acquiesced, silently, observing the exchange of clothes, wrapped efficiently into smart paper bags with the flex of black plastic that swept over the gleaming payment machine.

Grisela bustled her out of the shop, her words firing out as if she were expecting to face an interrogation, Rachel thought with amusement.

"Shall we get coffee? I'm simply parched, are you? I know a lovely place just nearby, you know," and so she continued, her voice an accompaniment to Rachel's thoughts. The coffee shop was indeed nearby, with outdoor seating and big bold prints on the walls.

Rachel settled herself at the table by the wall, bags around her, letting her stepmother order and bring the drinks. A thought crossed her mind as she remembered the book that was in her bag.

Would her stepmother not enjoy reading it? After all, her father loved Oliver Twist. Perhaps if she read it, too, then she would be able to go with him to the theatre. *You were right, Meredith,* she thought to herself. *I certainly did know the right people to give these books to!*

She reached into her bag, finding the wrapped book and placed it on the table. What a present for her dear stepmother, she smiled to herself. It just worked perfectly.

SYMPATHY TASTES SO SWEET

Tick, tock, tick, tock, tick, tock.

In the Bookshop that was populated with numerous black cats, invisible clocks started to sound, rattling, beeping and squawking from respective corners, nooks and bookshelves. The cats squealed and ran, diving for cover, escaping into the dark quiet of the backroom, disappearing from the noise that expanded to fill the space. The cacophony went on, polluting the shop with noise for a torturous sixty seconds until they stopped, synchronised, leaving a humming in the air.

Silence reigned, that kind of silence that only truly empty houses have, that silence that knows nobody is coming. But something in the bookshop sighed, a breath that gusted out in the shop, blowing open books and sending the pages into a flurry of movement. The zephyr moved around the building, dancing here and there, lingering on one spot, ignoring another, but wherever it went, the books shivered, opened and fell still.

Quiet entered again, an expectant silence this time. A hush. The wind slowed, returning to wherever it came from. And the book-shop waited.

Tick, tock, tick, tock, tick. The chimes were barely heard in the room, cluttered and untidy that it was in the gloom. The young man slept, head covered by a pillow, still in the clothes he had been wearing that day. His bag was barely unpacked. The room was packed with boxes, a hanging rail full of clothes, and old paintings. He slept on a camp-bed, his quilt askew. Gently a breeze blew in, making its way past closed windows. It blew through the clothes, the papers piled in one corner, and paused at the book that peeped out of the bag lying on the floor. The book was plain with a face on a black cover, matte, as is considered fashionable nowadays. Slowly, the book eased itself out of the bag, bending and stretching in ways that one might not expect from a book. The wind hovered over the book, blowing the pages as they flew, back, and forward. The man stirred, once or twice, his arm lifting to adjust his pillow, but he did not wake.

The wind picked up, whistling. The book lay open, the pages fluttering just at the edges. And from the spine, spreading outwards as if ink had dripped on the pages, the white page turned an inky black. The air began to vibrate, and the wind picked up, swirling and sighing in unearthly tones. At last, the young man woke, eyes wide with terror. He threw his pillow aside, trying to sit up, his chest working, his mouth opening. But no sound came out. The book flexed, and pulsated. The man's face began to lose colour, the pink tones seeping from his face as if he had been left out in the rain. As if his pages had become sodden. He gasped, wheezing, clutching his chest, whispering something.

"Help... Help..."

But nobody answered. The air grew thicker. There was a hum, a heat, in the air. At last the man's eyes rolled back in his head and he breathed in, wheezing, just once, his body strained, and then he collapsed to the bed, his mouth open, his eyes wide.

The book pulsated, growing thicker, older, growing veins, that flowed and wrapped tightly around the book. Quietly the wind waited, just a sigh in the night. At last the book shivered, growing still, and it closed, pages snapping shut with a wet, sticky noise. The wind died down, disappearing. And with it, disappeared the book.

Tick, tock, tick, tock, tick.

Nobody heard the chimes. They rang out quietly, muffled by elegant ornaments, nicely framed paintings on the walls, and elegant Egyptian cotton bedding that was draped over two figures. One was sound asleep, his hand almost reaching for his phone that was charging on the nightstand next to him. The other was lying prostrate wearing a black embroidered sleep mask, her face arranged in repose. It was quiet.

A breeze angled itself through the slightly open windows, meandering through the room. It paused over pictures, some knick-knacks, and a rather smart-looking bracelet lying on the ornate dressing table. It flowed past the sleeping man, and over to the adjacent night-stand, holding just a curved metal lamp and a book. It sighed, rustling the pages as they wriggled, opening in the breeze. The book fluttered, letting the pages fan out, subsiding back down. And then the book opened, stretching, opening at its middle.

The wind paused again, this time slowing into a shadow that formed at the bottom of the bed, head cocked, looking at the sleeping figure. It raised its arms, slowly. A wind picked up as the walls of the house moaned, the pictures rattling. The book spasmed, extending the pages, as dark blood-red ink spilled out on its pages, forming a slick sheen.

The figure with the mask gasped, gargling, her body taut. She stretched, her jaw straining, hands flying to her chest, holding it as if it was begging to be freed. Her jaw spasmed, her face contorting. The shadow watched. The book rippled, spurting burgundy ink. A gargle came from the figure, still masked, which was matched by a grumble from the body next to her, in unconscious repose.

The shadow watched as the body flexed once, twice, as the colour died from her face, leaving a waxy sheen. At last, the book slowed its fluttering of paper, its spreading of ink, and the cover slowly came to a close, settling still on the nightstand. The shadow figure stood, one hand reaching for the book, taking it in its hands. And then with a sigh, the wind exited the room, leaving one aghast corpse and one man who slept on.

The call came early. The tone sliced through the silence, discordant tones screaming in the silence. Rachel answered, hand reaching, ear on auto-pilot.

"Rachel? Rachel, darling, are you there?"

Her eyes snapped open as she heard her father sounding panicked. Had he ever been that?

"Daddy, it's me. What's wrong?"

He was panting. Something was wrong. Rachel sat up, pulling the quilt up close, feeling cold.

"What's happened, Daddy?"

Sobs skittered down the line, gasps of air punctuated by sounds that she had never heard before.

"It's .... It's Grisela, love. She's... she's ... oh, it's horrible! What do I do?"

Wakefulness rushed through her body and she sat up, alert. "Calm down, Daddy. What has happened with Grisela?"

He was crying, great sobs that hiccupped their way down through the phone. "She's... she's dead, petal. She's dead!"

Dead? Her fingers felt numb. The words that she wanted to say scrambled up and away from her.

"Petal? Petal? Rachel?"

His voice came through, tinny, and she realised the phone had almost dropped from her hand.

"I'm here, Daddy. I'm just processing. Are you sure?"

The reply came back quickly, outraged. "Of course I'm sure! Do you think I don't know what a dead body looks like? She looks.... she looks horrible!"

Rachel nodded, blankly. "Alright, alright. I'll get on a train this morning, I'll be with you in a few hours. I just need to pack some things."

"Hurry!"

"I will. I will."

She put the phone to one side, her eyes welling up with sudden tears. Grisela was dead? She had only just seen her a few days ago! Her Daddy's voice came back to her, panicked, upset. But he needed her. He had asked her for help. This felt.... perfect. A small smile spread on her lips.

"And black is one of my colours. That's lucky!"

That errant thought stayed with her as she got up, mentally planning what she needed for her mission of mercy. Her Daddy needed her. She would not let him down.

DADDY NEEDS RACHEL

Yawning, Rachel kicked her shoes off, crashing into the armchair. She had met so many well-wishers and drank so much tea the last few days, that she felt as if she would burst. Who would have thought that dear Grisela was that popular? And Daddy was inconsolable. Thankfully he was leaning on his daughter. She wriggled her toes, feeling the life return to them. What was it with those sensible types of shoes for funerals that always made your feet numb?

"At least that's over," she murmured to herself. "Back to reality soon."

What reality actually was, was a mystery. She had a leave from university on compassionate grounds and her lecturers had been kind, pushing back her outstanding assignments for another two weeks, and offering her any extra support over the phone that she could need. Not that she needed it, but a little time off would do no harm.

She made herself more comfortable in the chair, looking around the room. It was nicely designed, and that was thanks to her late stepmother's intervention, she acknowledged. She was an excellent homemaker. Rachel's eyes flicked to the bookshelves, immaculately dusted and arranged in a harmonious line of colour. She sighed, thinking of Quentin. She hoped that she would see him again soon. It felt like ages. She would have to stop back into the bookshop to see if there was anything else they needed. Hadn't Meredith said something about making it happen?

Rachel shut her eyes, blocking out the room. She concentrated on her breath, making it slow and even. She pushed her thoughts away. Slowly the image of a café with the beehive logo started to solidify in her mind, hazy and a little fuzzy at the edges, but it was there...

"Rachel."

Her breath flew out with an exasperated puff. Her eyes flew open, seeing her father there, stooped, tired. He looked purposeless. He looked smaller.

"I'm sorry, Rachel, darling, I didn't mean to disturb you. You must be exhausted."

He sat down gingerly in the chair next to her, looking as if he would be swallowed up in the padding of the cushions. He definitely looked smaller without his businessman bravado. That was interesting. Rachel raised her eyebrows, watching him wrestle with his thoughts. His brow furrowed, his mouth pursed a little, and he opened his mouth to speak twice, shutting it again. This was unusual. Daddy was never lost for words.

"I wanted to say, Rachel, that I am very grateful to you that you have been here for me, you know with, with all this."

He trailed off for a moment, his eyes looking suspiciously wet.

"I don't think I realised, you know, how much you've grown as a person of late. Grisela kept telling me, but I didn't listen... I just wanted to tell you that. I want you to have everything you need in life. I intend to make up for the times when I didn't do that. If there's something you need from me, you just say. It's your turn to be happy now. Alright?"

It was very alright. Rachel smiled, looking at Daddy, feeling a rush of something. Could he be finally accepting her?

"I know that, Daddy, that you love me. I did not know, that Grisela was such a champion of me. I ..." She watched him, seeing the play of pain cross his features. He loved her then, or thought he did. "She was wonderful. I am not surprised that she supported me in such a way. I hope that... I hope that I find someone like that."

Daddy squeezed her hand, eyes glistening. "I hope so too. I would give anything for that to happen, Rachel. Anything."

Yes...

Rachel squeezed his hand back, her thoughts a whirl of activity. She would see Quentin soon. Had Meredith not said so? And when she did, she would introduce him to Daddy. Everything would just work out perfectly. She would stop into the bookshop to speak to Meredith again. Just to be sure. Everything would be just.... perfect.

Rachel pushed the door open, feeling a rush of homecoming, a familiar air. She smiled as she stepped in, smelling the new books on the shelves. Two of the black cats approached lazily, tails waving, high, their green eyes knowing and mysterious. She bent to pet them, murmuring sweet nothings as she tangled her fingers into their fur. They purred. She melted. Truly, could a bookshop become an anchor in your life?

The cats, tiring of her worship, sauntered off, and Rachel straightened, her eye caught by a vivid book cover in the travel section. There was a train, crossing a bridge. and all around was snow. She felt a sense of déjà vu as she reached for it, her hands tingling.

There was something about it... She could almost hear the train whistle, the clatter of wheels over the bridge, the smell of freshly brewed coffee....

Meredith entered, her hands full of books, her perfect face turning to smile, lipsticked mouth curving. "What a pleasant surprise! The cats didn't let me know you were here this time. You must be practically family. Hi, Rachel!"

Her warmth was infectious. Rachel smiled back, her shoulders relaxing. "Hi, Meredith. It's good to be back. I was just looking at these travel books, here."

"Ah, wanderlust!" She put the books down, sliding them onto the counter and straightening them with one efficient movement. Wiping her hands on her perfect vintage slacks, she sauntered over, her eyes on the bookshelf. "Which one was it that caught your eye?"

"This one." She pointed it out, her hand greedily wishing to grasp it. Was she in the position to just go off and travel, and leave everything behind? She wondered if she was. Perhaps that was just what she needed. But what of Quentin? She needed him, too. Somehow. Even if somehow it seemed impossible that a book hero could step, whole and perfect, into this world.

Meredith walked over, touching the cover of the book gently. "Ah, the wonderful train ride through Switzerland. I can just see you there, sitting in first class, reading a paper and drinking coffee. And then a handsome gentleman asks if the other seat is free. A dark-haired, familiar, gentleman."

"Quentin," Rachel breathed, her eyes alight with dreams.

"Quentin," Meredith repeated, her smile widening. "I love that for you."

She turned to the bookshelf, pausing for just an instant and then she plucked it from the shelf, proffering it to her. "Here, I think you should have it. As a gift. From me. And the bookshop."

Rachel took the book, hugging it to herself. It felt like a treasure had been handed to her. "Oh, thank you, Meredith. This is exactly what I need! You understand me perfectly. I do need this, to complete myself. It's going to be perfect!"

Meredith watched, her eyes sparkling. "Yes, I think you would fit perfectly in that book, Rachel. You'll be just perfect."

BE MORE ALLIE

It was quiet aboard the Bernina Express. Or quiet certainly, in her carriage. She took advantage of the empty table to spread out her newspaper, eager to see what was happening back home. She did not intend to visit any time soon, but she liked to keep abreast of current events. Reaching for her coffee with long slender, manicured nails, she looked out over the bridge and sighed at the scenery, the mountains, the clear blue sky. This was perfect.

The carriage door slid open with a hushed swish, allowing in a tall man with dark hair and grey eyes. He was dressed impeccably, holding a small case which he stowed away. He glanced around the carriage briefly and then gestured politely. "Is this table free?"

"Of course, please, join me. I shall just move my papers."

She did, folding the paper and placing it neatly on the others in a pile next to the window. The headline blared out:

Local tycoon and daughter
found dead in mysterious
circumstances!

She did not look over at it, her eyes intrigued by the fine form of the stranger in front of her, wondering idly where his accent was from. He busied himself with his things, taking off his jacket and folding it next to him, and placing his glasses on the table in front of him. He smiled, his mouth quirking up slightly.

"It is nice to meet you. My name is Quentin. What is yours?"

She smiled back, charmed.

"You can call me Allie. What a wonderful name, Quentin!"

And she leaned back, eager at the possibilities in front of her. The train, the scenery, the coffee and now Quentin. It was just.... perfect.

"Waste no more time arguing about what a good man should be. Be one."

Marcus Aurelius

MATTHEW

"I am not a good man."

Matthew looked into the mirror, his face blotched, his eyes smeared with sleep. He needed a shave. He had exactly sixteen minutes to get scrubbed, caffeinated up and at the bus stop ready for the commute to work. But he remained at that mirror, looking at himself, into his eyes, making sure he was listening.

The moment passed, and he hustled off, preparing for the short bus journey into the centre of the city. It felt like he was stepping through a portal sometimes, from his rural spot outside Oxford and then being deposited unceremoniously outside the Council buildings in St Aldates a scant twenty minutes later. Perhaps he, too, metamorphosed, strapping himself into the smart suit, the dapper manner, and the smooth confidence, that his job needed. But the Council would not care if he was a good man or not. They cared about his appropriate assessment of data. And they paid him handsomely for it.

The bus arrived, and he deposited his frame into a sea of disembodied heads, ignoring the chatter, the hum of voices and fidgets and humming that seemed to populate public transport. Returning to a meditative state, he looked unseeing out of the window and thought.

What makes a good man? How did I miss out on it? Can I become one now? Is it too late?

Questions rumbled around inside his skull, with no way to leave. Perhaps he should wear headphones, numbing his ears with something so he didn't have to think. Maybe that's why they all did it, staring into lit screens or straight ahead, blankly, ears plugged with white plastic. Maybe it gave them some release. Maybe he was missing out.

He was not a good man. The thought stayed with him through the day as he paced corridors, analysed data, and managed teams. His voice rang out, making plans, being Matthew, but inside, his voice ran on, quietly. *I am not a good man. I missed out on something. Is it too late?* He shuffled papers, signed off on proposals, and encouraged young, ambitious faces. Was he too late to be a good man? What kind of man was he?

The day marched on, wearing away into evening, when the mood shifted, collars loosened, and minds started to turn towards Happy Hour, and making eyes over frosted glasses at your latest conquest. Not that anyone made eyes at him. He would have one drink to look friendly, then slip off home, unnoticed.

"What makes a man good?" he mused out loud.

"Eh, what?" his colleague asked absently, eyes not leaving the light of the computer screen.

Matthew blinked. He did not realise he had spoken out loud. "I have been wondering about it. It's a silly thing really. What makes a man, good? What are we beyond our jobs and responsibilities? Does any of that make us good? Or are we merely existing?"

The man pulled his face away from the screen, his expression focused. Leaning back in his chair, he stroked his beard for a moment, thoughtful. "Are you having a midlife crisis, Matt?"

He hated being called Matt. His name was Matthew. "No, not that I am aware of, Richard."

Matthew could hear the irritation in his tone and paused, reining it back in. "Perhaps merely an existential one. What do we do to keep us human?"

Richard stretched, his white shirt straining over his belly. "Well, clearly you don't do something to keep you human. Perhaps you should look at that. Do you have a hobby or an interest? You can't tell me you always had an ambition to work at the Council as a data analyst. What did you want to be, as a kid? What did you like to do?"

Matthew cast his mind back, feebly hunting through the debris of adolescent life, seeking out something that wasn't video games and lingerie catalogues. What did he do? He did not know.

Richard watched him, nodding sagely. "Maybe you need to find yourself a passion, my friend."

Matthew agreed, feeling relieved that he had not shortened his name again. That kind of advice made you beholden to someone, and you couldn't then correct them on something as tiny as a name. The adviser was in power.

But he was in a position of power. Why could he not be powerful? Maybe that was what his hobby needed to be. Being powerful.

Powerful. Yes, he wanted that. What kind of interest involved power? For that matter, where did you find a hobby? He did not know.

Making his excuses quietly as the group migrated towards the nearest bar, Matthew stepped into the street, not wanting to join the other crowds, those waiting for a bus, just yet. Perhaps he would wander for a while. Inspiration could strike. He chuckled at the idea of inspiration lurking in the streets of Oxford, but he persevered, putting his hands deep into his coat pockets, pulling his hood up to protect his hair from the drizzle and looked out at the shop windows.

What would he like to do? One shop mannequin gestured at him, resplendent in the latest fashions. He had seen young men like that in the office, or in the bars, leaning casually against the bar in a predatory fashion. If that was power, he did not want it. He wanted something else, something better, something life-changing. He wanted to watch, and see, but not be seen. He did not want to be on display. Pausing in the street, he contemplated that. That narrowed it down. What kind of hobby involved power and watching, that wouldn't get you arrested?

Matthew laughed again. It was time to research this, perhaps at home. He turned to cross the road, looking both ways to check for traffic, just as he had taught his children once, long ago, and he saw it, out of the corner of his eye. A smart black door with a brass door knocker, sparkling windows, and oak bookshelves lining the walls.

"The Black Cat Bookshop," he read, out loud. "Curious name for a bookshop. Why black cats?"

The bookshop must have heard him, as two cats leapt up into the window, eyes wide, staring at him. Matthew shivered. Perhaps it was the timing of it, but they looked sinister. Although to be fair, he was not much of a cat man. They always seemed to be judging him, silently.

A bookshop. That could hold some research for him. Surely people went in search of hobbies all the time. And it was still drizzling. It looked warm and inviting in there. He had always liked bookshops as a kid, sitting in the children's section with a pile of books, trying to choose the One Perfect Book that would go home with him.
His mind was made up. Crossing the road, he walked up to the door, ignoring the scrutiny, and let himself in. A bell sounded cheerily as he gently closed the door.

WHAT AM I, REALLY?

Inside was indeed warm. He looked around, admiring the aesthetic of the place. It was clean, organised and somewhat upmarket. It lacked the round, crowded tables that littered the place in Waterstones, but instead kept the books neatly arranged on the bookshelves. He scanned the shelves, seeing small labels denoting travel, self-help and New Age. He certainly did not need those. Well, the self-help, maybe, but he did not want to spiral further into indecision. He needed a focus. He felt a furry body brush against the back of his legs, slowly, the tail lifting and curling around his knee. He resisted the urge to flinch or hiss, but he moved his leg away, stepping forward to put some distance between him and the cat. The cat stared at him imperiously, green eyes narrowing.

Matthew heard footsteps and turned towards the back of the shop, where there was a low arch leading into another room lined with bookshelves. A woman stepped out, smiling. She was probably approaching middle-age, with bright red hair and red lipstick. He had always thought that redheads weren't supposed to wear red, but she seemed to look good with it. The woman stepped behind the counter, setting a small pile of books down and looked expectantly at him.

"Hello, I'm Meredith Smart. And I see you found my bookshop!"

Her voice was low-pitched, accent-less. She didn't have that nasal quality that natives of Oxford seemed to have, but she didn't sound as if she was from somewhere else, either. That was interesting. She raised a groomed eyebrow as she surveyed him, and Matthew realised with a start that he was staring at her in silence. He hoped that he was not looking creepy.

"Oh, yes! I'm Matthew. Matthew Walker. It's good to meet you."

Automatically he stepped forward, his hand outstretched, and she shook his hand. Her hand was warm and her handshake was firm. She knew her business, then. Her eyes were fascinating, pale with specks of gold, that appraised him carefully.

"And what can I do for you today, Matthew?"

Matthew's eyes flicked over the shelves behind her, then returned to her face, her eyes. Would she know of a hobby? *Would she know if he was a good man?* That question came unbidden and he blinked, confused.

"I'm not sure if you can; to be honest, Meredith, I came here entirely on a whim. I was thinking about taking up a hobby. I realised that I have very little to do outside of my work, and I feel a little..."

"Lost?"

"Yes, perhaps it is that. Perhaps I am a little lost. I want to reclaim myself a little. Am I merely Matthew the analyst?"

He paused, feeling embarrassed at the overshare, the words spilling out into the silence. "I apologise, I shouldn't put all that on you. I don't even know if this is the right place to find what I am looking for."

"Or perhaps you are in precisely the right place. Books are funny things," Meredith paused, picking up a book contemplatively, her manicured finger stroking the cover. "They hold many answers. After all, people write them, and they draw on their own life experiences to do so. Perhaps you will indeed find your quest in a book."

She looked directly at him, eyes glinting. "But which quest, and which book?"

Matthew wasn't quite sure what she was talking about, but he didn't want to leave. He felt as if he was in the middle of something important, right here, right now, and if he missed it, if he left the bookshop, he would regret losing this moment. He was meant to be here. He was supposed to be here.

"I want my life to have meaning, and I want to be powerful," he blurted out, surprised by the tumble of words that fell from his mouth.

Was this like being at confession? Spilling your secrets to someone who understands? Someone otherworldly. Someone who could change things.

"Power is important. It certainly gives meaning," Meredith replied, looking entirely unsurprised. "But perhaps you do not need a hobby. Or perhaps you do, but you will not find power in that. Meaning, maybe."

She put the book down, stepping away from the counter and towards the centre of the shop. "And what do you like to do, Matthew? What hobbies do you want to take up?"

Matthew stepped forward, wondering if he should follow her to the bookshelves or wait as if he were an interviewee or a supplicant where he was. He opted for the former, hesitantly moving closer, putting his hands in his pockets.

"I've been so busy trying to be a grown-up that I don't entirely know what I like to do. Am I old enough to take up gardening or woodworking? Must I put ships in a bottle?"

Meredith laughed, a tinkly laugh that sounded like bells. "No, you are not in your dotage yet, I think. And there are many more things a person can do. We are in the Golden Age of Inspiration and ideas, much as Rome was for a time, until their last great Emperor died."

She sounded pensive. Matthew strained his mind to recall his long ago schooling. "The Golden Age ended with Marcus Aurelius, right?"

"Right! Exactly. When he died, the Empire went from one of gold, to dust. They did not value him enough, yet they esteemed him greatly! What a wonderful man. Do you know him?"

Matthew faltered. "I am afraid I do not, I have always been meaning to read his work, but have never done so." He paused. "Should I begin with that?"

She narrowed her eyes, just for a moment, looking feline. Dangerous.

"You could. It might give you some purpose, but I think we need to look at the other element too." Pursing her lips, she tapped her nail against her chin. With a start, Matthew saw four black cats sitting around her feet in position, almost as if they had been carved there. He shivered.

"Are you creative, Matthew? You mentioned being an analyst, which can show signs of creativity. It's that seeing patterns and making magic from it. Musical, perhaps?"

He stifled a laugh. The idea of him being musical was laughable. "No. I have never shown signs of being musical, sadly. But I do like to listen to it."

Thoughts of the local band that played in the Sickle on a weekend flitted through his mind. Idly he wondered if Meredith would go to something like that. He suspected she might, but he was not going to ask her. He had come there for a book, not a pickup. And half of him wasn't even sure if he was supposed to be there. He felt uncomfortable, watched, under the quiet scrutiny of the cats. Guardians, he thought. That's what they looked like.

Matthew stepped back, getting some distance. "I'll just take the book about Marcus Aurelius, if you don't mind, Meredith. The idea of a hobby was a silly one, I think. And I really don't want to keep you!" His last words came out muffled in a nervous laugh, garbled. It wasn't like there were many in the bookshop to take up her time.

Meredith smiled back. "Of course. Perhaps the inspiration is yet to strike! Do you prefer hardback or something more suited for your bag, that you can read at your desk?"

He pushed back the idea that she could see into his world, and know his habits. She was just an excellent, insightful bookseller. "Perfect. Get me the portable version, thank you, Meredith."

She disappeared with a cheerful nod, and the cats followed, much to Matthew's relief. One of the bookshelves caught his eye, with a book that gleamed at him. Cosmic Consciousness, it said in the title. As his fingers reached for it, something shifted around him, something knowing, and he almost pulled his hand back. What was it with this place?

He shook his head. He was entirely given over to fancy of late. Pulling the book down, he scanned the back cover. There was the usual fusty fellow on the back in front of a bookshelf, looking wise in a tweed suit. Matthew scanned the back. Human evolution is a study of theology, and how our brains use consciousness in our everyday lives.

"Pseudo-science bunkum," he murmured, moving to set the book back on the shelf. But then he paused, keeping it in his hands. Perhaps he should read it. It might have something to teach him, after all. He moved to the counter, setting it down, looking over his shoulder to see if the creepy cats were there. They were not, much to his relief.

Meredith appeared, waving a pristine white book with bold black lettering on it. "Got one! I didn't want to get you the frightful new version, it is filled with silly observations from people who never knew the fellow. This one is much nicer." She paused, surveying the new arrival. "And this one? Excellent choice. The author is a bit cracked, but his ideas are sound. You're taking both?"

He nodded, watching her slim fingers wrap the books efficiently. He had not bought a book in aeons, and now he had bought two. Had he found a reading hobby, perhaps? Could that be a purpose?

Matthew took the bag gingerly, thanking Meredith as he stepped away, trying not to look too closely into her eyes. Something told him that if he looked too closely, his life would never be the same.

READING MARCUS AURELIUS - AND CHANGING

Rain pounded the bus windows, making the outside bend and twist, the car lights distorted in the haze. Matthew looked out, bag clutched close, thinking. It was all he had done recently, reading his books, and thinking.

Dwell on the beauty of life, Marcus Aurelius had said. So he dwelt on that for a while. Not that there was all that much to dwell on in a grey Oxford and a greyer office.

Create with your own mind, dwell on the infinite possibilities. Was he able to do that? Were there infinite possibilities in his rather cooped up life? Did he have a purpose? What purpose could a middle-aged divorced analyst actually have? The verve and passion he had in his twenties, when all seemed possible, was spent. How could he create with his mind, and dwell on the infinite possibilities?

He looked out of the window, watching the smudge of red lights against an ink-black surface. If he shut his eyes slightly, it looked like something else, like neon spots on an oil slick or something. He quite liked it. What if it was a different world out there, a world alive with information, with possibilities? He was but a passenger in a metal box, surrounded by people going the same way. What was out there on the information highway?

His mind opened with the idea. What if he was looking at this the wrong way? He was an analyst. He studied patterns for a living. What if his cosmic consciousness was already alive and well, in patterns? He looked out again, watching the dance of neon against the slick black smudge. He could paint that. He hadn't held a paintbrush in years, but so what? He wasn't doing it to be something, he was doing it to create something. A smile carved itself out on his face, focused, proud. Yes. He would paint. He would find his purpose, and create his own infinite possibilities. He would find the pattern of the beauty of his own life.

Yes, he thought to himself, victoriously.

Yes.

Matthew hummed absently as he tapped away at the computer, flow charts and ideas flowing into his eyes as he considered the data. Part of his mind, the colourful part, as he had begun to call it, was processing it, thinking about how he could translate it into paint.

He noticed a chip of red on his fingernail and he smiled. His new obsession was growing on him.

"You sound chipper, Matt!"

Richard sounded decidedly cheerful himself, his rotund face beaming over a stiff white shirt. Matthew smiled back. "I was just thinking. It's Matthew, though. If you want me to stay chipper, call me Matthew. I prefer it."

His colleague blinked owlishly. "I don't think you've ever told me that before. Have you been gnashing your teeth at my using the wrong name for years?"

Matthew decided not to open that particular can of worms.

He turned back to the screen, letting his eyes do the work, feeding the data to his brain. It reminded him of that film, the idea that they lived one life and there was another underneath. What could he do with it? With this life? He just needed to see the beauty in it.

"How does the data look to you, Richard? When you let it flow in your brain. Do you see it in colours or something else?"

His colleague did not respond for a moment, his hands stilled over the keyboard. Matthew wondered if he should ask him again, to check if he had heard, but then as he looked over he could see something, some kind of colour, swirling around Richard's head. Matthew's eyes widened. He waited, watching the colour deepen, settle and then disappear.

"I don't think I ever expected to hear something like that from you, Matthew. You have changed, lately. I think I see data as music, it makes sense to me like that. Some is smooth and flowing, some is fast and chaotic."

Richard turned back, his eyes alight with interest. "How about you?"

Matthew looked back at the screen. "I see images, a little, but mostly sweeps of colour. I'm starting to see them everywhere, the patterns of data. I've started painting, actually."

"Oh, excellent! Are you any good?"

"No. Or, I don't think so. I'm just splashing paint onto a board, really, but I'm enjoying it."

Richard nodded, moving back to his desk. "Well perhaps you'll show me sometime. You quite surprised me today, Matthew, I'll admit. I never realised there was this much more to you."

Likewise, Matthew thought, as he saw the colour come back, this time darkening, a flourish of something that looked almost like two eyebrows frowning. Richard was deep in thought again, but this time with his face in the computer, his nose almost in the screen. How was he seeing colour? What was he seeing?

He remembered a page in the book that he had been reading.

When we look at the heavens with the purpose of understanding, we see the reflection of our own souls.

Was this what this was? As he awoke to the world of data around him, was he seeing it as if it were a painting? His hand itched, wanting to clutch his brush, to hear the gentle sound of paint being moved on the canvas. He wanted to paint this, this scene, now. Capturing it in his mind, he put it to one side, the grey, the two people, the enquiring mind. Later he would paint it. He would paint the power of it.

"The soul becomes dyed with the power of its thoughts," he whispered quietly, not knowing where it came from. Puzzled, he pulled up the internet, searching for the phrase. Had he become poetic, too? It took just a second before it returned with results, linking it to many clichéd quote sites. Someone had said it before. Marcus Aurelius. He did not recall reading that phrase before. Strange.

But it fit him, somehow. His soul was becoming dyed by the power of his thoughts. And he would paint what he saw, and give that power, too. Joy ran through him, galvanising him. No longer was he merely a middle-aged analyst. He was a seeker, a seer of his time. He would be something. He would be remembered for something. The certainty of it dazzled him. He had a purpose.

Not that far from the office building, the bookshop twitched and sighed, as if it were a cat dreaming of something. It rumbled, happily. And the black cats stood, alert, frozen in their positions, waiting.

An Artist Without a Gallery

The canvases started to stack up in the room that he had hurriedly repurposed for a painting room. He still had books in the corner, but the rest of the furniture had been emptied. What need did he have for a desk that he never used? This was much better. He looked out of the window, recreating in his head the exact image that had captured him.

His brush was his pen, loaded with the power of his thought. His nose filled with the distinct fragrance of acrylic, an almost plastic fragrance that made his nose tickle. He loved that smell, seeing the flow of the brush on the canvas, the strokes leaving impressions of his thoughts. He swept upwards with the brush, feeling the flow in his wrist, how the person had looked when they were dancing. It was not just a blur. It was two halves meeting.

He painted it, frenziedly. Shades of blue for the woman who skittered through life, mouse-like. Shades of cadmium, slicing through the palette like the citrus of its name, bold, sweeping strokes of joyful dance. Her hair had spun out, her eyes closed, as she danced, unaware of who saw her. Uncaring, perhaps, in the moment. He painted it, the rush of seeing igniting his blood.

Is that how voyeurs see the world? Is being the observer so potent?

His brush flowed, hands busy, his eyes glazed, face ecstatic, as his hand created beauty. He was the viewer, and he was the power. He was the Seer. At last, he had a purpose. Slowly, the flow took shape, creating the light and shadow that he craved, the outer and inner self of the person. He breathed out, remembering the look of joy on her face. The painting tingled, taking on the substance of the feeling. Matthew's eyes widened as he looked at the beauty, the reality of what he had created. How had he been missing out on this for so long?

He put his brush down, gently, reverently, in its allotted saucer on the side table. He would wash and dry all his brushes before bed. The art shop owner had given him instructions and he would fulfil them to the letter. But for now, he would admire the painting, the encapsulation of that moment.

"Yes," he sighed, his heart full.

Yes, sighed a bookshop, far away in the bustling lights of the city. *Yes.*

It was the first time that he had visited the shop in a while. As he pushed open the door, Matthew wondered why he had taken this long to return. What a very cheery bookshop it was! Even the bell was lovely. He really should come back more often. After all, wasn't he a creative, just like the esteemed people who had put their books on these very shelves? He was one of them. It was practically a home to him now.

The cats arrived, their eyes unblinking, as they walked slowly from the back, tails high. He shivered inwardly. Why would such a wonderful bookshop have cats? Unhygienic creatures. Resisting the urge to shoo them, he walked over to the shelves, his eyes following the call of the books. They were just very nicely arranged. He ran his fingers lightly over the covers, wishing he could paint the sensation of unyielding paper, of linen covers, and strong book spines. The cats trailed behind him, their soft paws barely making a sound on the polished wooden floor.

The smell of books mingled with the sweet aroma of fresh brewed coffee and he shut his eyes, enjoying the flavour, the atmosphere of it. Books, and coffee. This was perfect. A cover caught his eye, with a striking monochrome design. The cats watched, unblinking. Matthew looked back at them over his shoulder. What if their gaze had a deeper meaning, or a secret that they wanted to share?

He shook the thought off, with a shiver. Foreboding did not belong in a bookshop. He wandered further in, letting the colours guide him. He stopped suddenly in the corner near the stairs, seeing glossy pages, hardback covers, and famous paintings. The images were vibrant, captivating his artistic sense, and he reached out again to touch the glossy spines. Taking a book, he flipped through the pages. The pages came to life, paintings swirling, strokes of paint lifting from the paper, demonstrating the technique, blending with colours right there on the page. His jaw dropped, and he staggered, nearly letting go of the book.

The cats drew closer, circling him, brushing against his feet. Were they the guardians of creators? Perhaps he was hasty to judge them. Matthew looked down, feeling the warmth of them against his calves, and felt some kind of connection come to life. Perhaps they were there to affirm his own artistic journey. He clutched the book to his chest, feeling the power of it, desperate to look inside again. The cats looked up, startled, and scattered, leaving him alone.

"Coffee! Hello, cats! Hello, Matthew, dear! I brought coffee. I hope you like cappuccino!"

That was Meredith's voice. Matthew started, wondering if he looked like some kind of stalker, hiding amongst the shelves clutching a book. And how did she know he was here? Well he couldn't hide behind the shelves forever. Holding the book tight, as he wasn't letting that treasure go, he stepped out, smiling sheepishly. There she was, hair dressed up in some kind of clip, with her black glasses and red lipstick. She held two reusable takeaway coffee cups, one with a green lid, one with a coral one.

"There you are! I was just waiting for coffee when I saw you come in and I thought I would get you a cup. That's alright, isn't it?"

Matthew was overwhelmed by her thoughtfulness. "Yes, it is," he stammered. "Very kind."

He reached out for the cup, trying to move the book from his chest into a more inconspicuous spot, by his side, perhaps. Meredith handed it to him, eyes landing on the book. "Have you chosen something already? You are fast. You won't need me at all at this rate. What did you get?"

Matthew hesitated. He couldn't say that he found a magic book that showed him how to paint, and he didn't know what the title even was. He held it up in front of him, resisting the urge to screw up his eyes in shame. She would think him a complete buffoon. But Meredith nodded, pursing her lips as if she was impressed. "That looks great. I must say I don't know much about art. I know what I like, of course, and have had many commissions made in the past, but I have never been able to create. Is this your new passion, Matthew, do you think?"

Her tone was encouraging, interested. He exhaled in a rush, relieved. "I think it might be, Meredith, yes. I've been painting rather a lot, and it's waking me up. I feel like I can see more, the more colours I paint into the world. I don't suppose that makes any sense."

She raised her eyebrow and smiled, red lips curving up. "Oh, I think it makes all the sense in the world. Can I see any of your paintings? Have you found a gallery yet?"

"A gallery? Goodness gracious, no. I've barely managed to set up in my spare room, and I doubt any proper art people would want to look at my art!"

Matthew paused his babbling. Meredith's mouth lifted further, hazel eyes twinkling, and she laughed, a small sparkling sound that made him laugh too. "Well, as a non proper art person," she paused for a moment to laugh again, "I would happily have a look. I am sure that you are better than you think, anyway! Could you bring some in?"

"Nh, I wouldn't want to waste your time, honestly. I have taken a couple of photos though, to show my children. They weren't much interested though. I can show you those and then you can tell me what you think?"

He did want to know what she thought. Even if she pursed up that pretty mouth and told him that he was absolutely no good, he wanted to know. It wasn't like he was doing it to try and make his fortune anyway. What if he was entirely unoriginal? What then? He reached into his bag, fumbling around old papers, files and keys until he found his phone, neglected at the bottom. It was scuffed, the screen a little smudged. Matthew brought up the photos, handing it over to Meredith. "There, just scroll through those, just like that."

She nodded, absently, taking the phone carefully, her eyes fixed on the screen. Her expression was myriad, shifting from one to another. He was fascinated. His eyes flicked up to see the now customary aura when someone was thinking, but there was nothing. How strange. Was she not as absorbed as she appeared, perhaps? A stab of worry pierced his heart. Perhaps this art thing was more important to him than he had realised.

At last, she looked up, her eyes serious. "I am not an expert but I think these are very good. Can I show them to an art friend of mine? He owns a gallery just nearby, not far from the Nuffield, I believe. Perhaps I can send the photographs?"

Matthew quaked inwardly at the idea of someone seeing his scratchings. But he put on an air of artistic ennui as he agreed, directing her to the email where she could send them. She did so, deftly, with an economy of movement that Matthew could never achieve. He laboured over technology, to the amusement of his children, who often seemed to think that he came from another planet. A lesser one, probably.

She lifted her eyes up from the phone, locking the screen and passing it back. "I'll let you know what they say when they come back to me. The gallery doesn't usually open till 11 am. But do not be surprised if it's a yes! I think your style, that movement in the composition, is just what they are after."

Matthew did not know what to say. He did not dare to hope such things. Nevertheless, there was the small beginnings of excitement brimming in his belly, a tiny flame of hope. He wanted to dance, to leap, to shout. Instead, he meekly followed the bookshop owner to the front of the store to get his book scanned and bagged, ready to take home. And then he could paint again. A smile spread over his face.

Dwell on the infinite possibilities. Wasn't that what he was doing? It certainly felt like it. As he took his purchase reverently, holding it again to his chest, he was observed closely by the cats, tails high, eyes unblinking, as they watched the tableau beneath them. This time, Matthew did not shiver at the sight. He smiled.

POWER IN PAINTING

Hello Matthew, it's Meredith from the bookshop. Magali just got back to me and he wants to see all your work; or as much of it as you can bring. Could you drop by the gallery around six? I'll attach a pin of the website address. Let me know how it goes!
M x

Matthew stepped out of the taxi into a wide street, rushing with cars. The driver waited impatiently as he hustled out three canvases, leaning back in to pay the fare and add a tip. He was sweating under the jacket that he probably shouldn't have worn, but put on again at the last minute. What do you even wear to go to an art gallery, for pity's sake? Nobody taught him this stuff when he was doing Careers Guidance at school.

He looked at the smart-looking gallery with big windows, fresh paintwork and a black door. The name of the gallery was in gold lettering, gleaming at him in that obnoxious way that rich things seem to do.

Well, there was only one thing to do. He had to go in and meet this Magali. He took a deep breath, grabbing the canvases in one hand, and pushing his shoulder bag back up with the other. He could do this. He could do this. He walked forward, pushing the sleek black door open.

Inside was much as he would expect from a gallery, not that he had ever been in one. The walls were white and perfectly smooth. That was better to offset the paintings, perhaps. The ceilings were high and the light was .... perfect. It wasn't in your face, or overly bright, but every painting was subtly lit with a glow.

Whoever this gallery owner was, he knew what he was doing with light.

Matthew looked around, seeing nothing but fancy art and smart sleek wood, feeling the canvases dig into his legs. What on earth was he doing here? He wasn't art gallery material. This was ridiculous. No, he would just turn around and go home, and not visit the bookshop again. There were hundreds of bookshops around. He didn't need to go back to that one. She probably forgot, anyway. Yes, it was just fine.

Matthew turned, clutching the canvases, wishing he had asked the taxi to wait a bit. He didn't fancy lugging them to the nearest taxi rank, wherever that might be. A clack of heels and a swish of dark raven hair caught his attention. A very tall, very smart woman all in black was scrutinising him, one hand on her hip. "Are you here to see someone?"

Her tone was clear that she didn't believe he was, that she thought he had just appeared here as a gallery-less hopeful. Her eyebrow hovered, waiting to fire out the putdown, the, oh, I'm sorry, but –

"I was invited, er, I was sent here by my friend, Meredith. Meredith Smart? She said I should come by around six, that Magali wanted to see me."

The eyebrow stayed raised the entire time, hanging in the air like it was imitating a guillotine. As soon as he mentioned Magali, her expression changed, from a little hostile to surprised, perhaps. She even managed a ghost of a smile, her lips moving while the rest of the face stayed perfectly in place.

"Yes, wonderful," she sighed, sounding as if it were anything but. "I'll just call Magali for you, I am sure he is thrilled that you came by. Just, wait there, will you?"

He waited where he was put, as if he was a disobedient dog who had been out in the rain. Perhaps in this perfect aesthetic world, that was exactly what he was.

Matthew gently rested the canvases against a wooden table and placed his shoulder bag on top. He hesitated, wondering if he should take off the jacket. No, leave it on. No, off. No, on.

He sighed. This was ridiculous. Leaving the jacket on, he cast his eye around the gallery wall again, this time using his art eye, the one that saw the lights, the plumes and flashes of colour. The new lens slid into place, overlaying the usual world with something else, his Seeing, as he had begun to call it.

Not all that original, but he was going to leave the writing thing to those who could.

The first three pieces of art were beautiful, monochrome pieces of stylised snowflakes or something, arranged artfully. He got nothing from them, so he moved on. There was a rather nice dark green abstract art, framed in gold, which gave off something interesting. He paused, hearing strains of music, the sound of a kettle, and footsteps. That was interesting. Stepping closer, he looked to see if he could see those elements within the painting, but his normal seeing eyes just saw intricate brushwork and perfectly blended colours.

A painting two frames down caught his attention. It was a stormy green, with suggestions of waves and a thick texture of paint. It was like someone had taken a piece of bread and slathered the spread on so thick that it was making peaks and mountains fit for a snowboarder, if one could ever be found in these parts.

He pulled on his Seeing Eye goggles, feeling his mouth take a sharp intake of breath as the entire painting just exploded outward with colour, light and something else, some kind of cosmic movement that he did not understand. There was a great deal of depth here. The green abstract had feeling, but its feeling was akin to a puddle compared to this. This painting had towers, and glaciers, and valleys, brimming with feeling and light. He stepped closer, his hand aching to touch it.

"Ah, you have good taste. I was driven to touch this one too."

Matthew paused, hand almost at the painting, and he turned, feeling as if he was a cat burglar caught in the act. A man stood behind him, resplendent in a black tailored suit and a very sharp hot pink shirt. He was tall, muscular, and... Matthew paused as he took in his face, handsome.

Matthew had never considered himself to be anything but straight. He liked the look of women, their soft edges, their smiles. But this man was beautiful.

It struck a chord in him somewhere that threw out threads of gold, weaving, dancing. It was not lust, maybe, but something else. There was something special about this man.

Matthew was staring, but for once he didn't care. The man's hair was plaited, tucked into neat strands, hugging his face and his ears. His face was strong, with a full lip and expressive eyes. Matthew knew that he would have to paint him later. He cat-alogued his face, his expression, shamelessly. The man's mouth quirked, his eyes amused, as if he knew, but did not mind.

He put his hand out. "I'm Magali. You must be Matthew."

Matthew felt buoyant. "I am Matthew. Meredith sent me."

Magali looked into his eyes, searching, his eyes entrancing, a smile playing on his lips. "So she did. And you have some art for me?"

"I do!"

His exclamation came out almost like, I do? Matthew winced, clearing his throat. "I do, Meredith sent me. I already said that, didn't I?"

Magali smiled.

"I'm a little nervous. I'm sorry. You see, I don't really know why I'm here. I went to the bookshop and met Meredith and she advised that I find a hobby, and I started to paint, but I don't think I am good enough for this. I'm worried that I'm wasting your time."

There was a pause.

Magali did not speak, studying him, cocking his head just slightly. "You did not think you were good enough, yet, you are here. I think that is good enough for me. Come, show me your work."

Matthew obeyed, stepping back from the exquisite painting and moving towards his canvases, still stacked against the table. His hand shook as he reached for them. Was it this important? Perhaps it was. He took each canvas, placing it on the trestle table, picking up another, then the last. He stepped back, wondering if he should try to sway him with the small ones in his bag. No, let it be.

Magali looked, his tall frame powerful, leaning over the table, eyes intent. "Is this all you brought me?"

Matthew inwardly squeaked. *How did he know?*

He scrambled to the table, opening the satchel and spilling out the remainder, watching them scatter, domino-like, bumping into the others and leaving the frames askew on the table. His fingers twitched, wishing he could set them right, and make them aesthetically pleasing. It was too late. Magali was looking at them all.

Magali studied each canvas, his gaze lingering, hand hovering over the brushstrokes, as if he were following a melody that only he could hear. Matthew held his breath, awaiting Magali's judgment. The silence in the room was palpable. Magali moved from one painting to the next, his eyes intent, his face serious. Finally, he straightened up and turned to face Matthew.

"You have talent."

The statement fell like cold stones into a hot room, the meaning lifting slowly. Matthew stared, disbelieving.

"There is emotion and a unique perspective in your work. It speaks to me."

Matthew sagged, his knees feeling weak. "You really think so?"

Magali nodded, his eyes crinkling in amusement as a smile played at the edges of his mouth. "I do. Your paintings have a sense of depth, of storytelling. They have that element that will captivate the viewer. You have great potential."

Matthew smiled, his mouth reaching wider than he thought it ever had, perhaps even more than when the twins were born. This was something he had achieved, at last, despite being afraid. He had potential!

"I can offer you an opportunity," Magali continued. "I am planning an exhibition next month, and I think your art would be a perfect fit. It's a chance for you to showcase your work to a wider audience and receive recognition. I suspect your work will sell rather well."

The words echoed, around and around. His art was actually wanted? He had talent, maybe. He could be in an exhibition.

His chest swelled, as he took in a deep breath. Magali was waiting for an answer, his hand on the table, delicate bones splayed out against the wood. He looked at his canvases, the paintings that he did not dare call art. What other answer was there?

"I don't know what to say." Matthew paused. "Would yes suffice?"

Magali placed a warm hand on his shoulder, squeezing gently. "Marcia will fill out the paperwork for us. There is a fee that we pay for exhibited art, so we will need to take all your details. There is time, as I must still organise the exhibition and set up the gallery space for you. I really have a vision of this, of your work, and who I want to see it. I have such plans!"

His voice rose, ricocheting from the walls and lifting up towards the ceiling. Matthew watched him in awe. His vision shone from his face, in blazing beams of light. This was a creative man. This was a man who knew the waters of the art world and could guide him in it. Magali could be a mentor. Ideas flashed behind his eyes, of people dressed in black murmuring to each other while looking at his work, and he would stand in the corner, dapper in his suit, drinking champagne and talking to beautiful women. He could listen to the conversations, and see how they interacted, how they viewed his work. And he could then later, paint their emotions, their shock, and begin the process all over again. His breath caught.

Magali looked at him and smiled. "You see it too, Matthew. I can see this. I think this is part of a great journey for you, for us both. Consider this gallery to be your artistic home. Create art that resonates with people. And together we will explore those themes. We will light up people's lives on a level that they have never understood before. Your transformation is not yet complete. Just imagine how perfect you will be!"

Matthew took a deep breath. As he went to speak he stopped, choked with emotion. He nodded instead, putting his hand to his chest. Magali placed his hand on his shoulder, squeezing gently. "This is your home, Matthew. Now, leave these with me. Go home, and paint me some more. I will arrange your exhibition. And then you will transform."

He turned, his arms rising, his aura deepening. "You will transform!"

As his words echoed in the tall room, alive, dancing, the bookshop stirred in its sleep. And the cats watched, eyes wide, ears alert. Waiting.

AN EXHIBITION

His coffee was cold. He glanced at it, irritated for a moment, at its presence. How long had it been there, cooling while he painted? He did not know. His arm ached, and his hand was stiff. Carefully placing the brush down in its saucer, he stepped back, head to one side, inspecting the painting. This time he had painted angrily, layering on colour with a heavy hand, letting the swirls and turns lift out from the canvas. He liked it.

The white paint was stark against the black centre, and the red pulsating heart. He could feel the movement, as if the entire painting was a black hole, a vortex, waiting to swallow someone up. He reached for the cup, frowning as the cool liquid met his parched lips. "You will fit in nicely with Magali, my dear one. You, the vortex. What should I call you?"

The painting did not answer. He gulped down the coffee, eyes resting possessively on his art. He really should go and eat something, and check his emails, maybe. All he did lately was paint. And prepare for the exhibition, of course.

Magali had phoned a few times, his velvet voice wrapping its way down the phone line and into his mind, taking up residence there. The man was fascinating. Matthew hoped they would spend some time together at the gallery tonight.

His phone flashed, neglected on the side table. He picked it up carelessly, smiling at the message. Bren was going to come to the exhibition. Clearly, he had achieved some coolness at last! He briefly considered inviting Meredith too. But would it be awkward with his daughter there? Perhaps. He smiled. This was the day when he could transform.

It was evening at last, as the sky darkened a little, the Sun dying in degrees, dropping flames into the sky. Matthew was already dressed, artfully arranged in the new shirt and trousers that his daughter had picked out for him. He felt sleek, armoured. Or his body did, anyway. Inside his heart was pounding as if it were about to stop.

He got up, marched about, and sat down again, only to repeat the process. He checked the time on his phone every few seconds. Would Bren be here on time? She wouldn't be late, would she? What if they were late? Were they supposed to be late, or was that just the case in the films?

His phone flashed up, the display showing a message, and he grabbed it, feeling like a dying man in a storm. It was Bren. *5 minutes.*

Well at least she wouldn't be late. He sat back down, finger to his collar, loosening it. Did he have everything? He just needed his wallet and keys today, he didn't have to bring paperwork. Just bring yourself, and your artistic genius, Magali had said on the phone, smiling.

Matthew could tell when Magali smiled. It felt like everything in his voice lifted.

He looked back up at the dying sun and wished he could paint it. There was something sad in sunsets, as they seeped away, but they still went out with a bang, with magnificence. He could understand why people craved the golden hour to paint. It was perfect.

Bren's battered red VW pulled up outside the gate and she waved to him from the driver's seat. Matthew got up from the window, waving back. If he got millions from his art he would have to buy her a new car. How much would he be able to actually earn from his art? He had no idea. Magali's assistant had run through percentages but he got lost. He would wait till they sent him a bill. Or perhaps they just wired him money. He would find out.

As he climbed in, his daughter eyed him critically. "You look sweaty. Nervous. The shirt suits you, though."

He stammered thanks as he settled himself in, admiring how her capable hands handled the wheel, her eyes on the road. She was a sensible young woman. Perhaps all those years at university were good for her. He reined in his questions, knowing that if he asked, that small frown would reappear on her forehead and she would purse her lips slightly just like her mother did. If she wanted to share something then she did. Otherwise, her life was off-limits.

"You look nice, Bren," he managed. She did, dressed simply in a grey silk dress with a black jacket over the top. She had put her hair up and a little makeup on, some silvery stuff that made her look a little bit faerie, perhaps. She smiled and reached over, patting his hand.

"Thanks, Dad. Let's get you to the gallery in time, OK?"

"OK," he replied, knowing she wanted the peace to concentrate. She was a nervous driver like her mother, although she didn't seem to panic like her mother did. He watched the green hedges flash by as they approached the city. Is this how it was for other people, coming to the city at night to look at art and talk about mysterious things? He felt like he was at last opening the lid on life, finding something that he had missed.

Dusk drew in, and the street lights slowly winked on, dim, still. Lights in houses were welcoming beacons, signs of life in brick boxes lining the roads. Matthew wondered what they were doing, what their dreams were. He wondered what their auras were like. He sneaked a look at Bren, wondering if he could see hers, but all he could spot was a faint sparkle of light around her hairline as if she had dusted glitter there too.

The road was busy by the gallery, with cars rushing to and fro, some parking, some leaving. Bren found a spot at last, carefully wiggling the car in with her tongue sticking out of the side of her mouth. Matthew watched her, smiling. What a moment to share with her. The gallery blazed with light, the door wide open, and there were people dressed in black already inside. Were they late?

Bren looked over at him. "Don't be nervous, Dad. We're not late. Shall we?"
She held out her hand as if she was the parent, and he was the child. But he nodded, climbing out of the car and offering her his arm. Tonight was going to be perfect. He was an artist now. Nothing could stop him.

Together, they walked into the gallery. The white walls gleamed with the light that criss-crossed from the ceiling, artfully displaying Matthew's canvases. They looked incredible. Matthew gasped as he looked, his eyes wide. Bren took a breath as she squeezed his arm gently. "Dad, these look really good. Are they all yours?"

Matthew gazed around, counting his artworks, big and small, arranged perfectly. Thirty-three pieces. "Yes, love, they're all mine. Do they look alright?"

Bren laughed, her eyes on the walls. "They look alright. They look more than alright. I liked your paintings at your house, you know, but here, seeing them here, they've got something else. They look like real art! I mean, sorry, Dad, I don't mean -"

Matthew laughed. Nothing could detract from today, not even the doubt of a daughter. He glanced around to see if he could spot the striking figure of Magali, but he was nowhere to be seen. He did see a young woman with a severely short haircut, dressed in black, handing out drinks in fluted glasses. He went to take two, glad to have something to do with his hands. Bren took hers with a murmured thanks and moved away to examine the art.

Matthew was alone. He stood self-consciously, wondering how an artist should stand. Should they be humble, or arrogant? Something in between? He did not know. He wished that he could have picked someone's brains beforehand. More people filed in, looking at his art. Some hovered in front of one piece for a while, some passed them without even a cursory glance. Bren lingered a while in front of a colourful piece that was inspired by the sunflowers in the neighbour's garden.

He heard a voice at his elbow.

"Congratulations on the exhibition," the voice said. Matthew turned to see a man with dark, intense eyes and a warm smile. He looked elegant in a tailored suit, giving off an air of sophistication. He clearly belonged here.

"Oh, thank you," Matthew replied, trying to hide his nervousness. "I'm glad you could make it."

The man extended his hand. "I'm Renner, a friend of Magali. He asked me to come here today. Your work is quite impressive, I must say. It has a captivating energy."

Matthew shook his hand, feeling a rush of excitement. "I'm Matthew. It's an honour to have my art displayed here."

Renner nodded, still smiling. "The honour is mine. I can tell you put your heart and soul into these paintings. They seem to tell a story."

Matthew hesitated for a moment. Should he open up to this stranger? "Yes, they do. I've been going through some personal changes, and these paintings are a reflection of that journey."

The man raised an eyebrow. "Personal changes? Would you care to share?"

"Well, I used to paint in a more restrained, controlled manner. But lately, I've been letting my emotions guide my brushstrokes. It's been cathartic, to say the least."

Renner nodded, his brows drawing together as he thought. "Art is a powerful outlet for emotions. Your paintings evoke a sense of depth and intensity, like there's a hidden world within each canvas."

"I'm glad you see that," Matthew replied, pride spreading through him. "I've poured a lot of myself into these pieces."

Bren joined them, her eyes curious as she looked at the stranger. Renner bowed slightly as Matthew made brief introductions. "I am glad to meet you. Your father's talent runs in the family, it seems."

His daughter blushed and looked away. "Thank you, I think. I am very proud of Dad, he's been brave to come here. He is inspiring."

Renner smiled again, his mouth curving slightly while his eyes remained intense. "I agree. Bren, would you mind if I stole your father for a moment? I want to hear more about his inspiration with these pieces."

"Not at all," she murmured, stepping back. Matthew felt a jolt of anticipation. This exhibition was about him, and people wanted to know HIM. The power rose, zipping through his blood. "Which pieces do you want to see, Renner?" he asked, stepping towards the paintings. Matthew hoped that he would pick the vortex one, but the man pointed instead to a series of three, ranging from the lightest blue to the dark. "Can you talk me through these three, first?"

Matthew bowed his head in acknowledgement. "Of course." Magali appeared at the corner of his eye, looking resplendent in black and white. He waved, his eyes sparkling, and swept Bren up in conversation, walking her over to a group of young people. That was kind of him. It was as if he knew everything about people.

Matthew turned to the art, watching the man inspect the pieces with a studious air. He examined the pieces himself, trying to switch on the inner eye, but it did not seem to work for his own art. The brushstrokes stayed static, frozen in time. Matthew sighed inwardly. It would have been nice to see that.

"What inspired this particular piece, Matthew?" Renner asked, not looking at him.

Matthew paused for a moment. "I have been painting a lot from the emotions that I see around me, from other people, you know, but these were more from how I saw myself. I've been on a journey, as I said, to go deeper with my own emotions and paint them out. This set of paintings were finished over a period of time but they felt together. They felt as if they belong together."

"Hmm. They do. They certainly do." Renner remained looking, hands clasped behind his back. Matthew peeked at him, looking for the aura that people had, but he could only glimpse stars and shadows. That was odd.

"And what emotions were you feeling when you painted these?"

"Grief," Matthew answered simply. "The first is my grieving my old life, the mistakes I made. The second is grief for my own passing, the running away of time. I am only just discovering myself but it feels as if it is too late."

Matthew stopped, thinking for a moment. Silence fell.

"And the third?"

"The third is grief of the universe." His reply fell from him, from his lips, and he wondered at it. What did that mean? But Renner did not look puzzled, he just nodded and looked again, stroking his beard carefully.

"I may speak to Magali about taking some of your work for my gallery. I work overseas but I spend some time here. I think I have the perfect buyer for your Grief pieces. Do you have a name for them?"

"No, no, not these ones. I don't name most. Should they have a name, do you think? Do they sell better?"

Renner chuckled, shaking his head. "Not always. I don't think my customers will be fussy about a name. Come, I see Magali is waiting to introduce you to people." He steered Matthew back expertly, moving across the floor to a smiling Magali, his face lit up with humour and pride.

"Matthew! Ah, my prodigy. Welcome to your first Exhibition!" He wrapped an arm around Matthew's shoulders, drawing him in, close. "I have sold many of your paintings already," he said quietly, "I think you will be in great demand. Your work will be hanging in many homes by the end of tomorrow. And you seem to have impressed Renner! You should be proud of yourself."

With a free hand, he whisked two more glasses from the waitress, handing one to Matthew with a knowing glance. "Here. Drink to your art. To our partnership."

Matthew raised his glass, his eyes on Magali, who followed suit. Expressions played over his face, amusement, satisfaction, and something else that Matthew could not identify. He felt that pull, again, as he slowly drank his drink in a silent toast.

"To my transformation!" Matthew said, lifting the glass again. Magali's eyes grew darker, like ocean pools at night. "I shall indeed drink to that. To your transformation." He sounded out the syllables carefully, slowly. It felt like he was making a vow. The world felt as if it slowed, quieted, and it was just the two of them, standing in a circle of light, as the art spiralled around them.

"Is it always like this, Magali? The creation, the feeling, the power?"

Magali leaned a little closer. "It is when you have the magic, Matthew. When you create with your mind, and you feel the power of possibilities. Then it feels exactly like that. It is the ultimate feeling for people like us."

Matthew wondered what he meant, but he did not want to break the spell. He enjoyed his closeness, the warm rush from the alcohol, and the buzz of the excitement, of strangers discussing his work. His life had meaning. He had found power, of sorts. Silently, he lifted his glass again for one more toast.

To Meredith, for helping me find the way. I appreciate you.

An image of her standing in front of the bookshop formulated in his mind. He would have to go back and thank her some time, take her a painting, perhaps. Who would think that a bookshop could bring so much change? At his side, Magali laughed and waved and directed the show, and in a flowing circle, the people swirled around the art. A glorious choreography. Matthew looked on, seeing the colours and the shapes of inspiration, of the focus the art pieces had, and he itched to paint it. But for now, he let himself get caught up in the frenzy of it, and he laughed and nodded and smiled. He had found his place, now. That was all that mattered.

PAINTING WITH PURPOSE

It was a Saturday morning, and Matthew decided to spend it in the proper manner, indulging in brunch, coffee and newspapers. It felt like a suitable thing to do for an artist, and the sizeable payment he had received for his art so far made him feel buoyant enough to splash out on some luxuries for a change. He planned to speak to Bren during the week about getting her a newer car. Nothing too fancy, mind, but something a bit more up-to-date. She deserved some thanks for looking after him at the gallery.

They had both stayed till late, talking to art people and making arrangements for drinks, and more exhibitions in the future. Matthew could see a new world opening up to him, one that was full of nuance and colour. At last.

It was sunny outside. He opened the windows, laying out the food and the coffee in an elegant fashion, arranging the newspapers in a pile. He wondered if he would be in the newspaper, or the gallery at least. Wouldn't that be something? Perhaps there would be something in the local papers.

He poured out the coffee, enjoying the aroma, watching it mingle with sunshine and a lazy day. There was something about the seeing that brought an added aspect to everything he saw. He did not always want to paint it, but he loved to see it. To see something nobody else saw.

The papers were a mix of the usual happenings, the good, the bad, and the celebrity. He glanced over the airbrushed faces and stark gowns, wondering why anyone wanted to look at that, why they were interesting at all. If people wanted to find connections with people, why read about people you would never meet? It was better to meet what you know, paint what you know. But they were beautiful, he allowed. Beautiful like a sculpture or a painting that did not move.

He put them aside, thinking. Something felt off, or as if he were missing something. He had the creative outlet, he had a future selling art, he was able to help his children a little, he could work at the office less if he wanted. But he was still waiting for something. What was it?

He shook his head. Perhaps he was just lonely. Thoughts of Meredith flitted through his mind. And then of Magali, his face alight with passion. Both were intriguing people, people he could learn from. Could he be more in their lives?

He made a decision, dashing off a quick email before standing, leaving the brunch where it was, virtually untouched. He reached back and snagged the coffee flask in his hands. He could use that. His art was calling him. He would find purpose in art, and paint his feelings, and from there, he could find whatever else he wanted. If he could paint himself successful, he could paint himself into love. Or a lack of loneliness, whatever it was he wanted. He imagined the light striking from Meredith's hair, and then he thought of the deep richness of Magali's plaits, of how soft they looked. He would paint. He would draw the magic, and he would transform, just as Magali had said.

He chose the big canvas this time, his hands working mechanically. They knew what to do. He half-closed his eyes, overlaying the white canvas with the vision that he needed. Infinite possibilities. He needed to paint his dreams this time, fulfil his own hopes. He started in the middle, feverishly slathering the surface with paint, making it deeper, needing the texture, the depth. This was him, really, at his heart, a vacuum, a void, a black hole that desperately wanted to be filled, to be seen. He painted it, the dark, unheeding of the tears that fell from his face, dropping into the painting. He did not see the canvas absorb the tears, swallowing them up.

He paused, his brush hovering, wondering what it was he wanted to add, what it was he dreamed of. Did he want love, or companionship, or inspiration? What would fill the void? Magali, perhaps. He remembered his hair, his fathomless eyes, his wide smile. Unbidden, his brush began to paint oceans of gold starlight, taking the shape of a face with shadows in his eyes. That was his wish.

He dropped his hopes into the painting, one by one, and the paint thickened, swirled under his brush. This was his dance, his journey, his power. As he painted, he felt the connection between his arm, his brush, and the canvas, and he moved to the left, adding green, shadows, and a secret enchantment. This was his knowing, this was how he would achieve everything that he wanted. At last, as the sky darkened, he paused, looking at the canvas. A whirlwind of colour and shape confronted him, from the black at the core to the gold and the greens, pushing at each other. He was in the centre of it all, a vortex, a whirlpool of need.

He signed with a flourish, then stepped back. "What a man wants," he said at last. "That's what I will call you."

A breeze flew in from the open window and swirled around him, taking his wish away. As he gazed at the painting, he thought he heard a sigh, no more than a creaking of pages, a rustle of paper. And then it was gone.

Not that far away, in one of the expensive suburbs outside the city, a painting was delivered, wrapped carefully and carried into a very well-kept house. The owner, a tall woman with perfectly coiffed hair and black spectacles on a chain, anxiously directed the delivery person to where the painting was supposed to be, wringing her hands as the man deftly opened it. As the painting was revealed, her face went slack, her eyes absorbed.

"Yes, it's perfect. Hang it there, would you? Yes, just right there, I've already had the fixings put in place. Be careful, now, don't touch the surface. That's it. That's it."

The picture settled itself into place, swallowing the sun shadows from the window, glinting. The woman did not take her eyes from the painting once, not even as she thanked the man, handing him three crisp notes as a tip. She did not look up as he hurried away, slamming the door shut behind her. She did not move, not even a finger, not even a blink, as she gazed at the painting. At last, as a key jangled in the lock and the door swung open, she turned away, blinking as if she had been asleep for a long time.

She leaned in to touch the painting, reverently, then turned to climb down the stairs. "Oh, Devon, our painting has finally arrived. This new artist has done wonders! You must look at it later. And how was the office, darling?"

Her husband answered in muted tones that did not carry up the stairs, setting his things down and moving further into the house. The painting started to swirl and move, the colours shifting and glistening. The shadows in the hall began to creep, moving towards the painting. As the painting moved, the shadows curled closer, sliding into the canvas, and disappearing. And then at last the painting moved again, showing a cruel dark face in the depths of the black. The face looked out, straining against the surface, rippling. It looked to the left, to the right, and then it smiled, before disappearing again, moving back into the painting, letting the art slip back into place.

WINE AND ART

Matthew was going on a date. Or, perhaps not a date, but a drink, anyway, in a nice wine bar, with an interesting person. Did that count as a date?

He arrived early, not wanting to be considered fashionably late. The wine bar was still quiet, and he took a spot by the bar, nodding to the tall man behind the counter. He looked around, enjoying the look of the place. There was exposed brickwork, and stacks of wine bottles resting in wooden shelves set into the walls. The floor was tiled and the tables were solid oak, scattered about artfully, giving enough space for conversation without having to bump legs with strangers. It was understated, classy and not pretentious.

Matthew nodded thoughtfully. He was learning a lot more about Oxford since branching out into the art world, and he approved of it. Why go somewhere that was the same as everywhere else? This was much nicer.

The man approached, rolling his shirt sleeves up. He was tall, with short dark hair, and he was covered in tattoos. Matthew averted his eyes, not wanting to stare. But one bold, black tattoo, caught his eye. He pointed. "Nice art," he mumbled self-consciously.

The man laughed. "Thanks. I enjoy using my skin as a canvas. Can I get you something, or are you waiting for someone?" His voice was low, cultured and warm. It fit here, in the place.

"Yes, yes," Matthew began, then hesitated. "Yes, I am waiting for someone, but would it be rude to get a drink while I wait? I'm out of practice with these things."

The man winked. "No, it's not rude. Perhaps just get something small while you wait."

Matthew peered around, hoping to see a menu. "I'm not really sure what to order, I don't make a habit of coming to wine bars. Um. Can you recommend something? A beer, maybe?"

"Sure. I've got you. You just relax."

As if he could relax! He fidgeted with the corner of the beer mat, his finger pushing at the edge, wanting to worm its way through the surface of the wood. If he didn't look up, nobody would know he didn't really belong there, after all. The barman returned with a bottle of craft beer, placing it on the counter with a grin.

"This one's a local brew and quite popular. I think you'll enjoy it." He reached up, bringing a sparkling clean glass down to join the bottle. "My name's Alex, by the way. It's a pleasure to have you here."

"Thanks, Alex," Matthew replied, mustering a smile as he poured the beer. "I'm Matthew, and I appreciate the recommendation!"

Alex nodded in an affable fashion, moving off to serve a couple who had come in through the other doors. Matthew sipped his beer, glad to have something to occupy his hands. The wine bar began to fill, seats and tables being taken and conversation rising interspersed with gentle laughter and a clink of glasses. Matthew checked his watch. Magali was late. Had he changed his mind about meeting him?

The door opened, ushering a cool breeze and a fragrance of something mysterious, something wild. Matthew breathed out a sigh of relief while busying himself with his drink, trying to give off a sense of nonchalance. Magali arrived at the bar, murmuring an apology, brandishing that mysterious smile of his like a dark flame. Matthew immediately forgave him for his tardiness, feeling as if all his Christmases had arrived at once.

He looked around carefully, noticing eyes landing and resting on his friend, of people, men and women alike, giving him that speculative look. And here Matthew was, with him. With him. Magali had the wine menu in his hand, eyes focused as he read. At last, he looked over it, meeting Matthew's eye.

"Do you like wine? Shall I order for us?"

Matthew did not really drink wine at all but did not like to refuse. He nodded, relieved that he did not have to navigate the choppy menu waters of types and years of wine. Magali summoned Alex the barman effortlessly, pointing to the menu and asking for two glasses. Setting the menu down, he turned his whole body towards Matthew, resting his elbow against the bar. He was dressed perfectly, as ever, in a long grey coat, a white shirt, and grey jeans. His long hair was plaited and draped over one shoulder. A smile played over his lips as he enjoyed Matthew's scrutiny.

"So, Matthew. How are you enjoying life as an artist? Have you finished with your day job yet?"

Matthew paused, putting his beer back on the counter. "I didn't know you knew I was considering that, Magali. Did I tell you that?"

Magali laughed and waved away the question. "Perhaps. It's a logical progression, maybe, now that you are successful with commissions. You don't need to stay working at the office. There is no need to hoard the work, is there?"

"No, maybe not hoard. But I might keep a few days at the office, just to be cautious. I can build up a good nest egg and then retire earlier, perhaps. And, I like the work. I like being around people. It helps me think."

Magali watched Matthew as he traced his beard thoughtfully. "Yes, I can see that. Being around people and seeing their emotions helps you frame the pieces that you then paint. It's as if you share in their emotion and put it into the painting."

Matthew shifted a little in his seat, discomfited. "Well, maybe. I'm not sure if I'm involved in their emotion. I can see it, like it's a shape around their head. Sometimes it's different colours, or a colour I have never seen before."

He paused. "I probably sound insane, don't I?"

"Not in the least. I am glad you trusted me with that, as it means I can talk on a deeper level with you too. That was what I was hoping to do, you see, Matthew."

Matthew liked the way Magali said his name, drawing it out with intention as if he was painting the letters into the air with a brush, or tracing them onto a piece of skin with his finger. He shivered. Alex returned with the bottle, set in ice, and two glasses. He moved to open the bottle and pour, but Magali turned and smiled, reaching his hand out for the bottle.

"May I?"

Taking the bottle carefully, he poured into two glasses in a practised fashion. The bottle was plain, not giving a hint of where it was from. Magali noticed Matthew's scrutiny. "I took the liberty of ordering a nice Italian white from Piedmont, a region in Northern Italy. It's always been well known for good food and vineyards. We must visit, one day. Perhaps we shall go and see some galleries, meet some art people, and do a wine tour."

The certainty in his voice conjured images of hills and rolling vineyards, and time to paint. He could almost taste the sun and the crisp wine. He blinked, banishing the dream. He was still in Oxford, and he was still Matthew. Magali passed him a glass, his eyes sparkling. "Drink!"

From someone else that could be a command, but the rich tone of Magali's voice made it become something else, an encouragement. Matthew brought the glass to his lips, feeling dazed. He drank. Flavours bloomed on his tongue, allowing his mind to expand, to explode. The wine was cool, fresh and crisp. He tasted flowers, then something lemon, tart and full of tang, and then it mellowed, the tartness falling away to leave something nutty, yet sweet. It was a revelation in a glass.

He paused, wondering if it would be rude to drink the whole thing. Magali laughed. "I love this one too. Please, drink, and relax."

This he could do, now Magali was here with him. "Are you something of a wine expert, Magali?"

Amusement lurked in his eyes. "I would not say so, but while I have been alive, I have enjoyed wine. And the ones I love, I remember. This one is dear to me. It's a very nice wine."

He took the glass in his hand, rolling it gently between his fingers, eyes not leaving Matthew's face. His eyes shone with promise, with mystery. And that smile played over his lips as he thought, the laughter dancing up to his eyes.

"I am glad we are here, together, Matthew. It is not often that I get to bond with people past a superficial level. Many have empty heads, and visions of impossible dreams, dreams that they will never fulfil. It's stifling, you know, to be around those people.

But you, you are different, Matthew. I knew it the moment I met you, when I saw you standing in front of that painting."

He leaned closer, lowering his voice. Matthew was transfixed, wondering what he would do. He could not speak, for fear of his voice squeaking out, mouse-like. Instead, he stayed where he was, clutching his glass, listening.

"More wine? Here, have more wine." He poured, letting the flow of wine be the only sound for the moment. Matthew could hear nothing but the wine falling into the glass, see nothing but the depths of Magali's eyes.

"You see I have been waiting for you for a long time. In my culture, we believe that there are people who can see past the mundane and can create great beauty with it. I look for these people, and I fill my gallery with their work.

I only take art from the most special of people. But usually they do not know, they do not understand, how they can create such marvels with a brush. They are artists who do not see past their canvas. It is a travesty."

Magali paused, his eyes pained. "But you, Matthew. You see! It has restored my faith in people, in my purpose here, on this earth. You can see the emotions, and you place yourself within them as you paint. You leave a part of yourself on the canvas, but you also take a spark of the moment, a snapshot of it. Your work is very powerful."

Magali raised his glass and touched it lightly to the glass Matthew was holding. "Shall we drink to that? To your power?"

Matthew drank, hiding his confusion. What was his power? Did he even believe in this stuff? Perhaps he did. Perhaps this was what he had wanted to find when he had searched through churches and gospels and holy places. He had been searching for meaning.

His lips trembled as he thought about what he wanted to say. "I do not know, Magali, if I see as clearly as you say, or if I am as powerful as you think. But I must admit that these are things that I have always craved. I have always wished that there was more, a hidden meaning, that only I knew about. It feels as if I am standing on the threshold of something. If you have knowledge that you will share, then I am all in, Magali. In whatever you have to offer."

The last words fell from his lips and he wished he could take them back. Would Magali know what he meant, that he was becoming steadily more infatuated by this life, by this man? Magali's eyes darkened, his expression intent, but he did not reply. Matthew waited for a moment, and it felt as if the whole world paused with him, holding its breath.

"I have secrets, Matthew. The art in the gallery, including yours, holds a power that goes far beyond what the human eye can see. There is a hidden world where creativity has its own will, and it grows there in the unknown. I am one of its Guardians."

Matthew's mind raced. A hidden world? Through an art gallery? This was a little more, alright, a lot more, than he had expected when he arrived at the wine bar this evening. But he did not move, nor did he make his excuses and head out into the cool night. He stayed, his eyes on Magali.

Magali reached out, placing a warm hand on his. Matthew shivered, even as he felt the heat from Magali's hand burning his skin.

"You have a gift, Matthew. I want to show you more, guide you, so you can begin to unveil it in your art. I want to show you the secrets of the hidden worlds."

Matthew turned his words over, thinking. What was power if he did not reach out to take it? How could he dwell on the beauty of life if he did not seek out the hidden depths of the unknown? Magali's hand still touched his, an invitation, waiting. He took a deep breath, turning his hand so that Magali's hand rested in his palm, and he curled his fingers around it. He looked up at Magali, into his eyes. "Show me," he said, not minding the tremble in his voice. "I want to know more."

Far away the bookshop stirred, whispering to itself, even as the noise in the wine bar returned like a bubble had popped, with everyone resuming their conversations, voices ringing out in the din. Magali smiled, tilting his head slightly, ordering another bottle of wine with merely a wave of his free hand. And Matthew leaned back, feeling dazed, feeling as if the world had become something magical, just for him. This was something just for him.

That night, when he returned to his home, he barely paused to remove his jacket before heading straight for a new canvas, his hands finding paints, his eyes glazed. Mechanically, he created, fashioning an opening in the stars, a dark space that yet held so much depth, so much intensity, that you could not help but fall into it. The stars were dimmed in comparison to what lay beyond.

What must it be like to be a Guardian? What are the secrets of the hidden worlds?

His paintbrush swirled, caressing the edges, hesitantly, even as Matthew leaned, wondering what lay beyond. The paint glistened, whispering to him. *Come. Come closer. Become one of us.*

Slowly, his face moved closer, his hair melding with the canvas, his eyes closing. His nose brushed against the wet paint and he stirred, confused. *Had he had too much wine?*

Laughing to himself, he put the paints away, carefully, reverently. He looked back at the painting with a critical eye. "The Guardian," he pronounced. As he turned away, the door in the painting expanded, trembling, and the stars began to wink out, one by one.

YESTERDAY'S NEWS

He woke as the newspapers landed on the doormat with a smart thud, punctuated by brisk footsteps marching away down towards the gate. He stretched, smiling, enjoying being at home for the weekend. The last two weekends he had spent with Magali, enjoying wine and evenings on a terrace, with conversation, and laughter, and – something. He hesitated to call it love. An interlude, perhaps? He did not know. He did not have words to describe it, or how to explain it to others. He preferred to keep it himself, a quiet silent treasure.

Magali was open and direct, but there was still so more about him that he could not understand. His house was beautiful but there was something strange about it, something that made a tiny part of him afraid. Magali was too big for him. Matthew knew that. He would take whatever he was given, and when it was gone, he would paint it.

Magali had sent his apologies for this weekend, accompanied by a basket of fine delicacies that probably came straight from Harrods. Matthew resolved to tuck into them as he painted, later. He had not painted in a while, having been absorbed in the present, in his own emotions. But now, at last, he could indulge. He needed to create. He collected the papers on the way to the kitchen, starting the coffee and dropping into his seat.

His kitchen was much more modest than the one he had begun to get used to of late, and he looked around it with a critical eye. Perhaps it was time to get it renovated perhaps, bring it more in line with his aesthetic ideals. He laughed out loud at himself, and shook his head. Aesthetic ideals indeed.

He plucked his coffee from the waiting machine and drew the newspapers to him, glancing over the headlines. One was the local paper but the other two were nationals. The nationals were ranting about which political party was scheming this time, and he had no particular interest in that. Politicians schemed. That was how they were made. Perhaps he should do an art series on them, and see how their souls looked like in paint. He snickered, taking a sip of his coffee.

The local paper had an interesting headline. His eyes skimmed it and returned, slowly. The Forsyth family had been found dead in what the police were calling suspicious circumstances. The man was a local businessman and his wife was on a number of charity boards. The photos that they had used showed a handsome woman with perfectly groomed hair, standing next to a man in the kind of suit that probably cost more than his entire house. He wore it effortlessly. His smile didn't reach his eyes. *Christopher Forsyth, prominent businessman,* he read. He searched for her name, fruitlessly. Why was she called Mrs Forsyth? Ah, at the end of the article there was another mention of her. Lilibet. For some reason, it felt important to him that he knew their names.

His eyes returned to the picture, his coffee forgotten, as he stared at their faces, smiling. Behind them was a grand fireplace, and above it was one of his paintings.

"Well, it's obviously just a coincidence, Dad. I think you're getting all worked up over nothing."

Her tone was impatient as if he had reached his dotage overnight. Matthew huffed to himself, listening to his daughter's tinny voice over the phone. The newspaper stared up at him accusingly.

"Yes, Bren, I know it's just a coincidence. It was a shock, you know? I felt guilty, almost."

"What would you feel guilty for, Dad? Did you paint it with poisoned brushes or something?"

Matthew laughed. "Well, no, although I wouldn't recommend anyone started licking paint as I doubt it would be any good for them. I think you're missing my point, Bren."

His tone sounded petulant, almost whining, to his ears. She always seemed to have that effect on him, as if he were the child. "I just didn't expect to see my art in a murder scene. Do you think they'll want to talk to me? I mean my name is on the canvas."

The exasperated noise that she made was an exact copy of her mother. Matthew winced. "Why would they want to talk to you, Dad? It's just a painting. I mean I KNOW that you're doing really well and people buy your stuff, but – it isn't a crime to sell a painting. I think you are blowing this out of proportion."

Bren sighed. "I have to go, OK, Dad?"

"Ok," he responded, but she had already gone. Empty air puffed up from the phone and he looked at it sadly. Was he blowing it out of proportion? He didn't know why, but he felt responsible somehow. He glanced again at the paper and shuddered. How did they die?

He did not want to know. He picked up the paper gingerly with his fingertips and turned it over. He would throw it later. It was just a coincidence.

He wondered for a moment if he should call Magali. But what would he say? No, it was nothing to do with him. He would carry on painting and not think again of it. He left the room, making sure that he did not look at the newspaper. But he could feel it burning into his back, as it watched his footsteps. As if Lilibet were watching him. Judging. He shut the door behind him, afraid.

PAYMENT DUE

The shop looked the same as ever. Matthew stood outside for a while, hands deep in his pockets, pondering his life. Pondering his reasoning. Was he being fanciful? It was almost as if every time he arrived there, something shifted, something changed within him. Here was where his life unstuck itself, where it unravelled better. A cat jumped up onto the window ledge, eyeing him knowingly. He shivered.

"Why did you come here, Matthew?"

His own voice surprised him. It sounded different, somehow. Had he lost some of his own accent, perhaps? He had been spending a lot of time with art gallery types lately, and of course, since leaving his old job, he wasn't around any of his old colleagues. He didn't miss it. They didn't have anything in their minds but how to spend their flexi-time or who to hook up with next. Matthew wanted to talk about art, about ideas, about the world around them, and their dreams, but they didn't understand. He was right to leave, quietly, without fanfare. They had done a collection for a leaving present, of course: and he was grateful for the whiskey and the paintbrushes, even if he would never use them. It's the thought that counts.

A woman shuffled by, her head bowed, carrying her fatigue around her like it was an extra overcoat. Matthew watched her, for a moment, entranced. What colour was her ennui? He turned his head to one side, looking for the colours. For a moment there was nothing but the rain-soaked streets, the black sheen of wet-on-grey. But then the colours sprang into life, showing her lines, her storm clouds of olive green that crouched above a grey-green sea. She was a maelstrom of it, sucking it in, taking it within herself. No wonder she walked as she did. He memorised the look, his hand itching to paint it right there and then in the street. She looked up at him then, flinching slightly and mumbled something to herself as she moved away. Matthew frowned. He should not have stared.

Inside the bookshop looked inviting, and warm. The cat had gone back in somewhere, to find a better reception perhaps. Matthew took a deep breath. It was time to revisit the bookshop. He did not know why, but he knew that. He crossed the road, the tired woman forgotten, and stepped inside.

The bell rang, echoing in the vastness of the building. The bookshelves seemed to stretch into eternity, somehow. He looked around, enjoying the silence, the smell of new paper and fresh polished wood. His eyes were drawn to the back room, with its lower shelves and dim lighting. Somehow it reminded him of something. What was it? He stepped closer, and again. It beckoned him. He walked forward, his leg brushing the counter to the right of him, but the back room was still just as far away. His brow furrowed in confusion.

Had he been overdoing it? Or was there something strange about the shop? How had he not noticed it before?

His eyes snapped back to the room in front of him, the one that called him but yet still remained far away. A darkness lurked at the edges, a secret. He watched the burnt umber edges of it, the smudges of something old, something quiet. This time his hand did not ask to paint it. This was something beyond his skill to represent. This was for him to witness, not recreate or preserve.

A figure appeared, walking towards him. She was clothed in black, her hair a flame against the stark sable. Matthew watched her, recognising her yet realising that this woman was more than she seemed. At her forehead, there was a flicker, as if there was something there that was being disguised. He looked again, this time using his extra sight, and he gasped. She was taller, her hair longer, but part of her hair was piled up around her head, secured by some kind of metal that looked smoke-like. Her features were finely carved, exquisitely so, and her face was serious. Her clothes were silk, flowing, and in her hand, she carried something that he could not discern. He blinked, watching her shape shift and shudder back to the form she wore previously, her eyes piercing.

"Hello, Meredith."

Matthew wondered if he should mention what he had seen. But she merely raised her eyebrow and nodded. "Meredith will do. I am glad you arrived promptly, Matthew. I do hate to wait after a summoning."

Wait, a what? Matthew opened his mouth to ask, and then he saw the expression in her eyes, her cold eyes, as her mouth thinned, quelling his questions. He began to feel nervous, his palms moistening and his mouth going dry. Why had she summoned him?

She stepped closer, leaning casually against the counter, and placing her fingers on the surface. Her eyes never left his. "You look good, Matthew. You look different. Do you think you look different?"

"Oh, I hadn't noticed. Do I look very different?" He stifled the urge to fidget. That was his old self, not him. Perhaps he had changed more than he realised.

Meredith appraised him, her eyes narrowed. "Yes, you do. You're thinner, and your suits are better tailored. Your posture is better, too. But there is something about your face. You look different. That's all that I can say."

Matthew pondered it. Even his face? He reached into his bag, rummaging for his phone. He pulled it out, remembering that last time he had shamefacedly produced an old and battered phone, not the sleek model that he had now. He had improved himself along the way. Was that such a bad thing? He opened it, bringing up the camera. The last time he had used it, Magali had laughingly curled up around his shoulder, tucking his face in as Matthew snapped the shot. He wanted to paint the essence of it, someday. He needed to paint Magali's laughter. His look.

He stared intently at his face. His eyes looked back at him, bewildered. They were the same. But his skin was clearer, not as patchy. His hair swept back from his head in that way that only rich people seemed to achieve. His nose was perhaps a little straighter than it used to be. His chin was stronger, and he had a jawline for the first time. He looked... younger. No, not younger. He looked more, more majestic, more beautiful. He had changed. And it had nothing to do with the nicer shirt, the fashionable jacket that had been chosen for him. It was something else. He looked different.

He closed the phone and looked back at Meredith. She read his face and nodded. "It suits you, though."

Some of her edges, her hardness, had softened a little, and she looked human again. Almost, human. Matthew could still see the slight shimmer around her silhouette as if she had taken a photo and superimposed it onto herself. He knew she wasn't just the person she presented as here. He knew she was something else.

"You said you had summoned me?"

A faint, barely there smile tugged at her painted lips. She looked at him for a moment, her fingers swirling over the counter. It was as if she was thinking about what she had to say as if she were making a decision. And then, her eyebrows drew together, and the air sparked, as if that was it, the decision had landed.

"I did, or you could say, that it was time for you to be summoned. You understand, I think, that there are layers to this world that not everyone can see?"

Magali's face rose in his mind, of his mouth as it paused in its tale, telling of the wonders and secrets of the world that lay untouched, in plain sight, that nobody ever saw. He swallowed, hard, and nodded. He did not trust his voice.

Meredith continued. "You were chosen when you came here, or when you were drawn here, perhaps, is a better description. You were looking for something. The bookshop granted it to you."

She paused again, her eyes bright. She was still now, one hand draped gently across her waist. But her eyes were still hard. Watching. Matthew did not move. He waited.

"You came seeking a purpose, a power. You needed something to complete you. And now, you are powerful. Do you feel powerful, Matthew?"

He began to shrug and thought better of it rather quickly. "You know, I'm not sure if I do, Meredith. I sought power to change something in my life; this is true. And I found painting. It turns out I am very good at it. It's opened doors to me, opened up worlds that make sense to me. Does that make me powerful? I do not know. But I do feel joyful. Do you intend to take it away?"

The last words fell from his mouth, unbidden, and he raised his hand to catch them from spilling out. He was too late. The question tumbled out, beseeching, and fell to his knees, disappearing in the echo of his shock.

Meredith watched, her cool eyes following the words, and tracking back to his face, his exposed shame, his fear. She did not smile.

"Gifts should never be taken away. It would be considered bad form. But I do ask for something, Matthew. It is within your hands, a trifle of a matter, really. I would like to see the influence of the bookshop spread, so that people can share in its gifts alike. I work hard, but I am only one person. Perhaps you could assist?"

It all seemed very reasonable. He felt moved to agree, to offer to help, but something small in the back of his mind urged caution. Nothing was what it seemed, today. "I would like to help, Meredith. The bookshop has helped me in ways I could not imagine. What does seeing the influence of the bookshop spread involve, exactly?"

The air around him shifted, and Meredith straightened, removing her hand from the counter. Her expression was serious, even earnest.

"Seeing the influence of the bookshop spread involves more than just a physical expansion. It's about fostering a community, igniting a love for literature and knowledge, and creating a haven for those seeking something in the written word. It's about bringing people together, providing them with the means to explore new ideas and perspectives, and encouraging a sense of wonder and curiosity."

She paused, allowing her words to sink in before continuing. "You have a gift, Matthew, not just in your art but in your ability to connect with others. Joy is infectious, and your passion for creativity is evident. If you could use your talents to help the bookshop become more than just a place for books, but a hub for intellectual and emotional growth, that would be a tremendous contribution."

He thought about her words, sifting them for a deeper meaning. Could it be that she simply needed him to be a beacon for the shop now that he had achieved his own platform? He could certainly do that. "I am happy, of course, to help. But I am an artist, not a writer. I do not know if I can reach the people who would want to come to the bookshop, but I can try. If that is worth something?"

Meredith stepped away, reaching for a book on the nearest bookshelf and turned, holding it in her hands. She took a breath and then waited for a moment, weighing her words. Matthew's feelings of unease intensified. "We also need to protect the bookshop's legacy, Matthew. It holds secrets and treasures that must be guarded. You can ensure that the right people find the bookshop, and the wrong people stay away. This may require some discretion. It may require you dealing with those who misuse the shop's gifts."

"May I ask how I would deal with those who misuse the gifts, Meredith?"

Meredith laughed. "You don't need to worry about that yet. For now, I want you to do what you have been doing: painting and creating beauty. I want you to focus on finding people's wants and desires, and paint those into being. And perhaps when you do interviews, now you are a rising artist, you can reference this bookshop as your inspiration."

Matthew nodded in relief. "I can certainly do that, Meredith. I was starting to worry that you would want me to start manhandling bad customers!"

She laughed, putting the book back carefully. "Oh, no, Matthew, I wouldn't ask you to do that. But do know that you might have to make hard decisions for the sake of your art."

Matthew glanced at her sharply. What did she mean? Meredith smiled again, her eyes remaining cold. "There's always a payment due, Matthew. You'll work out what's more important to you in the end."

"A cost? What do I owe?" A thread of panic worked through his voice, making it waver. The air felt thick and cold. Waiting.

"Every gift has a price, Matthew. The more you step into this world of mysteries, the more you will understand. As you make choices, your choices define your path. But as long as you intend to protect the Bookshop, protect its treasures, you will not go wrong. But please, do not concern yourself now. Paint people's desires. Paint your own. And spread the word. That will be enough, for now."

She nodded to him in quiet dismissal, and Matthew turned to leave, his head awhirl with foreboding and fear. What would he need to pay? Why did Meredith want him to paint people's feelings? He thought again of the newspaper, of the painting, of the woman called Lilibet, dead, a stranger that had somehow touched him. No, that was ridiculous. That was nothing to do with him.

He would talk to Magali and see if he could tell him more. As he stepped out of the bookshop, the door closing behind him, he wondered again what he would be expected to pay. And if he would be able to pay the price that she would exact.

BETRAYAL

"So, what did she say, exactly?"

Magali was perfect, as usual. He ushered him in, sitting down in front of him with a studied air. He went there straight from the bookshop visit, worried that he had bitten off more than he could chew. Already, Magali's calm presence had soothed him. He wished he could reach out and touch his hands, or step into his body, claim some of his confidence as his own, but Magali just looked perfect, there in his linen top and pants, his hair tied loosely, his beard beginning to grow. He was perfect. He did not dare to muss him, to change him.

Matthew let his fingers drop into his lap, only reaching for the tea that Magali had poured. Tea for the nerves. His eyes were on him now, concern brimming in the depths. Matthew picked up the teacup, feeling his hands shake slightly as he tried to hold the delicate cup. His fingers were fat, swollen with fear. Or was it greed? If he had taken something from the Bookshop, should he not pay it back? Was that not reasonable? Why did he feel rattled about it?

"Well, she was different to normal, I can tell you that. She said that I was summoned today, and that I have to pay something back for what the bookshop gave me. And, honestly, Magali, on one level she sounded normal, but on the other, she sounded scary. She definitely meant stuff that she wasn't saying. She said -"

He paused, sipping his tea. Magali leaned forward, resting his chin delicately on his steepled fingers, balancing his elbows on his knees. His eyes were meditative, clear. Matthew could drown in those eyes and he would not regret a thing.

"I'm sorry. She said that I would have to make hard decisions for the sake of my art, that I had to give the bookshop something. I already said that, didn't I? She mentioned the mysteries. Is she a Guardian, too?"

Magali looked into the distance, his eyes narrowing contemplatively. "No, Meredith is not a Guardian but she is something similar. But she does understand the world that I have described to you. And the Bookshop is a hub for mysteries, but in a different way to your talent, it is about knowledge, secrets, not capturing emotions. You see more clearly, I think. You have a skill that the world needs for the future. I think Meredith is more of a Protector of the past. Of the old ways."

He smiled, gently. "You do not need to worry. Whatever she asks you to do, it will be enough. And if it is too high a price, I will simply intercede for you. After all, I want you here. I shall be selfish!"

Matthew laughed, feeling somewhat reassured. Of course, it wouldn't be a high price or more than he could pay; he was just being dramatic. Settling back into his chair, he looked around at the room, enjoying the space, the calm.

The newspaper article shot back into his mind, startling him, and he sat bolt upright, spilling his tea into his lap. Magali reacted slowly, raising his eyebrow and grasping a napkin to mop up the pooling damp on Matthew's pants, face openly curious.

"Did you forget you had to be somewhere? Did you get a better deal? Or did a painting call you?"

"Perhaps the latter! I just remembered. I saw one of my paintings in the newspaper only a few days ago. When you were away. No, no, not in a good way," Matthew blurted out, seeing Magali smile and move to congratulate him. "I saw it in a murder scene. In an article about a murder scene."

"What do you mean, Matthew?"

"I mean that a couple were murdered in very strange and brutal circumstances, and there was one of my artworks on the wall. I know it's a coincidence, but -"

"Oh, that happens sometimes." His tone was nonchalant, careless. Matthew felt cold. He looked up, hesitant. Did he mishear him? Magali was empathic, caring. Did he just say that? His question was unspoken, but Magali responded to it, his brow furrowing. "Art and pain go hand in hand, Matthew. When you use your emotions and paint it, that is potent. Sometimes it attracts darker things. People who buy art, they are seeking something. A release from pain. You see?"

Matthew pondered his words, wishing that Magali would sit closer and reassure him that he was just being very silly. But he did not. He sat, waiting, his eyes agleam with interest. Waiting for Matthew to understand, perhaps.

"What is the bookshop, Magali?"

As his mouth issued the words, his brain was on its knees, begging silently that Magali would not know what he meant, would not open up another conversation about this mysterious world. But his eyes watched Magali, who paused, stroking his beard thoughtfully, and he wanted to cry. He did know. It was something.

"That's a good question, Matthew, and I am not sure if you are ready for the answer. Meredith is, as you know, a Guardian of sorts, but not in the way that I am. She is a Protector. Did you ever notice anything strange or out of place in the bookshop?"

Matthew started again, cursing his openness. He was like a young boy around this man. Every expression was a sonnet, every sigh was a verse. And it was there for Magali to read so easily.

"Ah, you have. The Bookshop is more than just a building, it is a conduit for something. It is alive, you could say. It gathers wisdom, it attracts seekers. But at its heart, it is rageful, it is hungry."

"Wait, wait. Are you saying that it is alive? The Bookshop is alive?"

Matthew began to laugh. But Magali just nodded. "After a fashion, yes, it is. It is old, certainly, not as old as some of us, but it has been alive for a long time. I do not know where it originated from, but I would think that it was born from a collective event, one that wiped out great wisdom and many lives. And their purpose gave birth to what is the Bookshop."

His eyes hurt. He put his fingers up to rub them, feeling dizzy. This was too much. How could Magali speak casually about something like this? It didn't make sense. Nothing made sense. But Matthew knew what he saw when he painted, and that was not of this world. What was happening to him?

Matthew made a move to stand, then sat down again. His legs were like jelly. Magali moved to sit nearer, but Matthew put his hand out, warning him away. "No. Tell me about how this links to the paintings. It does, doesn't it? Tell me everything, Magali."

Magali paused. "You are definitely not ready for this answer, Matthew. Can you not just not ask, and we'll have tea, and enjoy our day? Must you ask questions that you are not able to hear the answer to?"

"I need to know." His answer came out in a whisper. He felt like he was drowning, somehow.

"You are the link to the paintings, Matthew." Magali's words came out in a sigh. "Where did your skill come from? It did not come from you. You didn't grow it. You probably had the talent lying dormant in your brain, but you did not take the years to finesse it. How many books did you read about art before you produced the masterpieces that you do? Do you know how many artists are out there studying and bleeding for their craft who would give up a kidney for the talent and skill that you have? And you got it overnight. Without any effort. And then Meredith put you in touch with the right gallery owner, who catapulted you into a comfortable lifestyle doing your painting. Do you think that is normal? Do you think that you earned that?"

Matthew closed his eyes. He was right; he was right about all of it. But it did not help the rage that rose. Did he not paint the paintings? Was he not to take credit for a thing?

"So, are you saying that this is not real, that the bookshop granted me a mystical power, and that I am not an artist at all?"

He felt Magali's touch, just a brush of the fingertips, before he withdrew. "Even if the bookshop had granted you the talent as well as the skill, it would still be real. You paint. You are still an artist."

Matthew did not open his eyes, but he extended his hand, reaching, finding Magali's hand, and he squeezed, once, hard, in thanks. Magali squeezed back. He understood.

"If I am right in what you are saying, the Bookshop opened a talent in me that I did not know existed, and that is why I see the emotions in people, and I can paint them. And this is the gift that was bestowed upon me."

He paused, rubbing his chin. He felt nauseous. If one was true, then his other, darker fear could also be true. Could he be -

He cut off the thought.

"And now the Bookshop wants something back? Am I right in thinking that? This all-powerful being cannot do anything without interfering in humans' lives and then demanding something back?"

Magali arrived in a whisper, moving close, his arm enveloping him. "Hush. If the Bookshop demands something, I will get involved. You did not ask to get entangled and I will intercede."

Matthew leaned in, needing to smell his scent, his unique fragrance. He kept his eyes closed. "What more could the Bookshop demand, Magali? Did it kill those people?"

He felt the sigh, the breathing out, and it broke his spirit even before Magali replied. "It's how it lives, Matthew. It needs those people and their emotions. It acts to survive, just like everyone else."

Matthew stood, blindly, his head swimming. "I need – I need a moment, Magali. I need some air." His hands warded him off, mapped out his distance, the space that he needed. He heard Magali sigh as he stood, stepping back. "Of course. Have a moment."

He stepped away, his quiet steps barely audible in the thick carpet. "Wait."

Magali paused. "Yes?"

"You said – not as old as some of us. That the Bookshop is old, but not as old as some of us."

Silence fell for a long moment. Magali spoke again, more quietly this time. "Yes."

Yes. The word weighed on him. Yes. Was everything a lie? Matthew opened his mouth to ask and then closed it again. That was one truth he certainly could not handle. He kept his trembling mouth closed as he stood in a pool of silence, listening to Magali quietly leave the room.

CHOOSING

Matthew left Magali early, not wanting to let him know what his intention was, not wanting to ask him for help. He knew Magali would, that he would have gone with him, represented him, not let him fail. Even with all the things that had not been said, the secrets, the untruths, he would have come to save him.

Was that love? He did not know. But he did know that he had to face the bookshop alone.

The door faced him, innocuous, almost nondescript. It certainly did not look like a sentient being, a force for evil. No cats showed this time, marring the quiet vista of windows and glass and books. But yet he was reluctant to open the door, hear the ring of the bell, and face his fate.

"Yet I must. Courage, Matthew." He would need it.

He pushed open the door. If he could do nothing else now, he could do it with conviction. The bookshop was quiet, and cold. By rights it should not even be open, as it was late at night, but Matthew knew better now. The Bookshop was always open for the seekers, the flotsam and jetsam, the ones who needed something from life. It was a world between worlds, not a shop.

Matthew stepped between the bookshelves, resisting the urge to touch the books, to pick them up, and imbue his scent into them. Nobody needed to know that he, Matthew, was there on this day. But a part of him did, resisted, mourned that he would be so easily forgotten. Would Bren forget him, or Magali? He wondered which would hurt more. Bren would not notice his absence. She was capable, very like her mother, tolerating his awkward presence. Magali did not need him. He was perhaps an amusement at best. It was better, maybe, that he disappeared quietly now.

He walked closer to the centre, fingers absently tracing the spines of books, breathing in the air. His reckoning would come soon enough. He did not have to call for it.

It did not take long. Meredith appeared from the back, almost as if she were just checking something, and greeted him warmly.

"Oh, Matthew! It is lovely to see you again. And so soon! How is the world of Art treating you?"

It was as if their entire last conversation was erased. Matthew answered in the same light manner, surprised that he could even emulate it. "Yes, it's very good, thank you, Meredith. Magali has been –" he paused, choking on his words. What could he say? "Magali has been kind."

Meredith smiled, her mouth curving even as her eyes remained flat, fixed on her prey. "He is known for that, I understand. And what can I do for you, Matthew? Have you had more thoughts about how to best support this literary cause?"

This was his moment. He could expose the shop and stop the force behind it. He faltered, looking around the shop, wondering. How did it come to this?

Can you hear me? Are you real?

Hardly had he thought the words when he felt the air quiver around him.

Yes.

Matthew felt the panic rising. Was he talking with a bookshop? But it had answered. It was real. It was alive. And now he had to do what he had come here to do.

But what should he do? He needed to be a good man. The certainty hit him as if an express train had driven through his ribs. He would have smiled, if his mouth had allowed it.

"I have thought about this, Meredith. And I would like to support you and The Black Cat Bookshop."

She didn't smile this time. But she moved closer, her eyes unwavering. "This is wonderful news, Matthew. We need that kind of support." She paused for a moment. "And what did you think you could offer to support us?"

Her eyes were unblinking, green, hypnotic. He stared into them, wishing that he could see something, some emotion, in their depths. It would make his next step easier.

"I am not an activist, Meredith. I cannot go to bat for a cause. My intellect might be willing but my body is not. Yet, I do not think that the bookshop needs me to fight for it. I think that the bookshop needs something else."

Meredith moved closer again. "What do you think the bookshop might need, Matthew?"

"I think it needs death. Sorrow. Terror. Souls."

Each word fell from his mouth, heavy with judgement, seeped with terror. She watched them fall, expressionless. She raised her chin and waited.

"How many has the shop taken from my paintings so far, Meredith?"

She blinked, lizard-like, and then stirred. "Let me see. I think just two, to date. Perhaps three. Your meteoric rise took a lot of energy, after all, and it gets hungry. But I am sure it will slow down now. It tends to get greedy then hibernates for a while. I would think that if you keep painting, and if you find suitable patrons for the Bookshop, that you might be able to avoid all – future unpleasantness of that sort."

Matthew felt confused. His mouth was slow to form the words, his brain spinning. "What kind of suitable patrons do you mean?"

Meredith cocked her head to one side and regarded him. "Well, it's quite simple, Matthew. The bookshop needs to be sated in order to spread good in the world. And it does get hungry. The more people you can bring to the shop as patrons who can realise their dreams, the better. And if you find people who are a threat to those dreams, people who lie, or cheat, or steal, you can offer them a visit here. We will look after them."

"Do you mean that you expect me to find you victims? Can you not do that by yourself?"

She raised her eyebrow archly. "That sounded rather rude, Matthew. I would be careful. I do not like rudeness. I said patrons, not victims. But we can use either word if we must.

These are your terms. You will continue to rise as an artist and reach critical acclaim. You can spend the rest of your life with Magali if you wish, and make enough money from your paintings to have a very comfortable life. You will be a public supporter of the literary arts and recommend this little enterprise often. And we will never have to speak of this again."

As Matthew listened, the image built in his head, dreamlike. He could travel and paint as he visited different cities in Europe, with Magali by his side. There he was, tootling down Italian roads, beeping his horn, stopping off at vineyards to drink wine, eat good food and paint. And all he had to do was find patrons who would find some joy in their lives before – no. He shut the thought down. The dream collapsed into bitter black smoke.

"I am sorry, Meredith. I cannot accept this offer."

For a fraction of a moment, her mask slipped as the overlay moved, showing her true self underneath. He felt the crash of steel and smelt an acrid tang of fire. He heard faint screams from far away. And then she was back, Meredith, with cold eyes and a set mouth.

"That is disappointing."

She turned on her heel and walked away into the back room, disappearing among the stacks. Matthew waited, feeling helpless, wondering if that was it. Should he leave? The room was darker now, with shadows pooling in the corners. One by one, the cats appeared, marching to a beat that he could not hear. They gathered in a line and then turned, eyes on him. They were inky shadows with fluorescent eyes, smudges of black against the gloom. Matthew knew they were there to witness something. His heart hammered in his chest, making him dizzy.

"Right, here we are." Meredith's voice spoke right next to him, making Matthew jump with a start. She was wearing her glasses on the end of her nose and had a stack of papers in her hands. "I need you to read and sign all these, Matthew."

As he stared at the papers, bewildered, he realised there was a pen in between his fingers, and his hand was moving towards the page, resolute.

"Wait!"

Meredith looked back at him, eyebrows raised. "What is it, Matthew?"

"Well, you can't just expect me to sign something before I know what it is. What is it for?"

She huffed. "I did say read and sign. Obviously, you have to sign with full knowledge of what you are doing. What a ridiculous concept. This is your bill and payment plan. You have two options. You must either agree to sign the debt on to someone else, which will be one of your descendants, or more than one, who will be expected to pay your debt. How they pay will not be up to you.

Or you can choose to give yourself up as payment. But you will have to pay, either way."

She waved to the papers. "What will it be, Matthew?"

His hand moved closer to the paper, the pen straining in his hand. He had no choice. The debt would be assigned either to him or one of his children, the grandchildren he did not even have. Could he condemn them to that? Could he live with that? Sweat trickled down his back and his heart pounded harder. His eyes burned with tears. She was watching, her face expressionless, her eyes gems of green glass.

"It will be me." His words whispered out, wrenched from his body. He felt wrung dry, defeated. His hand reached the paper and signed his name with a flourish that was not his. He supposed that it did not matter.

Meredith plucked the pen from his numb fingers and swept the papers away. "Excellent," she said. "At last, we have reached a solution. What a shame you had to get so... difficult about it for a while. But there we are. Come along."

His legs began to move, robot-like, and he staggered along behind her as she walked, her back straight, arms crossed in front of her. They passed the counter, where the papers sat, his signature gleaming wet in the dark. It looked like blood. And then they were surrounded by the smell of dusty paper, shelves and old books. The air was damp and chill, and he could hear the bookshop breathe.

Matthew. Matthew.

The echo slipped into his ears and lodged itself in his skull. His breath came out in small pants, leaving curls of mist. Meredith turned and surveyed him for a moment. "You will remain here, Matthew. Your price will be paid as long as you live, here in the Bookshop. You are charged with being a Guardian, of keeping the secrets safe. Do you understand?"

He nodded, too afraid to even speak. But she did not need to hear him reply. She turned around again, reaching for something on a shelf. "It was nice knowing you, Matthew. Such a shame it didn't work out."

His blood was roaring inside his head, getting louder and louder. Matthew shut his eyes, breathing faster, as the world started to spin. Pain radiated from his heart, bursting outwards in spikes of light, round, and round, and round. Faintly, he felt the rough surface of the ground as he fell to his knees.

"I'm sorry," he whispered. He watched the words float up and fly away. He hoped they would get to whoever they were meant for. For all they were meant for. The fire spread, his body aflame. He arched his back and bared his throat, gasping. The floor lurched, tilted, swallowing him up, as he fell backwards, eyes wide, sightless. It was finished.

MAGALI

"I want to see him."

"I'm sorry, you can't. He's indisposed."

Magali bristled, energy crackling around him like a dark flame. "Don't test me. I am not pleased with this development. You gave him to me."

Meredith faced him head on, chin raised, unafraid. "I did no such thing. Just because you got fond of your artistic plaything, does not mean you got prior rights. He had claimed his powers and he had to pay. If you had convinced him better, perhaps he would still be here."

Magali breathed out hard through his nose, shutting his eyes. "This has gone too far, Meredith. You can't just snatch people from the street. People will miss him. He has a family!" Shaking his head, he put his hand on the counter, leaning forward. "I want to see the paperwork."

Meredith laughed. "Your higher-ups aren't going to interfere on your behalf, Magali. My paperwork is watertight, and you know it. I know you are angry, and I know that you've lost a good artist. I'll send you the next visionary that I receive. Perhaps that one won't be so damn moralistic. I really did have high hopes for Matthew."

Patting his arm, she spoke again, gently. "I know you liked him, Magali. I think he liked you too, for what it's worth. It's hard when we get attached to them. It makes us feel young again."

Magali shook his head, the silver in his hair glinting in the light. "It was more than that. He had such an understanding of people, of emotions. I think that with time, he could have unlocked many secrets. He was the key. His art really made people feel something. And he was a good man. Just because I am what I am, do not think that I do not recognise a good man. That is what he was. You should stick to your thieves and cheats, the ones who actually deserve to be broken. There are few enough good people in this wretched world, Meredith."

Meredith listened, unmoved. Magali stepped away, his eyes flashing. "I suppose it is too much to expect a god of the underworld to understand morality. Know this, crone. You have crossed me, and I will not forget it."

The air quivered and the bookshelves began to rattle. Some of the books stirred, their pages whirring. Meredith looked round, and then back to Magali. "It doesn't like it when you are rude. And you don't want it to be angry when it has your little pet, do you?" Her words were saccharine sweet, mocking. Magali's eyes burned red with pent-up rage. But he said no more as he slammed his fist down, once, hard, and then stepped away.

"You win this time, Meredith. But I will not forget." He turned on his heel, walking away. Slowly, the books returned to their quiet repose, pages stilling. And all around, in the corners, in the shadows, the black cat guardians watched, eyes unblinking.

HE'S NEW

Siobhan spotted the bookshop across the road and sighed in relief. That saved her a trip on the bus into town to get a book for her friend Vicky's birthday, and she would be supporting a local business. too! She started to cross the road, eyeing the smart sign over the door and the big double-fronted windows. How long had this been here? She was sure she hadn't noticed it last week. But that was the way of things around there. Shops popped up in a jiffy as if they could move themselves in.

Siobhan jumped, startled, when a black cat jumped down from one of the bookcases, walking along at the bottom of the window. Cats! Heavenly! She would come here again.

She pushed the door open, hearing a welcoming ding of the bell. The cat walked around her legs, tail high, purring. She spotted another black cat in the corner, sitting by the shelves, pale eyes staring. "Hey, puss," she whispered. "Come and say hi."

The cat didn't move from his spot. "He's new, I'm afraid. He isn't quite used to people yet." A voice came from her left, and Siobhan looked over, startled. The voice belonged to a woman with long red hair and black spectacles. She looked like a bookshop person. Siobhan liked her instantly. She always had a good eye for people.

"Oh, is he new to living in a bookstore?" she asked, looking over at the cat.

"Who, Matthew? That too," the woman replied. "He's new to being a cat."

Siobhan laughed, and the woman smiled. "I'm Meredith Smart, owner of the Black Cat Bookshop. Or, Curator, you could say. Sometimes, the books own me! Now, what can I do for you today?"

DEATH BY PAPERCUT

Chris looked up, watching Mick try and climb through the window but fail. Stupid prat. Why did he always want to do the tricky bit when he was so fucking useless? He shook his head, resisting the urge to yell at him. It was a quiet area with very few houses but you never knew if a copper was walking about. There was no point pushing their luck. At last, he heard the click of the window, and the idiot climbed in, legs flailing. He looked like some kind of demented grasshopper, getting in like that. What a prat.

Sighing, he threw his cigarette to the ground, stamping it out with his foot. He eyed the drainpipe, considering if it would hold his weight. It looked sturdy, not some kind of plastic for a change. He climbed, slowly, until he reached the low roof that led up to the windows. He saw a shape behind the curtain, an arm reaching through and then the big window creaked open, with Mick's grinning face behind it. "Hurry up then," he said, as if he hadn't been the one to cause all the damn delays. Chris grunted in response as he climbed in, his eyes adjusting to the dark. The room was empty, with just a table, a chair, and two filing cabinets pushed against the wall. There was a dim light downstairs, and he headed straight for it. "So, where do we start, Chris?"

"You go straight to the till. Get whatever is in there. I'm going to look for any valuable books and see if there's a safe or anything. Alright?"

"Alright," Mick replied, as he bounced down the stairs like an excitable puppy. Chris shook his head again. He really needed to find someone more sensible to do these jobs with. Mick would get him in serious trouble one day. Following his idiot cousin down the stairs, Chris looked around, assessing the shop. It was new, obviously, and nicely ordered. Out in the front, where the lights were on, were the normal books, all shiny and new. He wasn't interested in those. They weren't going to bring him anything.

Mick was already behind the counter, fiddling with the till. That would keep him occupied for a bit, although he suspected a shop like this probably took more card payments than anything else.

He stepped into the back, almost tripping over a small step down. He felt eyes boring into his back. He turned around slowly. Two cats sat on the bookshelves, eyes unblinking, staring at him. He hated cats.

"Shoo!" he growled, taking a step towards them. They did not move. Well, let them stare, he thought, as he turned back to the back room. He was here for more important things. He recalled the interview that he had seen on TV about the Roman documents that this shop had copies of or something. Why a bookshop in Oxford would have rare papers, he did not know. Didn't they belong in a museum? But that wasn't his problem. The news chap had said they were worth a small fortune. He wanted a piece of that. A small fortune. A grin touched his mouth as he stepped further into the back of the store. It smelled funny in here. It was cold, too, and not as pretty as out the front. He shivered a bit.

"Hey Mick, are you done yet?"

There was no answer. The fool was probably fussing the damn felines or something. Or looking for porn on the bookshelves. Erotica, or whatever they called it nowadays. He rolled his eyes. So, where would a person keep priceless documents that are thousands of years old? He scanned the room. The ceiling was low and the room looked as if it was made of brick, maybe. There were more shelves here, making up passageways that stretched outwards, but they were not labelled. It was bigger than he expected in here. He stepped further in, walking down one of the book aisles and looking to his right. There was another room down there, with a narrow doorway and what looked like... glass cabinets, maybe. That must be where they keep the expensive books!

"Hey Mick! Come and see this!"

There was silence. He felt a chill of something, worry, perhaps. Had that imbecile gone and left him behind? Chris turned, wondering if he should go find him.

Nah, he'll just text him.

Chris pulled his phone out from his jacket pocket.

Bloody Nora. No reception. Of course.

It was getting colder in here. He shivered.

Let's just get the valuable book and get out of here.

He put his phone away and walked towards the room. This room was tiny, just one square with those strip lights that you see in old buildings. There were cabinets with documents and big books that looked old inside them. The cabinets were locked. But that was to be expected, of course. He could pick a cabinet or two. He leaned over, peering at the writing. He could hardly read it. Was this the Roman one or was it something else?

Chris dug into his back pocket, looking for his tools. Finding them, he pulled them out and started to fiddle with the lock.

What was that noise? He paused. It was some kind of thudding, some kind of weird vibration in the walls. What was that?

"Hey Mick, can you hear that?" he called. His words fell like stones around him. The room was getting warmer now; he could feel himself getting too hot in his jacket. He did not like this one bit. Feeling his heart start to race, he decided that he would just get the money from the till and send Mick in for the book next time, now he knew where it was. He went to step out of the room, and then he paused. The books were gone. The big room was gone. All that was in front of him were tunnels, tunnels of solid rock.

"What the fuck," he breathed, his voice just a whisper. He was scared now. "It's just a dream, you dick, or you're tired, alright? Just walk the way you came and then you can get out of this weird shop once and for all. Mick! Where are you?"

The noise was louder. It sounded like a rhythmic bumping, a beating. Like a heartbeat. He walked faster. He could hear his own breathing, his heart pounding in his chest. The noise got louder, quicker. It sounded as if he was inside a drum, the sound assaulting his ears. *Mine,* he heard.

You.... Are .... Mine...

Right, that was it. He was done with this place. It was time to fuck off out of there. He broke into a run, blindly racing forward, a long-forgotten prayer rising to his lips. He could feel the sweat pooling under his arms, and his legs began to ache. How big was this place? He could hear sobs coming from somewhere ahead of him, sobs interspersed with ragged breath, and he ran towards it. "Mick!" he shouted in desperation. "Mick!"

The tunnel was getting narrower. He ran faster, panicked. What was this place? The ground under his feet was sandy, the walls a dark stone. He found himself slowing, fascinated by it, despite himself. His hands reached out to touch the tunnel wall. It was warm. He could feel the stone pulsing under his fingertips. It was as if it was.... alive. The thought came to him and his blood stilled, terror overcoming him. The walls shivered, climbing closer, claiming him. *Yes....* the voice whispered. *Yes.... Mine...*

Chris wet his lips, his throat dry. "No," he rasped. "Help me..."

But nobody answered him. The walls curled around him, embracing Chris as he screamed again and again, the walls sighing with delight, heartbeat racing, as it constricted, bones cracking, crumbling. Blood seeped to the ground, black and wet, thick. And slowly the blood ran towards the walls, absorbed into the stone. The heartbeat slowed, and the whisper came again.

Yes... it breathed. *Yes...*

Mick made short work of the cash register but it was empty. Of course it was. Chris always took the good jobs; it was like he thought he was better, just because he was older. He would show him one day. He had plans to hit the factory with some of his mates next weekend, Chris would be mad as a bag of snakes when he saw what he missed out on. He shut the cash register and leaned against the counter for a moment. Chris had gone very quiet in the back. What was he doing in there anyway?

"What you doing, Chris mate?"

Chris didn't reply. That was weird. He stepped out into the back room, shivering for a second. They really needed to heat this place better. He called out again. "Chris?" There was no answer. "Come on, mate, don't take the piss. This place is giving me the creeps all of a sudden. Where are you?"

The room just echoed. He looked around, not wanting to go in further. It wasn't big in the back, just the extra storage shelves, some unopened boxes in the corner and a small door marked WC. Maybe he went for a shit. Mick laughed to himself. Turning back, he saw a line of black cats sitting so still, staring at him. Alright, that was creepy too.

"Be off with you, mogs," he called out a little unsteadily. They ignored him. Mick stepped around them, giving them a wide berth and looked up longingly at the stairs, at the way out. He looked back at the door to the toilet, the empty room. Where had Chris got to? The cats still stared at him. But now they were closer. He hadn't seen them move. This was getting seriously creepy. He started to walk sideways towards the stairs, eyes on the cats.

They watched him. He watched them. His hand reached the metal stair rail, and he sighed in relief. He would go back out and call Chris from outside. Or wait for him or something. Have a cigarette.

The cats were in front of him. Still staring, in a line, barricading his route. Mick felt the hair on the back of his neck stand on end. There was something seriously fucking weird about this place and he did not like it one bit.

"They're just cats," Mick said out loud. "Just walk through them. They'll get out of your way."

But he did not move. His legs felt like they had turned into stone. His hand was frozen, fixed to the stair rail. Only his eyes could move, but he dared not take his eyes off the cats. They did not take their eyes from him.

A voice spoke from behind him. "Well, what do we have here?" it asked. Mick could not move, not speak. His tongue was glued to the roof of his mouth.

The voice, it was a female, continued. She sounded amused. "Are you a thief, perchance? I am usually partial to thieves, but you don't seem to be a very good one. That's quite disappointing, really. What do they teach you nowadays? You really should try harder. But there you are. Now you are here and I suppose you are quite caught, the fly in the spider web, the thief in the trap. What shall we do with you?"

He could hear footsteps as the woman walked towards him. He saw her face loom towards him as sharp fingers clutched his chin, turning his head towards her. He saw a flash of cold green eyes, merciless eyes, which examined him and then let his face go.

His hand came free from the stair rail, suddenly, slithering from the metal as if it had been greased. His feet were freed from the floor and he stepped away from the stairs, gasping. The woman was nowhere to be seen, and the cats seemed to have disappeared. The lights went out. It was pitch black. Mick could not see a thing. As his eyes tried to adjust, he heard rustling, papery whispers from all around him. He reached out his hands, looking for the stairs, something to orient himself, but he was alone in the dark. The paper sounds drew closer, louder. *Mine,* he heard in a whisper. *Mine mine mine mine mine....*

Eyes wide with terror, Mick fell to his knees. He opened his mouth to scream as the noise grew louder, but all that came out was a tiny high-pitched whine that was drowned out by the sound around him. The paper was whirling around him now, creating a hurricane of paper wings, flapping.

He felt the paper brush against his face, books flying in circles, open, like feral birds touching his skin. And then the brushing turned into tearing, as the books started to cut his face, slicing, dicing.

Death by papercut... was the last thought that flitted through his head as his skin was sloughed from his body, dying as the books devoured him, dissecting him with blades of paper, their pages wet with blood.

"*Yes....*" came the whisper as blood seeped into the floor, draining through the carpet to the waiting stones beneath.

Yes....

"Everything we hear is an opinion, not a fact. Everything we see is a perspective, not the truth."

Marcus Aurelius

LUCY

The weather in Oxford was terrible. Cursing to herself, Lucy tightened her scarf and pulled her collar up to protect her neck from the wind. This was something she would not miss when she finally left this hellhole for good. No way. She was going to warmer climes, and she would be done with the place once and for all. She was not looking back.

Her right hand moved to her left wrist, pushing up the sleeve of her coat, and fumbled for the bands that took up permanent residence on her wrist. She pulled them, once, twice, three times. Once, twice, three times. Once, twice, three times. Her skin stung, and the bands vibrated, making her wrist quiver. That new therapist had said she needed to stop using rituals to control her thinking but then what did they know? It wasn't as if they lived her life. All they did was listen with lying eyes and take her money. Parasites, all of them. She could see through them all. She always had.

Holding her wrist tight, gently soothing the sting, she ran through her mental to-do list. Passport photographs, pick up her dry cleaning, and drop off her prescription. At least she did not have to visit Her. That was always a dampener on the day, visiting that soulless place. Lucy wouldn't miss that either. Crossing the street, looking both ways to make sure, she noticed a bookshop to her right. It had large windows set into jet-black frames, and the lights were on. It looked cheerful. Perhaps that needed to go on her to list as well. Travel research. She could do it on the computer, but perhaps getting some books was a better idea. She nodded to herself. Yes, this was exactly what she needed to do.

She put her hand carefully on the handle and opened the door. It was warm inside, and fresh, as if someone had actually invested in proper air conditioning for a change. The books were arranged properly on plain shelves, with enough room to browse. She cast an approving eye about. It was nice to see a bookshop that was not infested with kid-lit and overpriced coffees. This was much better.

She stepped further in, eyeing the bookshelves, wondering if there was anyone to serve her. The bookshop was empty, which seemed a shame for the staff. It was probably a boring job working in a bookstore, having to be nice to people. Perhaps they were too used to it to notice.

A taller bookcase with large books caught her eye and she headed towards it. That looked like travel books. Perfect. Now, she just had to choose where to go. Every single book was emblazoned with a glossy picture, showing off the destination with its best light. It was all fake, of course. They showed the extravagant buildings in sunset or sparkling rivers. If you actually went to some of these places they would barely resemble the photographs; they had been tinkered with so much. That was the problem. Nothing was real. She knew that.

Her hand itched to pull the bands again. It was too soon. She needed to wait longer. Pursing her lips, she stroked her wrist carefully. Just once. Just do it once to be sure. She needed a clear head to choose her travel destination.

Her fingers found the bands. Once, twice, three times. The sting cleared her brain and let her think for a moment. Good. That was better.

She cast her eye critically over the books again. There were footsteps behind her, quick, light steps. It was a woman. Lucy turned, plastering the faint, friendly smile on her face that was required for these hideous interactions. Her therapist had said she needed to familiarise herself more with social niceties. Her ex-husband would have snorted and said that she was an antisocial bitch. Fuck him. He would rot in jail. Let him be social with the pigs and the rapists. He deserved it.

The woman was tall and well-dressed, but with far too much makeup on. She looked like she was trying to dress up as a glamorous granny with her vintage spectacles and too-bright lipstick. But Lucy smiled and nodded. It wouldn't do to appear impolite.

"A new customer! It's lovely to meet you. I'm Meredith Smart, I am the owner of the bookshop. Are you looking for something in particular?"

Her voice had no traces of a local accent, low pitched and modulated. Meredith Smart might not have good fashion sense but she was educated; she would give her that. Lucy appreciated intelligence. "Hello, Meredith. You have a lovely bookshop here. I was very pleased to see something that isn't one of those awful chain brands! There seems to be a Waterstones and Blackwells popping up on every corner. It's very refreshing to see an independent business at last. I'm here to look for travel books. I plan to emigrate. Soon, as soon as possible, really. I just need to decide on where, and make the necessary arrangements."

Meredith beamed, her eyes sparkling behind those ridiculous glasses. She did have excellent teeth. Lucy sighed inwardly at the state of her own. British dentistry was never as good as overseas. Perhaps she should add a good dentist to the to-do list.

"That's a wonderful life plan, I love that! And do you have any idea of what kind of country you want to live in? Do you want a warm or cool climate? Do you want to be in an English speaking country, perhaps?"

Lucy waved her questions away impatiently. "Oh, heavens no, no cold places, please. I want better weather, not worse. I don't care about what language they speak. When money talks, they always use English, don't they?"

Meredith's mouth thinned just slightly, her eyes narrowing. "I suppose they do. Well, there are many options to consider. Did you want to live in Europe or further away?"

Lucy gasped. "Goodness, no, not Europe. I don't want all that nonsense. It's far too near to this country. I want to live as far away as possible. Somewhere warm, somewhere civilised. Somewhere different, you know?"

"Somewhere different. Hmm. Yes." Meredith moved around to the other side of the bookshelf, her lips pursed and her eyebrows drawn together. Lucy followed. This woman certainly liked to be thorough. This was a plus in her favour.

Her manicured hand brushed over the books, one big square one with a mountain and a lake on the cover – *far too cold looking* – and then she hummed to herself, picking two books: one with the ever-present backpacker looking at an airbrushed landscape, and the words Bucket List on, and the other was the quintessential sunset over big mountains cover.

Lucy rolled her eyes. These authors were always so predictable. But she waited, not wanting to dismiss her out of hand just yet. After all, she didn't know where she wanted to go to either. She may as well give this woman a chance to do her job.

Meredith straightened and turned back to her, holding the books to her chest. "These are both very good travel books, and they may help you. I think the Bucket List will interest you and the other might be where you would like to go. However," she paused, looking thoughtful. "I am not sure if they are exactly what you are looking for. You're looking for something else, am I right?"

Lucy gaped. This woman might actually know her stuff. "You are right, I do! I mean, I will trust your judgement, but these travel stories; they're not real, are they? It's all photoshopped madness, with embellished stories. They don't tell me anything real. I don't learn anything from it."

The woman gazed at her for a moment, her eyes considering the matter. "Are you wanting to learn something or is it that you want to know what is real? Because those are two different things, Lucy."

"I want to know what is real. I want something different." Lucy spoke decidedly, knowing that this was important. She felt as if she were standing on a precipice of some kind, about to discover something secret.

"Something different. Yes. Follow me." Meredith turned on her heel and walked towards the other side of the bookshop, her steps quick and efficient. Lucy followed, hearing her heels clack gently against the polished wooden floor. It was quiet in the shop, almost as if something was waiting to take a breath. It was colder in this part, too, with a slight draft that blew around her legs. Lucy felt a twinge of unease and wondered if she should just buy the two photography books and leave.

But she did not leave. Something kept her at Meredith's back, walking into a rather dim corner of the bookshop, where the books were not laid out neatly like before, but stacked more haphazardly in dishevelled piles. These books looked old, and they did not look as if they were meant to be lying in a bookshop, even one of those second hand bookshops where the books became the walls all around. These looked arcane. There were dark leather bound books, and some were etched with strange markings. The air smelled of old paper and something else. Lucy sniffed, hoping not to sneeze. It was almost like incense, or the essence of it. She felt as if she had stepped into an entirely different bookshop.

Meredith crouched down, examining the books with care, tucking the travel books closely into her lap. She was careful not to touch these books, Lucy noticed, almost as if she, too, knew they were different. Lucy watched the woman look over the titles, head moving as she read. "Ah! Here we are," she said, as she deftly plucked a slim volume from the pile. She stood, clutching the first books to her chest and handed the new one over. Lucy took it with confusion. When Meredith had taken it from the pile it had looked old, dusty, and with strange markings on the cover. But now it was merely a slim grey paperback with an abstract design and the words, The Reality Architect's Handbook, on the cover. It looked new.

Lucy met Meredith's eyes cautiously. "What is this book?" It felt warm in her hand as if it had just been printed. Her eyes kept looking down at it, itching to flip it open, and see what was inside.

"It is as you see on the cover, it is the Reality Architect's Handbook. This is a special book that is only accessible to those who really can see the illusions in this world. It is the book you want if you want to see the hard face of reality, and if you want to be able to bend existence to your will."

Lucy's eyes greedily took in the cover as her mind exulted. This was what she needed. She would be able to see reality at last!

"I'll take all three. Thank you, Meredith." Her hand clutched the book tightly, not wanting to give it up. "How much do I owe you?"

Meredith paused, her eyes glinting with a strange light. "The two travel books are, of course no consequence, Lucy, but the architect book is special. It can determine yours and other futures; it can even change your past. Do you understand what you are buying here?"

Lucy breathed out, feeling her frustration rising. "If you are trying to tell me this book is not for sale -"

"I am letting you know that power comes at a price, Lucy. If you can learn to manipulate reality, it can also learn to manipulate you. Are you willing to pay that price?"

Lucy resisted the urge to snap at the woman, or roll her eyes again. She knew she needed that book. "I'm buying it, Meredith. Put it with the others. Don't lay your misplaced concern on me. I will pay good money for that book and that is all you need to worry about."

Meredith nodded slowly and smiled. "Very good, then. It has been decided. If you'll come this way?"

Lucy did not let go of the Reality Architect handbook, even when Meredith needed to scan it. She held it out awkwardly as if it were a newborn child, ready to snatch it back. She barely listened when

Meredith packed the books into a bag, mentioning the quote that had something or other to do with the shop. She needed the book and there was nothing else to say. It wasn't until she stepped outside into the cool air that she remembered that Meredith had said her name. Lucy never introduced herself. How had the woman known that?

THE REALITY ARCHITECT'S HANDBOOK

The book gazed back up at her, design glinting. Its pages were already thicker, the spine bent. Lucy had read it three times since she brought it back. She had even started the Bucket List and was pleasantly surprised by it. It wasn't as fraudulent as she had thought. But the real treasure was the handbook. This was what she had needed. She sat down in front of the book, knees together, back straight. She took three deep breaths. Her hand moved towards the bands on her wrist, but she paused. If this book was the key, she did not need this ritual anymore. She already knew what was real now she had the book. Smiling, she carefully peeled the bands, setting them aside.

She reached for the book, searching for the page of the first activity that she wanted to try. The handbook was a mixture of theory and experiments, getting progressively more complex as the book progressed. She would start simply today, and then progress. Something small. Seeing something real, seeing something not real. Then, making something real, not real. Finally, you can make even the unreal, real.

Lucy scanned the page, moving the small sticky tab out of the way. Find the right time of day, yes, yes. The morning was better for seeing and dusk was better for changing. She had done that. Visualise clear sight. Make the gesture. She peered at the page, trying to work out how the hand was positioned. It didn't look as clear as she would have liked. Sighing, she put the book down again and went to fetch her glasses. Perhaps that's what she should do, improve her eyesight. She laughed to herself. Or her teeth! Now there was an idea. She returned to the diagram, looking closely. Ah yes! So, the thumb went to the centre of the palm, and the fingers fluttered in a slight waving gesture. Alright. Self-consciously, she put the book face down on the table and shut her eyes.

I want to see what is real. Open my seeing eye. I can see more clearly. I can see what is not real. I am a Reality Architect. I can see what is real. I can see more clearly.

The mantra calmed her breathing, letting her settle into her position. Keeping her eyes closed, she fumbled with her hand position, moving her thumb into place and fluttering the fingers. Was it right? Did it work? It seemed simple. But the book had said that it couldn't be done by accident, that you had to activate the process by reading the book first. She had done that. She held her breath and opened her eyes slowly.

Her room looked the same. The walls were still white, and the mirror on the wall in the dark heavy frame was still there. The armchairs remained in their places and the lone coffee cup perched on her pristine kitchen counter. It looked like her room. Well that was disappointing. She reached for the book, wondering if she had done something wrong. But as she lifted the book, she gasped and sat back. Her glass table was shimmering, and her reflection in it, though hazy, was wrong. She looked a different age, a different person. Lucy put her hands to her hair in shock. The reflection had her hair but even shorter, almost a pixie cut, and it was completely grey. Her teeth were even and white. Her glasses were dark and bold. She looked different. She looked better. Lucy made a mental note to get a haircut put on the to-do list. And an appointment with an optician for better glasses.

Standing up, she shifted the book into her left hand and resumed the gesture with her right hand, fluttering the fingers. If the table had shifted, then so might the mirrors, or the windows. Anything with glass. Her heart was pounding with excitement. She stepped towards the mirror, visualising hard. What would it be? As she got closer, she could see a gentle ripple. The mirror surface was moving, swaying. She wondered if she dared to touch it. A bubble formed on its surface, growing larger, then popped and receded. Lucy stepped back. Just in case, she would steer clear of the mirror. She looked around her apartment again, wondering about the windows. But they were all closed, with curtains drawn. She had not wanted anyone to see her practising with the book. Her neighbours were all far too nosy for their own good.

A shadow in the corner caught her eye and she focused hard, narrowing her eyes. What was it? She did not think it was a shadow. It was like a lopsided rectangle, partly draped onto the floor. She stepped over to it, kneeling down and looking closely at it. It was not a shadow, as it had not changed since she got closer, but it was as dark as one. Her face felt cold, and for a moment she wondered if she felt a breeze from it. Feeling chilled, she scrambled away. She did not know what it was, but she could just steer clear of that spot anyway. Lucy glanced at her watch, wondering if she had taken much time. But the watch whirred in a strange fashion, the hands flicking back and forth as if they did not know where to go. That was weird. Lucy shrugged. Perhaps it was the effect of the glass, rather than an effect on time itself. Time itself was a reality after all, surely? She realised that there were some things she did not need to know, and that was one of them.

The book was still in her hand. She flipped the pages to the next tabbed page, the exercise for seeing things that were unreal. That was the one she wanted. She knew what was real. Unreal was more interesting. She memorised the hand gesture and tried it twice to be sure. This was becoming easier.

I am a reality architect, a reality architect.

The words jumbled their way through her brain as if they were an earworm. She sang along silently to them, willing them to stay in her mind forever. Lucy Jones, Reality Architect. It had a real ring to it. She put the book carefully into her bag before closing the zip, and stepped outside. She wanted to see the fake people and expose them to reality. She was the Architect now.

As the door closed behind her, the bookshop shivered and sighed. The black cats twitched and shuddered, before melting away into the shadows.

She needed an itinerary, a list of places where she could find and expose people. Where should she start? She considered the Ashmolean Museum for a moment, then discarded it. It was a nice place to visit, but people were generally in contemplation there. She would go to Westgate first. No, this afternoon she would go there, when the schools were all finished. She would go first to the University, then people watch over coffee. Perfect. She tucked her bag in carefully under her arm, tightening the strap so there was no chance it would fall, and she climbed onto her bicycle. As she set off, letting the wind catch her short hair, she laughed.

The University grounds were fairly empty, with some people scattered about. Some were studying in the cool morning sun, others were milling around in conversation or just in their own world. Lucy debated what to do. What if there weren't enough people to analyse? But she was just practising. Perhaps a few would be better. Her hand itched to get going, starting from the palm, her thumb twitching.

Reality Architect Reality Architect

The words kept churning round. She was desperate to see the people in their true forms. Putting her spectacles on to see more clearly, she muttered her incantation with her hand already in position. She kept her eyes wide open. She needed to see what they were all really like. There were a group of young women clustered together by one of the nearer buildings. She headed straight for them, eyes fixed on their shapes. They looked just normal, really, with straightened hair, smart bags and nice jackets. Her lips thinned. This wasn't right. They could not be –

Ohhhhh her mind sang, as they began to change. Frosty Blonde at the centre started to shift her form, losing half of her hair length

Extensions! Fakery!

And her face began to blotch, showing patches of red. Her eyes were shadowed. She looked quite nondescript underneath the unreality. Plain, even. The swishy brunette with the smart jacket to the right of her started to shift as well. Her hair was real, much to Lucy's disappointment, as it was very nice-looking hair. But her nose grew a shadow, a bumpier, not such a patrician nose, appearing in front of her as if she had put on a prosthetic nose. Lucy had to stifle her cackle. Such a young woman, and she had work done! Oh, the fakery. She turned, desperate to see more.

There were more groups of people walking from the buildings, chattering earnestly. She marched towards them, eager. The men did not seem to change much physically, although one older man who was dressed smartly was clearly hiding his grey. But they had more interesting secrets. As one man was talking animatedly about his weekend, bubbles of black were popping up over his head. She cocked her head in amazement. What was it? What was his ruse?

She looked around to see if there were more bubbles coming from people. What could it be?

Further away there was a woman talking on the phone and she had black bubbles coming from the back of her head. Lucy practically sprinted over to catch up, then slowed down breathlessly, trying to eavesdrop.

Yes she had no shame but this was so interesting

"Yes, ma, I'm studying hard. Mm-hmm."

More black bubbles popped up. Could they be, something like her thoughts? Her mood? But others were talking and they didn't have them. The woman turned towards the coffee shops at the end of the street. "No, I'm just going back into lectures. Yeah." More black bubbles. Lucy raised her eyebrow. The woman wasn't anywhere near the lecture theatres, the sneaky little liar. The liar! That was it! The black bubbles were lies!

She hugged herself, keeping the excited squeal inside. This was wonderful. Everyone was fake! And she was the only one who could see it. She turned away from Miss Lie a – Plenty and surveyed the green in front of her. There were more people now, smiling, nodding, lying, and hiding their secrets. Elation flew through her veins. This was what living was about. This.

Clutching her bag hard to make sure she still had the wonderful book, Lucy decided to go and find somewhere to sit and have a coffee. She might need a notebook, too. She wouldn't risk annotating her precious handbook, and she had to make notes on what she could see. What if she wrote a book about it someday? Perhaps she would be famous. Perhaps she would be the one to rid the world of fakery. Such possibilities. Turning on her foot, she abandoned the crowds of students, heading for more populated spaces. Coffee and watching. Caffeine and exposing. And then, for the next exercise. Changing real to not real. The world would never be the same again.

Inside, she laughed again, but this time she let herself really laugh, setting it all free. This was her world, and she was the Reality Architect. She would recreate the Handbook. She would change the world.

MAKING REALITY, TAKING REALITY

Lucy's hand ached from taking notes. She had been writing almost non stop all day, observing, analysing and note-taking. There were bubbles for lies, as she had noticed, but there were also bubbles for memories that people had denied or had entirely forgotten about. Sometimes people walked with a shadow behind them, following them everywhere they went. She didn't like observing those, just in case it was something malevolent.

Some people had strange tics where they would keep moving through a loop of behaviour, over and over. That one was difficult to work out, until she got close to one couple and listened to their conversation shamelessly. He was an addict, and he kept going back to the drugs even though he had promised to stay clean. He wasn't lying as such, she could see no black bubbles, but he was replaying his actions over and over as if he was stuck. Perhaps he was. Perhaps that's what happened when they were in the loop. Stuck in a behaviour.

She went back to the handbook, hands shaking with anticipation as she looked for the next exercise. Making real, unreal. This was going to be interesting. What could she do? The possibilities were endless. And how long would it last? This one was more complex as it was an action, not just viewing, but viewing then changing. She had to go back to the flicker and add something. What did it say? She picked up the book, putting it almost to her nose to see clearly.

It was, or appeared to be, an anti-clockwise twist. Was it while doing the flicker or not? She would have to try it both ways.

Scowling, she picked up her coffee cup, eyeing the crowds of fakers. They were all moving very quickly, dashing from shop to shop, spending money they could not afford. So many had plumes of what looked like fear coming out of their heads, or perhaps stress. She had no sympathy. It wasn't difficult to live within your means. If you have no money to shop, do not go to the shops. Don't spend money on things that you do not need.

Lucy begrudged wasting her new talent on them. They had hardly anything real anyway. Why would she help them to be more unreal? But she could do it on herself. She was certainly real, and certainly more deserving. And then she could see how it works, before trying it on other people. She sipped her coffee again, musing. What should she change? An image of Meredith flashed through her mind, and then the image in the coffee table. That was something. She snatched the image back, examining it carefully. She could change her glasses, her hair, or her teeth. She could do all three. She knew it looked real. Yes. This was a plan worthy of the to-do list.

She put her cup down and flexed her fingers again. It was a shame that she had to use her right hand to do it: her fingers were stiff. But her thumb moved into position easily, as she placed her hands in her lap to ensure nobody could see. She doubted that anyone would look, or even deign to understand what she was doing, but it was better to be careful. Knowledge in the wrong hands was never a good thing.

Lucy whispered the incantation and moved her hands. She waited. Nothing happened. What had she missed? Panicked, she went back to the book, reading the instructions. Ah, the visualisation. She was visualising the seeing but not the changing. Of course.

She took a deep breath and tried again, holding the image in her mind. Would she get all three, or just one of the changes? There was only one way to find out. A small fear worked its way forward, squeaking its anxious question – will it hurt?

But her need to try the power was too strong. Ignoring it, she moved her hands again, willing her new face into existence. Flicker and ... twist. Change!

Lucy looked from left to right. Nobody was looking at her. Clearly, she hadn't exploded. But how would she see the change? She slid her makeup mirror from her bag, the one that she faithfully carried but never used as she never wore makeup anyway. At least it would come in useful today. She flicked it open and peered into the mirror. Her glasses were different, more modern and bold. They changed her face quite drastically, and she stared at them for a while. What a difference! Such vanity, but really, it was remarkable.

She smiled into the mirror, joyfully, and her eyes alighted on her straighter, white teeth. Now, those were wonderful. It was fakery of course, but it still was nice to look at. Pulling the mirror back, she enjoyed the look of her shorter, more modern haircut. This was an improvement. Lucy, Reality Architect, the new look.

And it didn't hurt one bit, she told the panicked part of herself. *Next time, don't be ridiculous. Have I ever steered myself wrong? Well, then.*

She snapped the mirror shut. Looking at changes was one thing, but she wasn't going to waste time admiring the illusion. She would appreciate her achievement in learning the skill and no more. But she did sit a little straighter as she picked up her now cold coffee, and she did allow her teeth to flash just a little as she smiled, watching her test subjects run around like panicked rats.

Lucy eyed the book. What was next? She did not know. She could change things, but what should she change? The handbook gave concepts about what big changes could do, such as disruption within society, but she did not plan to do that. She would merely tinker around the edges. But who to change next? And what to change? She did not know. But she did know that it would be happening soon. This power was becoming quite addictive. And she did not mind in the least.

Today had to be a To-Do List day. Lucy had been putting it off for too long. Sometimes, even Reality Architects had to face reality. But she felt rather sulky as she packed her lovely handbook away and organised all the paperwork that she needed. Would She demand anything more today? She certainly hoped not. Perhaps she could say she couldn't stay long as she had an appointment or something. She hardly noticed after the first few minutes of complaining. Yes, she would do that. She would make up a dentist appointment. Her mouth curled up in amusement, thinking about it. As if she needed one of those now. She could just change things whenever she wanted. She would never have to sit in a dentist's chair again!

It would be fine. It would be fine. The car trip to the first stop was uneventful, although Lucy could not help but change the car colour a few times, just for her own amusement. She made sure to do the outside, so the driver didn't notice, and left it the right colour when he finally pulled up. She did think it suited the silver grey more than the bland beige that it originally was, though.

She clutched her bag to her chest as she looked up at the building, and her stomach lurched. It wouldn't be long, and then she was done for a while. Perhaps, if she made up her mind about where to emigrate to, it could even be one of the last times she had to come here. That thought cheered her up as she trudged towards the gate.

Doors clanged and locks clicked. She followed the others, head down, as the guard locked them in and out of corridors, herding them along in silence, until they reached the visiting room. A woman offered them tea, served in polystyrene cups. Lucy refused, wordlessly. She was not putting that into her mouth. Others did, clutching their cups as if they were a protection, a talisman. Lucy put her hand instinctively to her bag, flinching when she felt the absence. It was only an hour. She could get it back. Her hand crept towards her wrist, but she slapped herself quickly.

No. Stop that.

She didn't need that kind of crutch anymore. She didn't. She was the Architect. She could change anything into anything she wanted; she didn't need a crutch to help remind her of who she was. She was. She straightened in the seat, bracing herself. Alice would arrive soon.

And she did, strutting in with that slouch that she had now, throwing herself into the chair, looking up at her balefully. "Oh, it's you."

"It's me. How are you, Alice?"

Alice snorted. "As if you care. Did you bring the stuff that I asked for?"

Lucy wrinkled her nose. "It depends on what you referred to. If you mean the new clothes, the writing paper, the quilt and the money, yes, I did. The money is with the authorities, and they said they would administer it to you."

Alice shrugged, her face impassive. "And the tobacco?"

She asked this every time. It didn't matter what else she brought; there was always something missing. "You know I don't approve of the smoking. I won't buy you tobacco. You can buy it in here."

Alice rolled her eyes, a flick upwards towards the ceiling that would be worthy of a capricious tween. "Well, at least you brought the quilt. I need that. I'm getting married soon, you know."

Lucy tried hard to muster enthusiasm. "Oh, you are?"

"You don't need to put on that face. I know you don't approve. I don't care. I'm stuck in here, and while I'm here, I'll get what's available."

"It doesn't sound like you plan to value your wife. Is it a wife that you are marrying, or have you found a husband?"

There it was, the flash, the sneer of disdain. "I don't need to find a husband. I already found yours."

Lucy watched her sister impassively. She threw out this insult every time. She wished it didn't still rankle. "I don't have a husband. I divorced him years ago."

"I heard," she said, finger teasing at a crack on the table. "He writes sometimes."

Lucy didn't know that. "Do you ever reply?" *Does he still want you?* The question hovered in her mind, but she did not let it spill out. She didn't care. If she said it enough, perhaps she would make it real.

"Sometimes I reply. Sometimes he sends me stuff, money, you know, if I reply. He's trying for parole soon. He might be out in a year if he gets it."

Lucy shrugged. "If he gets it."

Alice stared at her over the table, her eyes cold. "I bet you'd like that, if he got out and I was still in here."

Lucy stared back. "I would like it more if you both stayed in here. You did something terrible, and now you have to pay."

Her sister paused, her finger perched in a frozen position, pointing to the table. Lucy watched the finger, wishing she could change it to something else, make her sister gasp, scream, panic. But she did not move.

"I wonder about that, Lucy. You see, when you're in prison, you have a lot of time to think about things. I know that I was drunk at the time, that I was drinking a lot. I know that I have some gaps in my memory. But I still don't think it was me that did the arson. I don't think it was me who destroyed all those records. I think it was you. I think you did it to expose him and to put me in here. I know why you did that to him. He was doing bad things to his patients. But why did you do it to me?"

Carefully, Lucy put her hand under the table and made the gesture. It was becoming easier to just move her hand, and not even visualise as much. Reality popped up, showing her the thoughts, the bubbles popping up all around her, and Her, sitting on the other side of the table, her face set in lines of discontent. Lucy watched her face, unchanged, negative emotions swirling around her head. But she did not lie. Lazily, Lucy wondered if she should ask her questions, watching for bubbles as if she had a polygraph. But really, it didn't matter why Alice was the way she was. She was unpleasant, and now she was here. It was fitting.

Alice was still waiting for an answer, and Lucy was ready to go. She decided to treat her sister to one last parting remark to chew on. Smiling, she leaned forward.

"I did it because I wanted to. Goodbye, Alice."

She stood, slowly, watching the swirl of colours around Alice's head, wondering what they all meant. It didn't really matter, now.

Deftly, she switched her hand from seeing reality to changing it. Her hand moved smoothly, following the earworm that was back in her head; I'm a reality architect - that's me. She pondered for just a moment what to change in her world. And then she had it. It was perfect.

As she left, nodding to the dour guard who slouched at the desk, Alice started screaming, hitting the table as if she were possessed, sparking the guards to erupt in a flame of activity, dragging her out, ending the visiting hour before anything else happened. Lucy smiled. *Good luck reading my ex-husband's letters, now you can't see. All the best, little sister.*

ANCHORS AHOY

Life really was so much more pleasant with the Handbook in tow. It never left her sight, either. She was not taking any precautions, not allowing anyone the chance to steal the knowledge from her. Tucking the precious pages back into her bag, Lucy surveyed her to-do list.

This time, she had written it on the mirror, as it was pleasant to watch the letters flutter in the breeze from wherever the mirror went to. It was another dimension; she was sure of it, but she did not yet know how to get there. The Handbook made vague mention of further volumes, with more advanced exercises – she would be making another visit to see Meredith before she left for all of those. Or perhaps the next one, and she could send the rest over. Or something. Whichever way it happened, she needed the rest of the books. There was simply no way she would live without them.

She checked her watch. The travel agent person would arrive soon - she had best get prepared for them. It had been surprisingly easy to change herself into a more authoritative, more convincing person and the person on the phone into a more meek, accommodating person. Within minutes, she had got them to agree to change their normal routine and send someone to her to arrange her trip, rather than make her go all the way to them. This was an improvement. Waving a hand at the mirror to disguise her planning, she tidied, her mind running through what they would do. The travel agent would organise everything for the trip and for her first month there. All she needed to do was relax and enjoy the trip. That was all she intended to do.

The doorbell rang and she bustled to let the man in. He was slight, young, with a nervous air. That was perfect. Being nervous meant he would be easier to influence. He said no to coffee, his eyes darting about, not sure where to stand and what to do. With a slight shift of her hand, Lucy amplified her confidence and authority, and soothed his nerves just a little, turning up his desire to please. He was just so easy.

Within seconds, he was sitting in the spot she had designated, laptop out and ready, brochures at his side. He was back in his comfort zone, and he was ready to shine. Lucy looked on proudly. This was exactly how it should be.

"So, Ms Jones, I understand you're moving to South America, is that right?"

"That is right, Carl. Can I call you Carl? Oh. good, thank you. Yes, I think I will start in Colombia, as I have read that the climate there is very pleasant. From there, I will probably travel as the mood takes me. But for now, I will require accommodation and the usual preparations for a month, until I can arrange something more permanent while I am there."

"Of course. And your budget -" the question hung in the air expectantly.

"Unlimited. You do not need to worry about skimping. I intend to travel there in comfort."

Karl the travel agent basked in delight. She supposed there would be a good commission in it for him. All the better. It would make him work harder.

"That's excellent, Ms Jones, that makes things much easier. Now, if I may make some recommendations?"

"Go ahead."

"I have been reading up about Colombia, refreshing my knowledge, you understand, and I would suggest that you headed for Cartagena as your first stop. It's a port city, there is an airport, and it has some lovely beauty spots. Would you like me to go ahead and start you from there?"

Lucy vaguely recalled something about a walled city and nice sights in Cartagena, thanks to the books Meredith had provided. She was such an efficient woman. "Yes, that sounds very good. And where would I fly from?"

His fingers flew over the keys. "We can fly you from London Heathrow, that would be the most convenient. Would you, er," he looked over the computer owlishly at her. "Would you prefer a direct flight or a layover? The direct flight would be, hmm, let me see, around 11 hours, but there are indirect flights which, um, would take longer."

"The direct is fine. Book me a first class, please."

He gulped and nodded. "And when do you plan to leave, Ms Jones?"

"Make it in around two weeks, whenever there's a reasonable flight. That will give me enough time to prepare. What else do you need from me?"

"Well, we have to discuss where you want to stay, if you need a hire car, how much luggage you will need, and I need your passport details and -"

He paused, mouth going slightly slack as he met her gaze. "I am sure that I can take all that with me and just ensure you have a good time without having to think about any of these details, Ms Jones.

Shall we just say that I will make all the arrangements and ensure there are no problems for you to worry about?"

She did like that. "Yes, Karl. That will do very well. Shall I pick up the tickets before I leave or can you have them couriered to me?"

"Yes, I will arrange everything, Ms Jones, it will all be here. Don't worry about a thing."

Lucy beamed. "I leave it all in your capable hands, Karl. I'm very pleased."

She turned back to the to do list as he scurried out, an air of excitement trailing behind him as he ran out, desperate to finish finalising the details. This was the way to travel. Lucy wiped Travel Agent from the list and stared at the remaining items.

Bookshop

Airport

Revenge

She would enact them in that order. First, she would go to the bookshop to procure the remaining Handbooks. Then she would take herself to the airport to start her wonderful new life, far away. And finally, she would enact revenge. On everyone who had ever lied to her, first. Fakery had no place in this world anymore. And she, the Architect, would see to it that it was purged from the world. With fire, if necessary.

The mirror rippled, over and over again, as if someone was touching the surface of a lake. And far away, the Bookshop stirred again.

Yes. Lucy, yes.

PAYMENT DUE

Lucy arrived early, determined to get the list ticked off. She pushed the door open, glad to be out of the cold biting wind outside. Honestly, the weather in Britain was just atrocious. Why people continued to live here, she did not know.

It was warm in the bookshop, and quiet. She looked around, frowning when she saw the tail of a black cat swishing against one of the bookshelves. Unhygienic creatures. She hoped it wouldn't come near. It didn't, much to her relief, but it stared at her in a most peculiar way. Lucy found her hand twitching. Should she try and influence the cat to go somewhere else? Would it even work on cats?

Shoo, she ordered. It didn't move. Lucy rolled her eyes. Cats never listened to anyone. It was a wonder that they hadn't become savages with that lack of self control.

She stepped up to the desk, looking for a bell or equivalent that she could press. She did not have time to loiter in a bookshop, however pleasantly warm it was. The counter was empty. To her relief, she heard a light footstep, and Meredith arrived, resplendent in dark red. She did still resemble the mutton dressed as lamb look, but Lucy had to acknowledge that Meredith's confidence went a long way towards her pulling it off. She eyed Meredith's fashionable black spectacles, feeling glad that she had upgraded herself so nicely. Meredith smiled warmly and nodded to her. "It's nice to see you, Lucy. How are you getting on with the Handbook?"

She did get right to the point. Lucy liked that. "I am enjoying it, and am almost all of the way through. It mentioned that there are other volumes – I would like to order and purchase those today, please, and you can either ship them to me when they arrive or I will take them before I leave. I fly in two weeks to South America. Do you have the titles in stock?" Her tone was crisp and authoritative. Lucy was confident that she would not need to use more than that to get the books arranged with perfect precision, and she could be on her way. Meredith was, after all, a businesswoman, and she knew how to look after her customers.

But Meredith paused, pursing her lips in that way that meant she was stalling, or she didn't actually know the answer. That was absolutely not what Lucy wished to see. Lucy raised her eyebrows, rearranging her own expression into one of polite impatience. That usually did the trick.

"I would have to check what the other titles are, Lucy, but I would be concerned about the cost of purchasing them. They are more, shall we say, specialist, than the first one, and they require careful handling. I am not sure if I would be able to sell them to you."

"Alright, Meredith, name the price. You know I'm not short of money. If you're planning on whacking the price up to cover the rent on this place, fine. I'll indulge you. Name your price, ship me the books."

Her fingers twitched, itching to change Meredith and make her more timid, more biddable. But she was not ready to do that just yet. It was one thing directing Karl the travel agent, and it was in his interests to get it done correctly. He was also a weaker character, an underling, if you will. Meredith was not. It would almost be disappointing to put her under and change her into something lesser. This woman she could spar with on her own level. It was rare.

Meredith moved behind the counter, took off her spectacles and began to clean them, not looking at Lucy. Lucy waited. Sometimes it is better to not leap in, and not plead your case. Let them respond. Sometimes, negotiations were a chess match. She growled to herself. Her ex- husband used to say that phrase. He was right, but it didn't mean she wished to be reminded of it. Dismissing him, she shook herself back to her negotiation. She needed those books. And she was not leaving without them.

"Did you say that you've almost finished this book, Lucy?"

"Yes, I did. I've covered almost all the exercises, and I wish to look at the next volumes. Now, I appreciate your thoroughness but I really must be on my way. Order the books, please."

Meredith very deliberately put her glasses back on and looked up. Her eyes were unyielding, and cold. Lucy looked at Meredith's eyes closely. They were a remarkable shade of sea green. How had she not noticed that before?

"I think that I am not going to do that, Lucy. You haven't learned enough from this book yet."

Lucy bristled. She hadn't learned enough? There was one way to show her otherwise. She fluttered her hand impatiently and twisted, amplifying her own authority, her own power, and turning down Meredith's. That would do it.

"Order the books, Meredith. I don't have all day and I really do not wish to be impolite."

Meredith smiled. "I am afraid that your parlour trick won't work on me, Lucy. It does work on humans, of course, as you know. I've enjoyed watching your exploits and your increased confidence. You've really been an apt pupil. But you would not be able to influence me that way. It is disappointing that you even tried. But then, you always have been swayed by your own wants, haven't you, Lucy Jones. Or should I call you Lucy Pedori? That was your married name, was it not, when you were married to the famous, or shall we say, infamous, Dr Shane Pedori?"

Lucy's mouth hung open, flapping aimlessly. "I, how, how?"

"How do I know? Is that what you mean?"

Lucy nodded. Her capacity for words had left her entirely. She felt quite dizzy. Nobody knew her married name; nobody but her sister even knew who she had married, and she was locked safely away. How did this stranger know?

"You know, Lucy, I make it my business to know what people do, especially when they commit crimes. And you committed a few crimes, didn't you. Shall we talk about them? Now, I must say, you did well in not getting caught. That, I applaud you for. I wonder if you are so fixated on what is true because of exactly how far you went in framing both your husband and your sister for their crimes. For their crimes against you. Did you know, Lucy, that your actions brought about the deaths of three people?"

Meredith paused, studying Lucy's face. "Perhaps you did not. You did leave the town very quickly, which the authorities seemed to sympathise with. Your attempt at arson spread to another building. Two children unfortunately died."

Lucy felt as if cold water had been dashed in her face. She spluttered, her mouth working. "You said – you said, three."

"Oh, very good, Lucy! I did say three. Good observation skills there. Yes, you killed two children with your fire. An accident, of course. But one of the women you exposed when you framed your ex-husband, killed herself after. It was quite the tragedy at the time. Her husband left her during the scandal, and she then opened her wrists in the bathtub. She was very young still. Barely in her thirties. So yes, Lucy. You have three deaths on your hands. And of course, your husband, sorry, former husband, and your sister are in prison because of you. Was your sister pleased to see you yesterday?"

Lucy flinched. "We are not close."

Meredith threw her head back and laughed, baring her long, slender neck. "No, you certainly do not seem to be. I was impressed at your response to her, blinding her like that. It isn't the way I would have dealt with it, but it certainly showed a sense of style. It's a shame, really. You could have been quite the benefactor for the bookshop."

"What do you mean? If you want a benefactor, Meredith, I can still be that even from South America. I want those books. I don't know how you know all this stuff about me, and frankly, I don't want to know. Can we just settle this?"

The smile on Meredith's face chilled Lucy to the bone. It wasn't just cold; it was feral, without humour, without humanity. "I thought that is what we are doing, Lucy. You see, books like the Handbook, they come with a cost. I did try to warn you that you would have to consider the cost of what you were doing with it. You dismissed me as, of course, you thought you knew better. You let the handbook control you, not the other way around. You gave it access to people; you let it work through you. You let it feed."

Lucy was frozen in place, a statue, her eyes moving to watch Meredith, who was moving with inhuman grace. Her fear washed over her, drenching her in sweat. She had never been this afraid before. Not even when she struck the match, setting light to her husband's office, not even when she had watched their trials in court, expecting at any moment to be exposed. This was something different. This was not something she could win.

"You cannot have the other books because you cannot afford them. You must pay still for this book, and I will take payment for that momentarily. But you cannot have the others because you would be drunk on the power. You would be a liability. Your plan for revenge is self-centred and short-sighted. You, Lucy, are a monster."

Meredith moved closer, her face shifting, her skin developing a metallic sheen, her tongue beginning to develop a fork at the very end. She was taller, and her garments had shifted to something more akin to a silken gown, rippling as she walked. Her glasses had entirely disappeared. Lucy began to breathe in short pants. This was not how she had expected the day to develop. Not at all.

"Are you – are you going to kill me?" Her words slipped out reluctantly from frozen lips. Meredith paused to study her again. "Kill you? No, I don't think so. You don't serve me as a corpse. But

I cannot let you leave as you are. You, after all, Lucy, are such a purveyor of the truth. You despise all things falsehood. Am I right?"

Her voice had become lower in pitch, quieter. The thing that was Meredith moved closer. "You despise all things untrue, yet the first thing you did when you got the handbook was to cloak yourself in unreality. It is almost as if you judge others for it while indulging yourself. You judge others for being false, yet you walk with a stink of lies that will never leave you, not as long as you live. I think people should know what you are, Lucy. I think you should be honest in what you are. I think your face should show what your rotting soul looks like. I think people should see that."

Something shadow-like wound around her legs, solidifying into an opaque smoke, holding Lucy still. Looking down, she watched the smoke move, slithering into place, swaying back and forth. It multiplied, whipping out soft grey tendrils that spread up her body, holding her in a vice-like grasp. She was swathed in it up to her neck. Tears ran down her face, and she started to whimper. Meredith ignored it, bringing up her hands, which had lengthened into long, sharp fingers that seemed to end in points. In claws. The Meredith creature looked at her dispassionately, tilting her head slightly as if she were inspecting a painting.

"Thank you for your payment, Lucy," she breathed as she slashed out with her claws. The fingers moved quickly, then slowly, as they tore through flesh, ripping open valleys in Lucy's face, burning through the muscles in her cheeks, scratching at her bones. Lucy screamed and screamed, feeling the veins in her neck rage and flex, her throat wide and raw. The claws continued, swiping, drawing, ripping, clawing her skin. Her face felt as if it were ribbons dangling from a pole, swirling in the air. She was invisible, just strands of skin; floating.

She was the centre of the pain, the dark moment where the scream never ends. And all she could see was Meredith's eyes, that cold sea green, looking into hers as if they had just met, as if they were dancing, as if they could never leave.

The claws slowed, and fingers replaced them, shaping the strips of skin and pressing them back onto pitted bone, spreading them over keening muscle. The pain eased, climbing into her hot skull, lying there as a reminder. Meredith stepped back, her face a mask of polite satisfaction. "Yes, that will do nicely. Well done, Lucy."

The smoke sifted away, unwinding itself from her legs and her body, then slid away, moving as if it were blown by a wind, slowly melting away. Lucy did not move, her body still frozen in place. Meredith offered her hand to shake and smiled a tiny smile. "It was nice doing business with you, Lucy. Don't you have a plane to catch? Please, don't let me keep you. You must have a lot to do."

Lucy found herself nodding, thanking Meredith and shaking her hand before her legs walked her out, lurching, staggering, but moving inexorably towards the exit. She left, feeling the sharp pain of a cold wind on her cheekbones, and she gasped. Her hands went up to her face before she stopped, afraid to feel, afraid to see. It was dusk, the clouds gathering, and nobody was on the streets. Carefully, she reached for her hood, lifting it to cradle her face and protect it from the cold. Just to protect it from the cold. She needed to get back, get home, and start her new life. It would be fine. She didn't need the extra books anyway; she had this one. She could work mastery with this one. A cold fear struck her. What if – her hand clutched instinctively at her bag, and she sagged in relief, feeling the paperback inside. Meredith hadn't taken her book. She still had her book. It would be fine.

She needed to call a taxi. Or hail one down, perhaps. She began to walk towards the busier part of the road, deliberately not looking back. The bookshop had given her what she needed. She still had everything else; her money, talent, and Architect ability. It was a fair price. And she could always get surgery if she wanted, later. Why not? After all, she needed to start a new life. Why not start it with a new name and a new face? A taxi pulled up quickly, slowing down at her signal, and she slid gratefully inside, her hood still up. The driver did not even look at her, taking her instructions with barely a nod, eyes on the road.

In the quiet shadow of the back seat, Lucy took the book out carefully, stroking the now worn cover and bent pages. It was hers. It was her handbook. Hers. She flipped through the pages, absently noticing that one of her fingernails was ripped and bloody. She moved it away from the pages, not wanting to soil them. At last, she opened the book wide, expecting to see the close-set text, the diagrams, the drawings of the gestures. But all there was on the page was a picture, a picture of her. A picture of her as she was when she looked into the glass table. Panicked, she turned to the next page, and the next, and the next, and the next. And as she flipped, her breath coming in gasps, the picture opened its mouth wide and screamed.

"Death smiles at us all; all we can do is smile back."

Marcus Aurelius

BRANDON

I am the silence.

Brandon wondered if he had read that somewhere, on an advertisement perhaps, or a newspaper. But it had wormed itself into his brain and taken a life of its own there. *I am the silence.* Was he that? He did not know. He was pacing through life, going through the motions. But he was not completely alive. He hadn't been since he turned away from his old life. He did not understand why doing the right thing and acting according to the way society demanded, meant he lost something of himself. But that was how it happened. He was lost in this world, still trying to find a foothold. And he did not know how to do that.

He reached the meeting place, looking around for somewhere visible to wait. Shawn was always late. It was his superpower. He always appeared with breathless apologies and an amusing story about why he hadn't got there on time. Brandon didn't mind. He tended to compensate for it, arriving late himself, or at least not early. And sometimes, it was good to just stand somewhere and think in silence.

Shawn had suggested a few drinks in town this time, which was unusual. Shawn didn't usually drink. But as a result, there was nothing but a couple of lampposts or shop doorways to loiter in while he waited. Brandon didn't fancy either as an option.

Was there a coffee place or similar that he could wait at? This part of Oxford wasn't familiar to him. He wouldn't even venture here if it wasn't for his best friend asking him to. He liked to know where places were, so he could bolster his armour and prepare for pitfalls. Damn Shawn. Brandon sighed. But that was who Shawn was, and he knew better than to arrive too early. But sometimes, just sometimes, he wished that he would not have to fend for himself for a while.

Most of the shops were closed, with shutters lowered or their lights out. But one shop still gleamed out with warm lights in the windows, glowing out onto the pavement. Brandon studied it, wondering. He could not read the sign from where he was standing. But it wasn't such a hardship to waste a few minutes wandering over to investigate it. The shop was new with fresh paintwork and clear windows. It stood out among tired businesses that didn't care to make themselves look presentable after a while. Some of them had their quota of faithful customers and did not need to spruce themselves further to keep bringing people in. This place had to be new. They still cared too much.

As he neared the shop, he saw the gleam of warm lights and carefully arranged bookshelves. It was a bookshop. He hadn't been in one of those for years, but he had spent a lot of time in the library when he was locked up. Somehow, books had become a comfort to him and he had looked forward to his weekly visit. Perhaps he could just step in and see what was available. Shawn would be a while still and he could see right across the street. He opened the door with resolve.

As he walked in, a black cat jumped down from the counter, eyeing him boldly. Its tail was high as it walked past and disappeared around a bookshelf. Brandon smiled as he watched it go. Being dismissed by a cat was always a plus in his book. He looked around, wondering where the fiction might be. Wasn't it usually put front and centre as that's what everyone bought? He wished that the cat would come back so he could ask it for directions.

He turned back towards the window, deciding to just go to a bookshelf and see what it had. It was better than shuffling about awkwardly as if he was asking for a job or something. A flicker of movement caught his eye, and he paused. A woman stepped out, smiling, holding a stack of books. She spoke, but it was indistinct, rushed, and she wasn't looking at him. Wiping her hands, she came towards him, eyes expectant.

"I'm sorry," Brandon said. "I don't know what you said, then. I'm hard of hearing. I need to be able to see your face so I can lipread."

The woman frowned, her brow furrowing slightly. Then her eyes widened. "Oh, it is me who should apologise! I am sorry. I was distracted with some paperwork and didn't think to look properly at you. I was asking if I could help you. My name is Meredith, I am the owner of the bookshop."

Her words were enunciated clearly, her mouth moving not too fast. She didn't speak with the closed mouth and set lip that was typical of the locals. Brandon wondered where she was originally from. "I'm Brandon. Thanks, I just stopped in to look around. I'm supposed to be waiting for someone."

She watched him with interest as if he was the only person in the world. Brandon wasn't sure if he liked that. People who paid that much attention usually had an ulterior motive. "Do you have any fiction books? I should pick something up while I am here."

Meredith smiled again. "Of course! Do you have a preference on genre? What was the last book that you read?"

Brandon hesitated. "I am not sure, it has been a while. I read some, er, a few years ago, but it was in quite a small library. I enjoyed some science fiction, and I did read some books about spies. I can't remember the author's name. I'm sorry."

"No, don't worry. That gives me plenty to be going on with. I think I know just the book for you. I'll be fast and then you can get back to your friend."

Meredith turned on her heel and marched away before he could respond. He waited awkwardly, not sure what to do next. He turned back to the shelf, wondering what section it was. All the books in front of him seemed to be ones for clever people, with plain covers and smart titles. A book caught his eye, and he looked more closely at it. Eloquent Empathy. Well, that was certainly not fiction. Brandon picked it up. Under the title it read, How to build better connections using and reading nonverbal cues. He mused for a moment. This could actually be very useful. He was used to watching people, of course, but he did not always know why people acted the way they did. And he was certainly lacking in connections, especially since starting afresh. He made his mind up quickly, taking the book to the counter. He looked over his shoulder briefly to check if Shawn had arrived yet. The road still looked empty. Damn Shawn.

Meredith returned with a paperback in her hand. It looked interesting, with splashes of orange on black. She put it down on the counter and tapped it with her fingernail. "I think you'll like this one. It's the author's first novel, but he did a good job with it. It's quite an intelligent story." She eyed the other book and looked up at Brandon. "And what do we have here? This looks right up your street!"

Brandon smiled in response, but that slight edge of unease returned. It was as if Meredith was just a little over-familiar, a little too keen. He watched her steadily as she packed the books into a cloth bag. She presented it to him, showing him the quote that was emblazoned on the front. "Death smiles at us all; all we can do is smile back. Marcus Aurelius. "

"I like to add literary quotes to my bags: it's a little touch of whimsy. Are you familiar with Marcus?"

He shook his head. "Not especially, no. Was he a great writer?"

"Yes, he was!" Her face was enthusiastic, smiling. She spoke a little quicker, but not too fast that he couldn't follow. He appreciated that. "He was a great Roman commander and later an Emperor, but he was also a scholar and a writer. Based from his readings, he was thoughtful and compassionate, it seems, even by today's standards."

"A Roman emperor. He certainly laid his legacy down, then, if we still remember his words."

Meredith nodded, her eyes sparkling with what could have been approval. She had very pretty eyes, Brandon thought, and an unusual colour. "He certainly did. We have a lot to thank him for. I should let you go and not talk your ear off, Brandon, I am sure your friend is waiting!"

Bemused by the dismissal, he took his bag and looked over his shoulder, out of the window. Sure enough, he could see the slight figure of his friend lounging against a lamppost across the street, idly smoking a cigarette. The lit ember of the end blazed out against the dim grey of outside. Brandon turned back, confused. Hastily, he pulled some crumpled notes from his pocket and nodded his thanks to her, holding his bag carefully. These were perhaps the first books he had ever owned. It might mean they were significant. He felt the eyes of Meredith on him as he walked, but he did not turn back. That lady had secrets, and he did not want to know any of them.

"Ah, there you are! Did I keep you waiting so long that you wandered off to find pleasures elsewhere?"

Shawn was in his dandy phase tonight, gesturing dramatically and smiling a lot. He would call him milady if he got away with it. Brandon wondered if that was why he had suggested drinks. Was he hoping to take out a friend and bring in a conquest? He did not know. He smiled, and presented the bag. "I found a bookshop, just over the road. I hope I didn't keep you waiting."

Brandon wished that he could point out that he wouldn't have been IN the bookshop if Shawn was ever punctual. But it was who he was as a person. And Shawn was his friend.

So he said nothing, and smiled again. "Where are we headed then? I assume you have a plan?"

Shawn grinned, his face alit with mischief. "I certainly do! We're going to visit some pubs with quirk and some pubs with mirth. And then finally, we might find some conversation that fits... our worth!" He laughed ferociously, his head thrown back, his face animated by his own joke. Brendon wished that he could step into those moments, rather than just hover uncertainly on the side-lines. Why did he hesitate so?

Brandon nodded, trying not to be too awkward. "Well then lead on, O mighty guide. But I'm not staying out late. I'm absolutely not!"

Shawn laughed again, but it sounded more like a cackle than a laugh. He pointed to the building ahead of them, a rather imposing looking building that crouched under a bridge. "You will not stay out late. I promise!"

He leapt ahead, dancing as if he were a banshee, and Brandon wondered how much he had drunk already to reach this level of merriment, this unbridled joy. But he followed, a smile tugging at his lips, and he tucked his books into his pocket for safe-keeping. He didn't want to lose them. A book was precious for taking you out of this world. He understood that magic. An image of Meredith's eyes rose up before him and he shook his head, pushing it away. She was a mystery but it was not his business. He did not need to know, and he did not want to know. He was meeting his friend, and that was far more important. And tomorrow, he would work on his new task: mastering empathy.

The door of the bar opened, letting errant notes of a live rock band spill out onto the slightly wet pavement. Shawn looked back, his smile so wide it could split his face. Brandon shook off his day and set it aside. It was a Thursday evening and he was with his friend. Everything else could just wait.

ELOQUENT EMPATHY

The books were on the table where he had left them after stumbling in bleary eyed and drunk the night before. As ever, it had been a late one, despite his insistence on the contrary, but it had been fun. Shawn had not gone off to pick someone up, much to his surprise, and had opened up about his life and sorrows. Brandon almost told him about his past, but stopped just in time. He was glad of that this morning. He did not need an oversharing hangover to go with the cider hangover.

Shaking his head at the remnants of a kebab and a beer bottle on the kitchen counter, he got to work clearing up and making the place presentable. It was a neat and spartan apartment – Brandon did not know how to add those little touches to make it homely, but he supposed with time, it would happen. Perhaps he needed one of those fancy bookshelves, you know, for his two books. He sniggered to himself as he cleaned the surfaces down and set the water to boiling. He eyed the books from across the room. He must have tipped them out of the bag to look at them last night, because the bag was on the floor and the Empathy one was on the top. At least he hadn't tipped beer on them, he supposed.

Taking his coffee, he moved back towards the table, picking up the book carefully. It didn't look all that special, with a fancy design or anything. Brandon wondered if the author liked to be minimalist about this stuff. Maybe they didn't like to communicate either. He flicked open the book, eyes sliding past the author's note and all the acknowledgements. The contents page was quite lengthy, too. He sighed, wondering if this was even a good idea. He should have just stuck with the fiction book. It had been too long since he read a book, and even then, he was a slow reader. This type of text would take him centuries. He moved to put it down, defeated, then paused, uncertain.

Either he was losing his mind, or the book had begun to pulse, as if it had a heartbeat. He opened it again, letting the pages fall open where they wanted. This time, he rested it on his legs, and he reached for his coffee, wincing when a little spilled on his hand. The book flared into light and he put the drink down hurriedly on the arm of the chair, gasping. The book was on fire.

The light faded, and the pages stilled.

Brandon held his breath, watching the book as if it were about to eat him. What just happened here? His heart was pounding almost out of his chest and his eyes felt like they were going to jump right out of his body. He took a grip of his coffee mug and brought it to his lips. If he was going to be murdered by a book, then he would be caffeinated as he went. If it wasn't the rule, it was now.

But the book waited meekly, not moving, not doing any freakish light show. Brandon clutched his mug to his chest and leaned closer, peering at the book.

The lines were close and dense. He couldn't make anything out. And then one sentence seemed to rise from the page, getting bigger and easier to read. He read it out loud, haltingly.

> In the shadows of our feelings, empathy shows the light within. It ties together our shared sorrows and joys. Understanding others lights up our own story with the ink of connection.

Brandon paused, his brow drawn together in worry. "What the fuck?" His words flew out of his mouth, scaring him in the sudden silence.

The book rustled, and the lines shone out again, but this time not as strongly. He froze. Words appeared on the page again, darkening.

> In the dance of pages, where words breathe and emotions weave, Eloquent Empathy awakens the dormant threads of connection. Within these leaves, your own story aligns with the symphony of others. Through understanding, the ink of shared experience illuminates the narrative tapestry. Explore, for the pages whisper the secrets of empathy.

This was getting ridiculous. And annoying. "I don't even know what that means. An ink of connection? A narrative tapestry? What are you, a bloody Hallmark card?" The book pulsed twice and stared back at him. Brandon felt almost amused alongside his terror. Was he arguing with a book? Had he finally lost his mind?

> In these pages, emotions come alive, connecting your story with others. Eloquent Empathy reveals the shared threads of experience. Explore, and you'll discover the secrets of understanding.

Well, at least it explained it a bit better. "Thank you," he said, feeling rather self-conscious. But the book lit up again, sending lights up over the page as if they were branches, then subsided again. Maybe it was saying you're welcome.

He put his mug back to his mouth and started when he realised it had already gone cold. That was weird. That was very weird. Putting it back on the table, he settled back into his seat, adjusting the book carefully. If this wasn't his mind going west, then something incredible was happening. Picking up the book, he examined it carefully, looking all over the cover and flicking through the pages. Now, he was not a surveillance expert, but he did not see how it could be anything but a book, and he had picked it up from the shelf himself. That would be an elaborate con indeed.

"Is this even real?" Brandon wondered aloud, not expecting an answer. But his eyes flickered downwards hopefully, just as the book pulsed and the lights sprang up again.

> Yes, this is real, Brandon, as real as words on paper can get. Or as real as your neighbour's cat who is pretending that they do not plot world domination. In the language of feelings, reality takes a holiday. So, is it real? Let's just say it's as real as your imagination dares to believe.

Brandon's eyes widened as he read. The neighbour's cat was definitely plotting something. He saw him every morning, giving him the look of death from the top of his owner's wheelie bin. He was absolutely planning world domination. He read the words again. It knew his name.

> Yes, Brandon. I do.

Great. It can read minds, too. Brandon glared at the book but it did not respond to his comment. The pages were still, quiet, but he sensed that it was waiting for something. For him. "Eloquent

Empathy. Is that your name? Are you... magic?" He paused, and took a deep breath. "Look, I'm not sure if I'm losing my mind entirely, or if I just drank too much with Shawn last night. If this is real, and I know you said it was real, and I know you know about the cat, but I knew about the cat, so maybe I'm making this up -" he shut his eyes, rubbing them carefully. "I don't know how to deal with this situation."

The book did not respond for a moment.

At least you're being honest.

Brandon blinked three times. Why did he have to get a book that was not only enchanted but was rude? But the rudeness was the tipping point. He would not have imagined a book to be impolite. It had to be real. It just had to be. His fingers moved toward the pages but paused, not wanting to be impolite himself. Two wrongs don't make a right, after all. "Can I, read you, book? What do I call you? Do I call you something? Book? Eloquent? El?"

The book flickered and pulsed rhythmically, and he smiled. If he didn't know better, he would think that the book was laughing. This was interesting. And he had to admit, it was a good conversation.

I think that I like this name, El. It's snappy. Yes, you can read me. I want you to read me. I am a book and that is my purpose. You wouldn't want to deny me my existence, would you? But we are going to go on a journey together, Brandon. I want to teach you about the connections that people make, and the experiences that they share with you. With me, you can find out anything about anyone, even make them do what you wanted, if that was your wish.

Brandon frowned. "I don't do things like that anymore, El. I used to be a bad person. I don't want to manipulate anyone. But I do want to be able to communicate better and connect with people. Can we do that without, you know, indulging in the Dark Side stuff?"

The book flashed and flickered uncertainly. Brandon watched the book ponder his words, awestruck. He was communicating with a book. It was talking to him. This was actually real. The book pulsed again, and the lights ran around in a tightening spiral before fading. He wondered what that pattern meant. They had to be patterns of feeling. Or emotions, perhaps. Were they separate from feelings? Was it a book expression? What was El thinking? He put aside the uncomfortable notion that he was already referring to El as a person, with their name. The book had named itself. It was simply polite to use the name.

> I think I understand. Dark is considered by some to be selfish or bad. Manipulation is not a negative force. It is necessary. When you dress or write, your fingers manipulate the object. Does it feel aggrieved by you using it for its given purpose? For becoming something more?

"I, er, don't think a pen thinks anything, El."

> Do I not think anything, Brandon?

And that was a touché moment right there. Brandon conceded the point. "Alright. Well, I am keen to learn nonverbal communication and build connections with people. I am disconnected, so separate from people – and it does not help that I cannot hear. People do not know how to communicate with me. I would like to do better."

That flicker came again, running up, down, then separating into small dashes that drew a symbol before fading on the page. It was definitely thinking. Brandon wondered if all objects were thinking. Were his clothes thinking about him right now? He shuddered. Best not to think about it.

> Why can you not hear?

Brandon laughed. That was direct. "I was born that way, El. I don't mind it. I'm sure some non hearing people would like to hear, but I like having my silence. I can put aids in to help me hear if I want to, but I don't usually. The world is quiet, muffled, as if I am still in the womb. It's like white noise for me. I find it relaxing. I don't need to hear everything. I enjoy having space and time to think."

The book pulsed again, the lights dancing in a tiny spiral. Brandon smiled. El understood.

"So, what's next, El? How do I learn about the ways of people? Do I read you first? I am a slow reader, I need to tell you that in advance. Don't get tired of me!"

The book lit up, one flash, then another. El was definitely laughing. He, she? They? Seemed to be a cheerful soul.

> Now, Brandon, we're going to go out. You can read me later. First, I want to show you how it is. Out there. Outside.

Outside! It's what the book ordered. Brandon scrambled off the sofa, picked El up gingerly, and headed out of the door. If El wanted to go outside, then they were going outside.

It was only a short walk to the shopping centre in Templars Square, to find crowds of people and have a practice. El had assured him that they would be perfectly fine tucked into his bag, but Brandon had wrapped the book up just in case. He wasn't sure how clean his backpack actually was, and the idea of a philosophical talking book being shoved into dust mites and receipts was embarrassing. He held the bottom of his bag close to his bag to make sure El wasn't being jolted. Which was a ridiculous notion, of course. But El was teaching him about empathy and El could think. So, he would keep the book safe and comfortable. And that was that.

Brandon reached the shopping centre nervously. It wasn't somewhere he went often, as there were too many lights and too many people, but it was a good place to start his practising. The doors shuffled open, admitting him into a white tiled hellscape of chain store shops, a bedraggled café and men sitting around in metal chairs and walking frames.

He looked around, looking for an empty bench to sit at. The one nearest to him was occupied by a tired looking woman, bags at the side of her. He walked on, behind the café and towards the stairs that led up to a deserted mezzanine floor. There was an empty bench which he occupied gratefully, throwing himself down and opening his bag up. El was, of course, wrapped safely inside.

He set up position, arranging El on the bench, putting his bag next to him and opening the book. A moment of stage fright overtook him. How would he speak out loud? Should he keep the book near his face? Did the book need to see things?

Stop panicking, Brandon. Your energy is all over the place.

"Easy for you to say, El. I'm the one talking to a book!"

Then you should be more discreet and not sweat while you stage whisper. People will think you are spying on them. Just think your thoughts and behave like a normal person.

Brandon bit back all of his retorts and took El's advice, as much as it rankled. Normal person, indeed. *Alright,* he thought as loudly as he could. *What do I do next?*

> Put your hand on my pages until you feel it tingle. I need to activate you. Then look around.

That didn't sound so bad. Brandon put his hand onto the page and then hesitated. *Activate me?*

The book pulsed just once, and the light turned a deep red. That was new. It had only been white light before. He looked around carefully, but nobody seemed to have noticed.

> Yes. How do you think these things work?

Brandon really wanted to roll his eyes. El was being aggravating.

> Likewise, Brandon. Let's get started.

He supposed that was fair. Brandon shrugged and pressed his palm into the book, feeling the page flutter and then warm up. Tingles spread into his palm, tracing lines back and forth, up and down. It was hot but it did not hurt. He looked right ahead, watching the crowds form outside the bakery, and hoped nobody would notice what he was doing. Perhaps he could say his hand had an itch? But nobody looked over, nobody challenged him, and slowly, the heat and the tingle faded. He removed his hand, turning it over to look at it to see if it had changed. It had not, of course. He placed his hand on the bench and looked down at the book.

What next, El?

> Look around, Brandon. Process what you can see. Tell me what you see, if you must. You should start to see… connections.

That sounded simple. He looked around, eyeing the redwood-stained benches, the white floors, and the glass-paned roof that lined the middle of the shopping centre. He looked at the people who were moving about, heads down, snaking into shop after shop, some laden down with bags, some with just one, or even none. Brandon knew that some stayed here all day. It was access to a toilet, to friendly voices, to a warm spot out of the rain. He knew that better than anyone. He knew how things that felt unimportant on the surface, became important when you had nothing else. You took nothing for granted.

His musing appeared in front of him, cloud-like. But it was a light, wispy cloud, not a stormy one. Brandon watched it move, transfixed. Slowly the cloud transformed into light and shot out, reaching other people and marking them with a splodge, a print. The mark blazed out in gold light for a moment and disappeared.

Brandon waited, his eyes wide. Something was happening, and he wasn't going to miss it. The people didn't seem to notice the light, nor did it harm them, as they carried on moving about, oblivious. He watched one figure, an elderly lady with a cane, slightly bent over, wearing a furred leopard print coat and matching hat. She had a plastic carrier bag hanging from her cane which she used as balance as she moved forward, not lifting her feet from the ground, walking slowly with purpose, almost as if she were skating.

As he watched intently, the light from the book skipped down to the floor and raced to her, playing with her ankles as if it were a young wolf, and ran back again. That was a signal, he thought. It wants me to watch her. I was right to pick her. So, he watched.

The change began so subtly that he might not have seen it if he wasn't watching. There was a flicker around her form, just for an instant, and then it faded away. A slight shadow formed behind her, one that looked like shadows of people. He leaned forward, staring intently. Yes, it was as if her shadow was made up of old photographs, dancing, moving, looking away. Brandon felt a stab of something in his chest, which then died away.

He put his hand to his chest absently, rubbing the painful spot, as he watched the old lady walk past. The shadows did not seem to touch her, not the ones from the bench, or from people, or where the sunlight hit from the windows above. He wondered at it. She walked alone, never touched by anything. The truth of it struck him, and he found himself standing, walking over towards her, hand out, before he even realised what he was doing.

Her head turned towards him, her face slack and frightened, and he saw the shadows turn, arching upwards toward her, almost as if they wanted to attack. A rhythmic pulse began in his ears, feeling almost like – he paused for a moment. It felt like a rapid heartbeat, that speedy flicker when a bird is close to death as fear overtakes them. His eyes were drawn to her white knuckles, holding tight to the cane. She was afraid. Of him.

Brandon didn't know what to do. *El! I saw the woman change, and I wanted to talk to her, but she's frightened. How do I set her at ease?*

There was silence. Of course there was. He could have kicked himself with frustration. El was on the bench still, where Brandon had placed the book. Waiting for him to come back. He was on his own. But he breathed for a moment, and looked again at her, the woman, her eyes. He smiled. She smiled back, just a ghost of a smile, but it was there.

"I'm sorry," Brandon said gently, "I didn't mean to alarm you. You, er, you looked like my grandma for a moment. I had to come and say hello."

Her smile broke across her face as if the sun had come out, her eyes bright, her mouth wide. She was beautiful. Light blazed out from her face. Brandon hesitated, dazzled. What had happened?

"Oh, don't apologise, duck. I was just startled for a moment. Aren't you a handsome young man! Do you visit your grandma often?"

"I don't, she died a few years ago. But when I could, I did. She always looked after me."

Those words were not meant to be spoken, but he did not regret letting them leave his mouth. He watched them fly, gold-edged, and saw her reaction, as joy erupted as birds around her face. She leaned forward, eyes crinkling, and stroked his face, just once, then withdrew. "She raised a good boy, that I can tell you. God bless you."

She went to move away, adjusting her stick and turning to carry on walking. Brandon stopped her, gently, with just one hand on her arm. "I'm sorry. Do you, need anything? I don't have much, I'm not rich, but can I help with anything? I would have wanted someone to help with my grandma," he added hastily. It wasn't about his grandma. It was about her, about the beauty of her spirit, but he couldn't say that. She wouldn't understand.

She smiled again, her teeth showing, her eyes sparkling. "No, duck, I don't need a thing. You coming over for a chat was the tonic I needed today. I don't ask for anything else. God bless you. You're a good man."

He stepped back as she left, watching her shuffle away, her shoulders bent and broad in her leopard print coat, her cane steady in her hand. She did not look back. But the shadows did not return, not the ones recording her past and not those that towered over her so ominously. Something had changed. And he suspected that that change was him.

DISCOVERING

Brandon couldn't stop thinking about that moment. Over and over, he replayed it, seeing the woman's face break into joy, just because he had SEEN her. It was literally that; he was sure of it. Using empathy meant that he could see people and bring them peace. He could bring everyone peace. He could go around helping anyone he saw and make them feel better about their lives.

"Shall we go back out again, El?" His words came out cheerfully, in a more natural fashion than he was used to. Normally he felt self-conscious, weighing each word before dropping it into the conversation. It was nice not to have to do that.

El hummed and pulsed before sending a line of lights up and down. They were red again. Brandon watched the lights thoughtfully, wondering what the change could mean.

Yes, soon. You did well earlier.

"Am I sensing a but, El?" Brandon chuckled to himself as he waited. It was almost as if El was getting more human-like by the minute.

> A but? Why would you sense one?   I am wondering how to track your progress. You did well today, and I know that you are happy that you made the woman feel less alone. This is a good thing and it is part of what empathy is: building connection through experience.

There was definitely a but coming. He shifted, adjusting his position to ensure he could better see El. Perhaps he should get the book a stand so it didn't have to lie down all the time. El pulsed again, shaking him from his thoughts.

> Joy is fleeting as an emotion. It is not as easily sustained as some of the others. So while you can easily bring joy to people through connection, you would have to remain with them for them to stay happy. And that would be impossible.

Brandon pursed his lips. "I don't think so, El. People keep their joy tucked away. They might not always show it, but it's there."

> Giving joy isn't always helping people. It doesn't last and they don't rely on themselves or communicate with others.

"What are you suggesting, El? What do you think is better?" The book paused for a minute, entirely silent. He began to worry. Had he overloaded El somehow? Was the book broken?

> It is better to use empathy to build connection through many emotions, not just making people happy. Sometimes grief or anger

are powerful motivators. You need to broaden your mind and understand what it is you can learn here, instead of taking the first exercise and stopping. I want you to grow.

"El, we've been through this. I don't want to manipulate people for my own gain." The book did not respond.

Sighing, Brandon picked it up, wrapping the book carefully, and left the apartment in silence. It was cold and crisp outside, with enough wind to let the leaves flutter and move. The roads were quiet for a change, and he decided it was a good time to walk and clear his head. Shoving his hands into his pockets, he set off down the street, aiming towards one of the parks. The fresh air would do him good. Turning down a passageway, he walked on, head down.

Was El right? Should he be broadening his mind? Was there a way to do that without hurting anyone? It seemed as if all the roads were turning crooked and leading back to his past. He did not want that, even if it meant he was diminished as a person. He could not possibly be, as he was living by the rules now. Surely that had to be better?

The passage ended abruptly, leading him into a quiet road lined with bare trees. As he turned, the door to the shop on his right opened, and two young people spilled out. They looked tall, perhaps already teenagers, with phones in hand and suspicious expressions. They looked at him and nodded. Brandon nodded back. There was no need to be unfriendly. They had all been kids once.

He trailed along behind them, wondering what they might be saying or thinking. It was hard to be a teenager, and even harder in this world. It was hard not to feel sorry for them. Light flared out of his chest and trailed towards them, looping around their leg and winding up their arms. One tendril stopped at the teenager's chest, the other tickled the ear of the tall one. Brandon smiled to himself. Empathy, much like El, seemed to have a sense of humour.

A dull black pain grew in his temple, making him wince. What was that? He looked over at the pair, who were still on their phones, lost in their own world. The tendrils had moved to the taller one now, so Brandon focused on him. The boy was feeling something strong. Brandon's vision blurred for just a moment, and when it cleared he could see doors trailing out behind the boy. Each door seemed to float in space, each one identical, a black door with a plain brass knob. They were closed. Door after door after door... he ached for the boy. He had many secrets and a great deal of pain. El was right. Joy wouldn't help this boy for more than a moment, and then he would be right back in his misery.

Brandon turned abruptly and walked on his heel in the opposite direction, wanting to get away from people, from the dull pain, from the doors in the teen's mind. Did he really want a lifetime of pain, of seeing people's pain, when there was so little he could do about it? What if he got tempted to manipulate people for money, just as he used to in the past? Conning was like a drug to him, the rush of seeing the trap set, and the victim walk right in, he knew that. It was a game of wits with high stakes. What was not to love? Except it meant hurting people, people who didn't know better, people who had more money than sense. Rarely did a con land on someone who truly deserved it.

But what if he could target just those who deserved it? What then? No. He shook off the idea. It may start that way but it would never end that way. And who was he to decide who deserved something or not? He was no judge. He did not want to be.

Keeping his eyes looking at the ground so he did not see more people and their secrets, Brandon made his decision. He needed to go back to the bookshop.

Brandon hadn't dared to open his bag and tell El that he was returning and giving the book back. He felt wracked with guilt. After all, it wasn't El's fault. They had simply picked the wrong person to teach.

It's not you, it's me, he whispered to himself. *I'm sorry, El.*

The bookshop looked even smarter in the daylight, with gleaming windows and a smart black door. This time, there was a cat perched proudly on top of a book display in the window, and Brandon noticed the sign. The Black Cat Bookshop. Well, that was why there were cats there. He wondered if that was the one he had seen last time or a different one. It was hard to tell.

He pushed his way in, hoping he could get this over and done with. He didn't want to just slap the bag down and leave, that wouldn't be fair on El. But he didn't entirely know how to explain to the shop owner that he had accidentally bought a magic book that showed him the secrets of the world and could read his mind.

Meredith would cart him off to the loony bin as quick as that. And he wouldn't blame her. Brandon rubbed his temples. He felt tired, all of a sudden, as if he was coming down with something. He sniffed and then sneezed. Was it the cats? No, he had never had an allergy before to cats.

Shrugging it off, he stepped into the shop and gently placed the bag on the counter. It looked up at him silently, without any lights to show that it was actually alive. He didn't know if that made him feel relieved or sad. He didn't want to say goodbye to El, but what choice did he have? He wasn't the one for the book. It was the right thing to do.

Meredith appeared, almost as if she had stepped out from a wall, and smiled. Brandon blinked in surprise. She must have been behind a bookshelf or something.

"Hi, Brandon!" She made a point of looking right at him, which was impressive. Most people took a moment to remember that he was deaf, if they did at all. He nodded sheepishly. "Hi, Meredith. I just wanted to, erm, drop this book off. It's not for me, I'm afraid."

"Oh, that does surprise me. Have you read it?" He nodded, and Meredith pursed her lips, thinking. For a moment, she looked like a cat, lost in thought, regal. He shook off the idea before it took root. He did not need to start getting empathy here. He needed to leave the book here and go back to his life.

"I am afraid I can't give you a refund for it, Brandon, as you have read the book, unless it was damaged in some way."

"Oh, no, I understand that. I don't need a refund, I just want to give the book back to you. Can you find a better home for it, perhaps?"

Her head tilted, eyes narrowing ever so slightly as she inspected him. "Did you like the book, Brandon?"

Brandon grimaced and squirmed inwardly. That was not the question he wanted to answer. "I did, actually, it's very interesting. But I think that the kind of person who would do best with this kind of book, is a person that isn't me. I don't want to manipulate people or make them change how they feel. I just wanted to connect with people, perhaps bring some peace to people's lives."

Meredith nodded, looking a lot like she knew exactly what he was not saying. "Of course. I understand completely. Sometimes a book isn't right for us at all, sometimes it just comes at the wrong time. I appreciate that you dropped it off and didn't just discard it. I can get this one into the proper hands, I promise you."

Brandon nodded, struggling to focus. His head felt strange as if he had a headache without a pain, and it felt like his skin was throbbing. What was happening? Meredith was still speaking, her mouth forming words, but he couldn't make them out. It was as if someone had cut off his brain, melding it into something different. Nothing made sense.

Out of the corner of his eye, he saw El light up, muffled by the bag. It was a white light again, flashing and pulsing at the same frequency as his skin. Without thinking, he stepped forward and placed his hand on the book, feeling the same strange sensation as the day before. Something curled into his palm, hot but painless. El was activating him again.

The fog cleared and he stepped back, bewildered. Meredith was looking at him, her brows drawn together in concern. But he did not look at Meredith. His attention was drawn to the bookshop, or more accurately, the thing that floated in the bookshop, that was looking right at him.

There was a swirling dark grey smoke hanging there, stretching like vines across and within the walls, around the bookshelves, and across the ceiling. It rippled, sending ripples of black stars up into the air. He had never seen anything as beautiful or as terrifying in his entire life.

Meredith moved, and his eyes tore themselves from the smoke to look at her. "You see it, don't you." It wasn't a question.

"I see it. What the fuck is that?"

"It is the bookshop. Or more accurately, it is what makes the bookshop special."

Brandon searched her face, looking for an expression or a twitch, something to show that she was lying, or getting ready to spring the punchline on him. But she did not. He looked back up at the smoke. It was definitely still there.

"But what... is it?" His words came out like a whisper, hissed into the silence.

She sighed. "This is a long story, and I do not care to tell it all right now. But I can tell you enough, as you have advanced enough to be able to see it. You deserve that. The bookshop is alive. It is a being that came about through great sorrow, when a wrong was done to a large group of people. Their collective sorrow, their collective loss of knowledge, wisdom and culture, gave birth to the bookshop. Or, the consciousness of it. To keep it from being destruction itself, I formed it into this. So it is lodged here, for want of a better word."

Brandon watched her carefully. That was not the whole story, but it was all he was going to get. His eyes shifted back up to the smoke, and then down to the counter where El still lay. Why had the book done that? Did it know that the bookshop was affecting him? It must have been the bookshop. Was it getting into his brain, perhaps?

"Before, when I came in, I felt a dull ache and a strange foreboding in my head, which intensified. El, the Empathy book, signalled to me to touch it and then it cleared. Was that the bookshop? Was it trying to do something to me?"

Meredith frowned. "If it was, it was moving very fast. You only got the book a day or two ago. That could be – concerning."

A sliver of worry worked its way up Brandon's neck. "Concerning?"

She shrugged. "It picks who it wants to keep, you see. It sounds like it picked you."

"You need to explain that, Meredith. Please." He added the afterthought hoping it would sound authoritative, but it came out a lot like a squeak. The sliver of worry had wormed itself into a stream of sweat, sliding down his back. He stepped a little closer to the counter, wishing he could ask El for some advice. Wishing he hadn't tried to give it up.

"The bookshop offers people knowledge, and it feeds from what you learn. It draws some people into itself because it recognises them as like, or because it wants to learn more about them. But everyone, whether they come to the Bookshop again and again, or just once, everyone must make a payment for the knowledge they have taken. Even you, Brandon. Even you."

"So, are you saying, even if I give the book back, I still have to pay – that?" He pointed to the ceiling. The smoke thickened and pulsed again, moving along the ceiling at an alarming rate. Brandon shrank back, his hand grasping the book that he was going to give up.

Meredith smiled sadly. "It seems so. You are in debt."

His mind spun like clockwork, flicking through the possibilities. He had to pay. And that thing up there wasn't going to play fair. He had to put his old head back on. And he needed an ally. Pulling El from the bag, he opened it to the pages.

"I'm sorry I tried to give you up, El. Can you forgive me?"

The book waited, then sent three dots in a straight line. Brandon felt the corner of his mouth twitch. Even in the middle of a crisis, El had to be smart.

"I think you were right, El. But I can adapt. Do you know what I mean?"

El swirled the light in a spiral and then went out.

> The dark side, Brandon?

Brandon grinned. "Exactly," he replied, resisting the urge to hug the book to his chest. He had an ally. A friend, perhaps. And he would not go down without a fight. Grimly, he turned back to Meredith.

"And what are the terms of my payment?"

Meredith paused and put her finger to her mouth for just a moment as she thought. "I am not sure yet. It normally becomes apparent as you develop your skills, but the bookshop seems to have taken an early interest in you. Perhaps you will have to wait."

"Or, can I perhaps, negotiate payment? After all, if the Bookshop has not decided, then I might be able to offer something it would like." El flashed the lights in approval, one line that ran up and down. That had to be a high five. If it wasn't, it was now.

He turned back to Meredith, waiting. He was on track, he knew it. Meredith smiled a half smile, her eyes calculating. "I knew you would be interesting, Brandon. You have such an interesting past. Alright, I will allow a revised payment plan negotiation, and the bookshop can agree the particular terms and duration. I will even get someone neutral to witness the paperwork to make sure everything is above board for you. If that's agreeable to you?"

Brandon shrugged, then nodded. He had regained some ground but not enough to really call the shots on this shitshow yet, and so for now, he may as well be agreeable. He wondered about the paperwork and the witness. He wondered if anyone would ever believe him about today. He imagined Shawn sitting down in front of him, listening to this story. The man would have a heart attack. He was surprised that he hadn't had one, yet. It had been an eventful few days.

"Alright, then." Meredith reached out and shook his hand firmly, taking him by surprise. She looked hard into his eyes.

"Be back here at nightfall, Brandon. You have some negotiations to prepare for. Good luck." The words resonated in his brain, edged with cold steel. He gasped, feeling her fingers turn into claws for just an instant, and back again. El pulsed in his hand as if it were reassuring him.

The light in the bookshop winked out in an instant, and then as if by magic, back on again. Brandon gasped again, clutching at his chest, wheezing. He was standing in the centre of his apartment, holding El in his hand. He was alone.

Negotiations with a Monster

Brandon's hands shook so badly that he wondered if he would be better off drinking his coffee with a straw. He glared at it balefully, before opening the fridge and getting a bottle of beer out. Desperate times called for desperate measures. Opening it, he took a mouthful, wishing it had an extra shot of tequila in it or something. He needed to get drunk more badly than he ever had in his life.

He was having a lot of firsts today. El was back on the table, sending off pulsing lights like they were at a rave. At least they hadn't learned how to do strobe lights yet. They gave him a headache.

Cutting that thought off, just in case El was listening and was feeling vengeful, he returned to his spot, determined to make a plan.

He had till nightfall. That was in three hours, according to his watch. Not long enough, anyway.

"I don't know what sort of shit you got me into here, El. I wasn't expecting this, you know."

El flashed up in what had to be an indignant red blotch, then sent the horizontal lines out.

> You picked me, remember.

El was still pissed. "I said I'm sorry, El. I just got overwhelmed by it all and didn't want to be seeing people's feelings all the time. It wasn't personal." Brandon sighed. "I was wrong, OK?"

El left the blotch of red on the page, blinking like one of the old-style answer machine lights. Leave a message, I'm not home... He sighed again. "Have you got any suggestions of how I get out of this mess?"

> I'm a book about empathy. Perhaps you should have chosen one about hostile negotiations instead.

Brandon laughed and reached for his beer. Definitely still pissed. "Well, I'm good with negotiating. I'm happy with you. You'll do."

The light softened and paled to an ethereal forest green light, then went out. Perhaps the book was appeased at last.

"So, what should I offer the bookshop, do you think? You might not be a hostile negotiations book, but you've got empathy. Like you said, with connections, we can make people do whatever we want. I reckon, we'll do better putting a plan up together. We just need to work out what it wants. And then make it think that what we offer, is what we want."

Brandon paused, raising the beer bottle in a salute. "I say we con the bookshop into letting us go free. What say you?"

El lit up the spiral, running from white to yellow to green. That was new.

"Classy light show, El. I like it. Does it mean you have an idea?"

> Perhaps. Meredith said that the bookshop offers knowledge and draws people into itself when they are alike, yes?

He frowned. "I think so. I can't remember the exact words. But it was something like that."

El vibrated and then sent lights that scrambled over each other like beetles. Brandon watched with concern. "Are you alright, El? You're looking a bit squiffy."

> "The bookshop offers people knowledge, you see, and it feeds from what you learn. It draws some people into itself because it recognises them as like, or because it wants to learn more about them. But everyone, whether they come to the Bookshop again and again, or just once, everyone must make a payment for the knowledge they have taken. Even you, Brandon. Even you."

> That was what she said. I did not know that I had that facility. Useful.

Brandon stared, not sure if he wanted to be sick at the reminder of Meredith's words or clap for El's new skill. He opted for the latter. "Hey, that's great! I bet that'll be useful. Do you know how much you can record?"

El blipped out light, almost as if they were hiccupping.

> No idea. Let's not push it. I prefer using my own words, not someone else's. They didn't taste good.

"I bet they didn't. Sorry. I won't ask you again unless it's absolutely necessary. Life or death." He paused. "I suppose it already is."

That was sobering. He gulped down the rest of his beer, again wishing that it was stronger. "Hmm. So the bookshop gives knowledge. That's you, and other books like you." Brandon stroked his chin, deep in thought. "Hey, are all the other books like you? In the bookshop?" In a flash, his eyes dropped to the other book that Meredith had chosen, with its bright orange cover and fierce machines. He moved to pick it up and paused, hesitant. Afraid. "Don't be a fucking coward, Brandon," he murmured, and grabbed the book, opening it wide. It looked like an ordinary book. He flicked through the pages, looking for lights or sounds or something else magical. Nothing happened. "That was a bit disappointing. I was expecting a Terminator or something for a second."

Terminator? I thought you didn't want to be killed.

Brandon laughed. "Pop reference, El. If we ever get through this alive, I'll be introducing you to the movie world. Starting with Terminator. But in short, it's a sentient robot in disguise as a person that comes back in time to kill the female main character, so she doesn't give birth to the man who brings down the machines. It's a good story."

He sat back for a moment, thinking. Perhaps the bookshop needed to be introduced to something like the Terminator. It might scare it into being a bit more human. That's it!

He leaned forward, knocking his drink over as he went. "I've got an idea!"

I don't think we can go back in time yet, Brandon. But the idea has merit.

He rolled his eyes, reaching for the beer bottle and putting it safely in the kitchen. "No, you exasperating smart-ass. A story is the idea." He retrieved a tea towel to mop up the spill and shook his head at the book. "What if, we give the book knowledge, knowledge of my life, knowledge of what we have learned, and build it into a story, that it listens to? I bet it would take that as payment."

El did the spiral loading symbol, letting the lights wink in and out as it went. Brandon waited. They had time, after all. Some time. He considered whether he should get another beer. He would need his wits about him later, but he would probably be that scared shitless that he would be instantly sober as a judge. It was worth the risk. He was about to get up and hit the fridge when El stopped the lights.

> Giving knowledge of your life in a story would be authentic, and storytelling is certainly a powerful tool. You could use it to deliver certain messages that kept the bookshop interested. I think it has merit, and it buys you time, which currently you, or we, do not have much of. I suggest you use this plan and see what the bookshop says.

Brandon smiled at the addition of we. It was nice to not be alone. "Do you know anything about the bookshop, El? Is it like, your father or something?"

The book did the strange rhythmic lights that he was sure was a laugh. Maybe they weren't related then.

> I am not sure what the bookshop is. I was not aware of it, that I know of, before we arrived at the bookshop today. And yes, I am still 'pissed' about you planning to leave me there with a monster. I assume that is a vulgar word for angry.

> I do not feel connected to the bookshop, but I suppose I must have been created there. I am eager to find out more about my origins

so will help you to get the bookshop to open
up to you.

"If you were created there, then we need to find out more about where you came from, definitely. Can we talk about how to use empathy with my stories? How do I make them irresistible? Do I just have to feel the stories? Is that it?"

El paused, letting the white light just simmer gently on the page. Brandon watched it, realising that the lights really were soothing. It was like a gentle lightshow, or starlight. It was nice to watch.

"Hey, are your lights creating the empathy, El? Is that what I am seeing? Are they your feelings?"

Something like that. You need to feel the
stories to make them come alive. And yes,
the lights are how I feel. My words are how
I think. Is it not that way for you?

He thought about it for a while. His words were how he thought, but he could layer his words with meaning that was not true. He could give his words no meaning, or let them fly high with his happiness. Did that mean his words were his thoughts, or were they always interconnected? Perhaps some emotions came through more strongly than others. He looked at the book. "Yes, it is like music, perhaps. The notes are the same but you can play it differently with different emotion depending on which instrument you use. My emotions are my orchestra, my words are my music notes. So I need to tell my story with an orchestra."

A symphony. It will create a resonance, if you
can make the bookshop understand.

Brandon decided he was going to get another beer. If he was going to be a fucking conductor for the night to bargain his stories as payment to some cloud demon in the ceiling of a bookshop, he may as well get a bit tipsy beforehand. "Alright then. I'll bring my guitar. It's a joke, El, before you take it seriously. Eh?"

He threw a grin over his shoulder as he watched the lights settle into the line of indifference. Ha! He was reading the book like a book. He was a pro at this stuff! "I'm coming to get you, Bookshop," he muttered to himself. "I might not have much, but I can convince a person of anything. Let's see what you've got."

His words were bravado, but for the first time, he could hear a soundtrack behind the words. It was a mix of fear, sheer fucking spite and a little bit of hope. It was his soundtrack and by fuck he was going to play it.

Twilight drew in faster than he had expected. But he and El were ready, standing at the window watching the sunset streak through the sky. They were both silent. El had run through principles of how to use empathy, and Brandon was surprised to realise that he had done most of it already when doing his former 'job'. That would come in handy. The book was the expert, but he was the person who knew how to do it in real time.

Books were all well and good, but sometimes you needed someone who knew how to do it with their eyes closed, who was not afraid to get his hands dirty. As he waited for the summons, El under his arm, he knew he was that person. It filled him with a faint note of confidence. Perhaps today, he was the best man for the job. That was worth saying out loud.

The room folded around them, snuffing out the light. Brandon waited, as calm as he could be under the circumstances, breathing through his nose, ignoring the pounding of his suddenly over-worked heart. In almost an instant, they were there at the bookshop, and the players were all assembled. He thought it looked a lot like a chess board all of a sudden: the Bookshop curled up in the corner like a sleeping sea serpent, Meredith, the Queen, her eyes flashing in amusement, and the cats, lined up on the stairs, watching the show. Her pawns, perhaps.

But there was another player, and one Brandon had not seen before. He studied him openly. Today, they played for different stakes, and he did not have to fumble around for politeness. The man was tall and exceptionally attractive. Brandon was not attracted to men, but he could see that this man could command attention from everyone. He was wearing a sharp three-piece suit with a white shirt that dazzled against his dark skin. His hair was long, reaching to his waist in long, smooth plaits. His eyes were dark, serious, and evaluating, his gaze fixed on him. Brandon did not know who this man was, but he was a player in this game. He just needed to know which side, and which piece.

Meredith began with her move, spreading her arms wide as if she was at a performance. Perhaps she was. "Welcome, Brandon. It is nice to see you again."

"Yeah, right," he muttered under his breath. El pulsed in response. "Nice to see you, too, Meredith. But please, don't put on a show for me. I don't need it. I'm just going to put El here, right? They want to watch the process, for book purposes, you understand." He could have sworn that the man with plaits laughed, but he didn't react. He kept his eyes on the Queen, letting his peripheral vision handle Magali, waiting for her first move.

"Of course, Brandon. This is how it will work today. You are here to negotiate a payment plan with the Bookshop, and they will either agree your terms or deny them. Magali here," she gestured dismissively to the man, "will be a witness to the process and add his signature to the paperwork when it is completed."

Magali stirred, clasping his hands in front of him, letting his sleeves ride up. He was wearing a very expensive watch. The man saw Brandon watching and winked, almost imperceptibly. Then he looked at Meredith, letting the atmosphere cool considerably. "So, that's what you're up to, Meredith. You called me here and caused me to cancel an important meeting with a client, to witness one of your victims negotiate a payment plan?"

Meredith smiled a smile that had no warmth or humour in it. Her eyes were like iced seawater, stormy, angry, and cold. "That's right, Magali. You can witness, sign, and leave. If we get this over with quickly you can even re-join your meeting."

"Oh, no, I've cancelled it. I'm at your leisure today, Meredith."

Brandon could read the polite words but the undertone that he could feel in the air between them was beyond antagonistic. Magali sent spikes with his comments, and Meredith was more than ready to return them. He wondered what had happened between them. Lovers, perhaps? Some kind of tiff?

Magali turned his attention to Brandon with a snap, making him jump. "Has Meredith explained the terms and my role here, Brandon?"

He could feel the tension rising from Meredith in waves. He looked over at El, who was perched against a book, meekly listening. *Do you think Magali could be an asset?* The book stirred and twirled the lights for a moment, then ran up and down. *Yes.* That had to mean yes. The book had seen what he had seen, then. He had a potential ally, for whatever reason. That was unexpected and entirely welcome.

He turned to Magali. "No, she hasn't. She said merely that you would witness the arrangement."

El flashed the lights three times. Brandon looked over, raising his eyebrows in a silent question.

Alright, I will allow a revised payment plan negotiation, and the bookshop can agree the particular terms and duration. I will even get someone neutral to witness the paperwork to make sure everything is above board for you. If that's agreeable to you?"

This time, the words were projected into the air, hovering above the book, ensuring that everyone could see them. Magali studied the text message box, then contemplated El. "Is that what Meredith said, exactly?" El responded with the lights, running up and down.

"That means yes, I think," Brandon offered helpfully. He was rewarded by the slightest twitch of Magali's lips and a crinkle of his eyes. "I see. Thank you. And thank you, Eloquent Empathy."

El responded with a twirl of lights in thanks. "The book likes to be called El," he added, amused. Why he was amused when he was facing imminent death, he did not know, but this was quite funny.

Magali eyed him again. "Right. Thank you, El."

He fixed Meredith with his hard stare. "You were evasive in your response to Brandon, which is careless of you. I expected more."

Magali looked back at Brandon, making sure that he saw him before he spoke. "Brandon, I am here to witness your negotiations and your payment plan for the bookshop. I cannot interfere with your owing of a payment because that is something sacrosanct. You were given knowledge which you have used, and therefore you must pay for that knowledge. But. And this is a big but. There are two other duties that I can impart for you. First, I can ensure that negotiations are held.... fairly." His eyes were full of meaning, and his words were measured. Brandon wondered what his voice sounded like. Was it deep and sonorous? Did he speak with an accent? He would have to ask El, later. If there was a later.

Magali continued. "And second, I can assist you in those negotiations." Meredith gasped and stepped forward, but Magali held his hand up to stop her. She stopped. Brandon watched with interest. Magali was a key player in this game, and he was not necessarily on Meredith's side. That was useful to know.

"What do you mean by, assist me in those negotiations, Magali?" Magali smiled, pleased with the question. "It means that I can insist you have more time to prepare, with more knowledge about what you are dealing with. I will help you with information gathering and with structuring your proposal. Do you accept my help?"

He paused. There was more to this than met the eye, and he did not entirely trust Magali. Yes, he had defended him to Meredith, and the man did not like Meredith. But that did not mean he was not out for something himself. Brandon looked at Meredith, who was waiting, absorbed in the interaction. Her eyes were ablaze, intent. El was doing the traffic light flash again. He ignored it. *I know, El. He's keeping something back. Keep an ear on things.*

He took a breath, forming the words in his mouth. Now was a time where he needed not only the words, but the symphony. He took a note of disbelief, a note of relief, and a note of suspicion. Then he added his intellect, just a drop, so Magali knew he had a brain. "And how much does your help cost, Magali?"

That was the right question. The bookshop smoke unfurled and curled again, the cats swished their tails in seriously creepy unison, and Meredith nodded, just once, so slightly that Brandon almost disbelieved that he had seen it. Why would she nod? Why would she care if he got help without fucking his life up more along the way? Magali smiled, his grin as wide as the Cheshire Cat.

"The price is not more than you can afford, Brandon. A friend of mine was taken by the Bookshop. I want you to help me get him back."

Well, that was a no-brainer. Of course he would help. But Brandon knew this game. He waited, feeling the pulse of the bookshop through his feet, feeling the percussion of hearts beating, waiting for his response. At last, he answered. "I accept, Magali. I will help you. And you can help me."

Time slowed as Magali leaned forward and shook his hand. "It's a deal."

MOVE THE MIRRORS, TALK THE TALK

Magali arrived early, looking fresh and ready to negotiate, carrying two cups of takeaway coffee and a briefcase. He was dressed more casually today, in a black jacket, jeans and a dark green sweater, but he still looked like he had taken fashion tips from Lenny Kravitz. Brandon chuckled to himself. All of these years of never noticing what a woman even wore, and now he couldn't stop looking at this man's sartorial choices. How the world turns. Perhaps it was a trauma response to approaching death by bookshop.

He nodded, handing the coffee over and scanning the room briefly. "Let's get to work," he said. Brandon resisted the urge to salute, putting the coffee down and opening El up so they could join in the conversation. They flipped the lights in a pretty pattern; to either say good morning or something else, he did not know. Magali hadn't moved, his eyes unfocused. "How many mirrors do you have in here?"

Brandon raised his eyebrows. That was an odd question. "Two, I think. One in the hallway, one in the bathroom. Why?"

Magali twitched slightly, his mouth thinning. "Remove the hallway one. Cover the bathroom one. Mirrors are portals, and the bookshop can use them easily. Don't leave yourself exposed."

Seriously? He blinked, and blinked again. "Are you serious? Portals? To where?"

Magali stared at him, his eyes serious. "You do not want to know. Cover the mirrors. Or better still, remove them both."

"Alright, alright. No smashing them, then? Is that still considered bad luck?"

"No, not bad luck. If you smash them, you just made more portals. Why would you?"

He was being serious. Magali was actually being serious. Brandon went to cover the mirrors, collecting a small towel and a sheet. He eyed the hall mirror with fear as he went past, resisting the urge to duck under it just in case. What if something was watching him right now? His bathroom was dark, darker than it normally was. He wrapped the sheet around it carefully, tucking it in behind the frame. When this was all done with, he might get rid of the mirrors entirely. How often had a creature looked at him from the mirror? It did not bear thinking about. Magali was right. He didn't want to know. He lifted the hall mirror from the wall in one smooth motion and hauled it outside, stacking it against the bins with the mirror part facing away from the apartment. "Bye, freaky mirror portal," he muttered as he left. What a world to be in. All he did was buy one chuffing book and all of a sudden, the entire world was turned upside down. He needed that coffee.

The coffee was good, nicely blended and rich, with just a little milk added. It was actually exactly as he always drank it. He lowered the cup, eyeing Magali with a little suspicion. "It's very good. How did you know how I drink it?"

The man responded with a very Gallic shrug. "Can I keep no secrets? I am just good at guessing, perhaps."

Hmmm. Brandon narrowed his eyes and returned to his coffee. As quirks went, it had a good outcome. He wasn't going to worry about it. "So, we had the idea of offering stories to the bookshop to pay my fee for the knowledge, but add my understanding of empathy to enrich the stories. What do you think?"

Magali listened, sitting opposite him in the only chair, his hands loosely clasped together. He ruminated for a while, statue-like, as El danced with the lights and Brandon sipped his excellent coffee. "I think it has merit. Although I think you should offer only one story. The bookshop will interpret stories in a different way to you. It would drain you dry. Give it just one, but make it the best story you have."

He eyed El for a moment, his expression thoughtful. "I do wonder how a wisp ended up in the bookshop."

A what? El seemed to have the same reaction as the lights turned from the usual rhythmic dance to the weird, chaotic beetle dash, with lights crawling all over each other. He tore his eyes from the book and stared at Magali. "A what?"

"A wisp. Foolish Fire, if you want the Latin word. It is a spirit of light that likes to lead travellers astray. They are known for being mischievous creatures." Brandon cough-laughed into his coffee. El returned to the line of indifference, smouldering away in a noxious angry red. *It's true, though,* he thought at the book. *You ARE mischievous.*

"Then El is a spirit too? But not made by the Bookshop?"

Magali rubbed his long fingers over his chin and beard in a thoughtful fashion. "No, El was not made by the Bookshop. Although they may have come into contact with each other over the last four centuries. That is why the book uses lights, perhaps. It is part of its nature."

"It hums, too. I can feel the vibration of it. I thought it used lights to communicate with me because I am deaf."

Magali nodded, still thoughtful. "It could be doing that, too. Although I have not met many helpful wisps. They are normally more interested in leading people by the nose through impossible tasks. A light of amusement entered his eyes. "But then, you are in an impossible situation. Perhaps this wisp is not that unusual after all."

An impossible situation? That wasn't encouraging. "I thought you were meant to be helping us out, Magali, not scaring me to death. If it's impossible, why offer?"

The man smiled, his eyes smouldering with humour. "It is impossible. How many do you think renegotiate with the bookshop, or even negotiate at all? Do you know what it does to people?" He paused, studying Brandon's face. "No, I think you do not. The bookshop gives knowledge, but it also consumes knowledge. It takes souls, their consciousness. The entity that is in the bookshop was a spirit created over four hundred years ago when a terrible event took place. Many lives were lost, many were burned."

Brandon watched, watching Magali's face. There was real pain there. It was as if he remembered it. "What happened?"

Magali stirred himself and smiled sadly. "You would probably know of it as the Witch Trials, right at the height of the Civil War. Over a period of twenty years, women were hunted, interrogated and killed in brutal ways. It was a very dark time. Much wisdom was lost to the fires. All that pain and fear began to manifest itself as a consciousness, a collective one of hundreds of souls crying out in anger and grief. It is why it manifests most as a smoke. It is what it was born from, from smoke and rage and pain.

But because of that, it craves it, in turn, to stay alive. It consumes those who seek knowledge; it swallows up the people who succumb to the power. I do not know how many people it has consumed over the years. Since Meredith claimed and confined it to these walls, it has been much less active, but it still hunts. At least now, it is more discriminate. But that is what you must face. A spirit that has festered in its own rage for hundreds of years, a collective soul of screams and smoke and cries. This is why I said it is impossible. However, before you drop your brave face and wilt, you do have a wisp on your side who seems to want to help you, for whatever reason. And I, too, have agreed to help you. I think that evens the playing field somewhat."

Magali reached for his own coffee cup, his fingers curling around delicately. Even his nails were smooth, polished and cut. The man was perfect. Brandon shook his head. "And what are you and Meredith? Because I know you're not human. Humans don't go around enclosing spirits in bookshops or bringing the perfect cup of coffee. Well, maybe they do if they know you, but you've never met me, Magali. Are you both the same? Are you the bad guys? Or something else?"

"No, we are not the same. Meredith has a human shape but she is actually a god."

Brandon spat his coffee out. It flew in droplets towards El, who sent up the flashing lights in alarm. Magali deftly pushed the book out of the way and smiled archly. "So wisps and spirits born of a tragedy are easy to accept, but a god is not? You surprise me, Brandon. I thought you people were all quite happy with accepting deities."

He fidgeted, wiping the coffee from his chin and his front. That was dignified. "Yes, on paper, but not in real life. I would rather they stay in books. Which god is she?"

"Her real name is Laverna, and her domain is the Underworld. She is technically a Roman god, so not widely known, but she keeps much of her power. She is actually patron for thieves and con-artists, which is an interesting detail, considering, you know." He waved his coffee cup expansively, looking at Brandon significantly.

"You know?"

"Your past. You used to be a con-man, did you not? I suspect she has a soft spot for you."

He laughed so hard that he started to cough, his eyes streaming with tears. Magali watched him quizzically, eyebrows drawn together in puzzlement. God, that man deserved to be in films. He would be a millionaire. Brandon bashed his chest with his fist, trying to settle his heart. It would be done with him in no time at all at this rate. "Man, that was funny. If this is Meredith's way of saying she's fond of me, I wouldn't want to see what she does to people she doesn't like."

Magali's eyes grew sad. "No, you don't want to see that." He paused, his eyes far away. "But she has given you a fighting chance. More than just a chance, really. She didn't have to summon me to witness. She knew I would be focusing on the contractual details. It makes me wonder if she's pulling the strings more than I realised here."

"Do you mean that this God, Laverna, helps criminals?"

The man leaned forward, his eyes bright. "That's exactly what I mean. The criminal quarter of Rome would leave offerings to her temples, which were tiny little boxes at the sides of the road. It was notoriously hard to catch a thief in Rome at the time. She was a very popular deity. She was good at her job, I suppose you could say."

"Wait," Brandon said. His head was swimming again. "You say that like you were there." He watched Magali, and waited for him to laugh, to scoff, to deny it. He did not. "It's like you were actually there in Ancient Rome. Like, two thousand years ago." Magali still did not respond, or disagree with him. Damn. He subsided into his chair. In the corner of his eye, he could see El, one green light blinking, as if they were intent too.

"What exactly are you, Magali?"

Magali picked up his cup again, eyeing Brandon carefully over the rim. At last, he spoke. "I'm a demon, if you really want to know. I've lived here for a few millennia. I've become quite attached to the place."

Brandon's mouth felt as if it had rolled onto the floor and stayed there. He remained where he was, blinking, trying to process the information. How do you respond to that? Yeah that's great, where are your horns and tail? Can you grant me a wish? No, that's a genie. What's Satan like? No, stupid, Brandon. Think of something!

Magali continued, delicately filling the silence so that he did not have to. "I don't know how familiar you are with demon lore, so I will assume you have little knowledge of it. Please forgive me if I am mistaken. Much of what we are has been changed or altered, over the years. We're fallen angels, really, beings that decided they wanted something more than was originally offered. We have a society, rules, and a hierarchy. Most of my kind get involved in legal matters and representation. I know of a few demon lawyers. It's quite common. We tend to gravitate to contracts, of course."

"Of course," Brandon echoed faintly, feeling incredibly stupid. But what else could he say?

Magali seemed to not mind the interruption. "Most demons prefer to stay out of sight. This means that we take on your forms, and live as one of you. We rarely meddle. But after a while, we get tired, and want to see more of the world. We connect with souls who can see the other meanings, who can have a deeper understanding of what there is, and we show them how the world can really be."

"And then you take their souls, right? Just like the bookshop." He did not mean the words to fire out as they did, because honestly Magali seemed to be a reasonable sort, but it rankled. The fear, the anger. It had to come out.

"Not necessarily, Brandon. We do not trick people into making unwise bargains. If someone comes to us, knowingly, and exchanges their soul for great wealth or whatever, we will not stop them. But they have to find us. We are not the evangelising type. It's not our style."

"And you buy babies' souls, right? I've seen enough films. You'll snatch babies if people offer them to you."

Magali's face became stern, his eyes blazing red for just one moment. "I would not believe everything you watch, Brandon. We do not take other people's souls in a bargain and we never take innocents. This is why I offered to help you, and I was clear about what I needed in exchange. My friend was taken by the bookshop, and I believe that he was an innocent. We do not touch those who are considered to be innocent. He did not use his power to corrupt or be corrupted, and he gave himself up to spare more lives. I wish he had let me help him. I want to help him now."

Brandon wasn't convinced. Magali seemed to be genuine, but he was done with taking anything on face value today. "I thought demons were supposed to be evil."

Magali laughed quietly. "We are. We have no concern for your lives; we do not care if you kill yourselves or wipe yourselves out with pestilence and famine. And indeed in that sense, anyone not considered to be an innocent is probably fair game for a demon. But that does not mean that we would hunt or torture you. Why would we need to? We have a morality of our own, and we stick to it. It might not make sense to humans all the time, but it is still there. And I, as do all demons, stick to my word. I am not trying to deceive you. I need you to help me get Matthew back, so this is in my interests to help you. Do you understand?"

He cast his eye back to El, who was still in green light listening mode. *What do you think, El? Can we trust him? As much as we can trust someone, anyway. An ally for now, until we get rid of this enemy, type of ally?*

El did the whirr of lights, then ran up and down. *That's what I thought too. Let's do this then.*

"Alright, Magali. First, I want you to tell me all about Matthew. And then I want you to tell me everything about what you know the bookshop does. And finally, I want to know how you think I can present this to the Smoke Witch Demon that's waiting to eat me."

Magali reached for his papers, spreading them out on the table. "This will take some time. Get comfortable, you two."

It had taken some time. Brandon felt positively wrung out from the talking, the information that he had been given. El looked tired too, their lights languid and faint. In a matter of hours, Magali would return for them to take them to the bookshop. By car, this time, he had said. He wasn't being summoned by magic anywhere! He chuckled. He would like to see anyone try to summon a demon like Magali.

The TV flickered in front of them as it played the first Terminator film. El seemed to be absorbed, but he was struggling to focus on it. Is this how it was for the characters in the films when they were facing overwhelming odds? Of course, they always prevailed, and if they didn't, they went out in a heroic blaze of glory. He didn't think he had that in him. El could, maybe. They had more spite than he had.

"Hey, El?" he called over quietly, not wanting to disturb the book. It had so quickly become his friend that he didn't know what he would do without them. But he had to ask. He waited for the book to flicker in response. "I've been thinking about what Magali said. About you being a wisp and being trapped by the bookshop. Do you want to, you know, be rescued? Do you want to stop being a book and go back to being a wisp?"

El thought about that for a moment, quietly letting the lights whirl around. The green light stayed on, though. Clearly they were becoming an Arnie fan.

I do not know what it is to be a wisp. I have no memories of before I was a book and woke up when you bought me.

Brandon thought about that. Why did they have no memory? What happened? He half hoped that El would want to stay a book, and stay with him, absorbing trash movies and people-watching. But he knew, really, that they had to be set free. Even if they left. Even if he didn't survive it. They had to go first. El and Matthew.

"But you were captured into the book. You might remember if you were freed. Perhaps someone can help you remember. Isn't it better to be you?"

> Am I not me now?

"Oh, come on, El. You know I'm not one of those philosophical types. I didn't even pick up a book to read of my own choice until I ended up in prison. You're you because you are. But don't you want to be free? Maybe you can turn yourself into a flying holographic book or something if you're a light spirit. I don't know. I just don't think you should be tied to the bookshop. That's all."

There was a long pause. El's lights did not even flicker.

> I think what you mean is, you are worried about who will look after me, my book, when you are gone.

Brandon winced. "You could have sugar-coated that a bit, you know. I mean, yes, I am facing almost certain death. Would it not be better if we got you free? Maybe you could hang out with Magali. You could critique his dress sense."

> That isn't funny.

Brandon laughed. "Well, I thought it was funny. I'm a dying man, you can laugh at my jokes!" El just put on the line of lights. He rolled his eyes. "Think about it, OK? I want to get you out. I want to add you into the negotiations. But I won't unless you say I can. This is something you choose. But I do think you should be free to be a wisp. Be... wispy."

The book did not change, but he felt the disapproval emanate out in waves. He laughed again. "Humour a dying man, El. Just think about it. OK?"

> The future has not been written. There is no fate but what we make for ourselves.

Brandon gawped for the second time that day. "Are you quoting The Terminator at me? Man. Now I have to survive so I can make

you watch some proper movies. You're going to be ruined. Big time."
He shook his head. "And hold fire on, I'll be back. We might need
that tomorrow." The book laughed back, just the lights in the dance,
before the green light switched back on. He smiled. He never expected to be watching a robot movie with a book that had a wisp
trapped inside, but now it was happening – it was exactly the right
thing to do. He thought of Magali and his pained face when talking
about his friend. He wondered what Matthew was experiencing,
trapped in the bookshop. He wondered if it would take long to
locate him.

*I'll find you, Matthew. I promise. I'll do what it takes. Just hang in
there. I'll be coming for you soon."*

Brandon rested his head back on the couch, eyes on the TV. He
didn't even need the subtitles for this one anymore. He knew what
they would say. Was he a hero like them? Or was he the Terminator?
Time would tell. It always did. Comforted, he closed his eyes.

DECIDING THE PRICE

The drive in Magali's car was an experience. He knew Magali was rich, from the way he dressed, his air, and that magnificent watch. But this was a NICE car. He ran his hand down the soft leather seats, admiring how it moved, silently, like a black cat in the night. It suited Magali, who drove like he handled everything else: a ton of focus, a dash of amusement.

Brandon looked around the inside of the car. "Hey, I thought mirrors were a no-go?" He pointed to the interior rear-view mirror and raised his eyebrows. "Is something going to come out of that?"

Magali shook his head, amused. He pressed some keys on the dashboard, and a screen came up. "Dictate," he ordered. A flashing icon came up, waiting. Brandon pursed his lips and nodded, impressed. That was some fancy gadgetry. "I live in the human world," Magali said, and paused. The words deftly appeared on the screen, running across in clear green print. Magali looked at it and then nodded his approval.

I have to follow the laws of the land! But with these," he passed his hand through the mirror with ease, "These are an illusion. I do not need to see with them, and nobody knows better. It works for me."

"How do you adapt to the changes, Magali? If you've been here for thousands of years. Do you get tired of it? How do people not notice that you're not ageing? How do you get to grips with new technology?"

"If you are alive for a lifetime and it doesn't matter really, how long that lifetime is, but if you live for a lifetime, you have to adjust. If you do not, you are left behind and eventually, you die. Each leap forward carries its own technology, its own ideals, and even its own language. After a while, you grow to love it. As to your other question – people see what they want to see. Some see me ageing at the same rate as they. Their brain cannot grasp an alternative. So it makes up a fiction to explain it."

That made a lot of sense. Brandon could see that himself, as the internet took hold, and everyone moved to emails, texts, and written speech over calling. Suddenly he was, in that sense, in the normal range. Nobody wanted to talk on phones anymore. People preferred to see the words. They stepped into his world. And he didn't mind in the least.

Magali looked over at him, just briefly, but the expression was loaded with meaning. He wanted to ask a question. Something difficult. Brandon braced himself for it. And sure enough, Magali tightened his hands just slightly on the wheel, then let them relax, stretching out, before he asked, nonchalantly, "Have you decided how many stories you will offer?"

He knew what he meant. Had he composed a story for Matthew? "I have. I know how many stories I'm going to offer."

Magali looked over again and frowned ever so slightly, but he did not respond. Perhaps he wasn't worried about it. Did demons have special ways to recover debts? Or did they have to rely on the usual agencies like everyone else? The image of some debt collector call centre handling a demon debt tickled him and Brandon had to stifle a giggle. Not even a manly chuckle, but a full-on giggle. He wiped a tear from his eye. He was probably crumbling from his brain downwards. This was just more than his mind could take and he would disintegrate into a giggling mess of shit jokes and tears. It wouldn't be the worst end, really.

Magali was still looking at him with mild concern. Brandon pulled himself together and patted the very quiet El. "So, how alone will I be in there? I mean, I know you can oversee if the bookshop accepts the offer or not. If it does, what then? Are you allowed in?"

The demon focused on the road, more than he had to, considering the traffic was light. Eventually, Magali replied. "I doubt that I can. I would be seen as interfering, and my boss, so to speak, would not look kindly on that. I suspect that El will have to stay outside as well. I will take care of them, though, with their permission."

Brandon brought El up to his lap. "What do you say, El?"

El set off the lights, up and down. Clearly, they were not in the mood for talking. Magali saw and nodded, his eyes on the road. "So be it, then." As the words fluttered past on the screen, the car fell into silence. There was nothing else to say. Brandon focused on the road and the trees straddling the road, rushing by in the dark. He used to watch these forests, or forests like these, probably as a kid, imagining that there were a ghostly group of horsemen riding alongside, watching him. Now, he just wished that they would find peace somewhere and leave humans like him alone. He sighed. Magali reached his hand out, brushing Brandon's hand gently and moving away before it looked like something more lingering.

"It won't be long," Magali said. "You might want to run through your stories, just in case."

He nodded in agreement and put his head back, closing his eyes. But he did not need to rehearse his stories. If he got a shot with the bookshop, these stories were ones that he had lived, seen, and experienced with his soul. He would never forget them. If the bookshop wanted emotion? It was going to get it.

They pulled up quietly. Magali put the handbrake on slowly and took out the keys. He looked out of the windscreen for a long moment before he finally turned. "Are you ready, Brandon?"

Brandon wondered if he should make a quip about being born ready, but it really didn't feel like the time. Magali was on a knife's edge, his eyes worried, his hands tense. Even El wasn't doing their usual rave dance of the lights. He could joke all he wanted, but deep down, he knew that they were concerned for him. He, who had never had anyone worry before. How did he end up with this, where a sentient book, or a wisp, he amended, and a demon were here with him, fighting for his welfare?

"I'm ready," Brandon said quietly to the night. "I'll get Matthew back for you. I promise."

Magali reached a hand out, squeezing his shoulder. He didn't look at him. "I think you should get Matthew out second, Brandon."

Brandon looked up, startled, meeting Magali's eyes in the rear-view mirror. He had not mentioned his plans out loud. But Magali nodded, just once. *Give El a chance at freedom first, Brandon. Matthew chose his fate. El did not choose theirs.*

He heard, or felt, the words within his brain. It did not feel similar to when his hearing aids were in, and sounds were bombarded at his skull. It felt more like his inner voice, but not one that he knew. He knew it was Magali. He nodded, eyes meeting Magali's. *I promise,* he thought. I promise.

Magali opened the door, letting the cold night air invade, and the spell was broken. Brandon breathed in deeply. All of his life, all of his experience, and all of his dreams. For whatever reason, it was for this moment. Now. And for the first time, he was fighting for people other than himself. For the first time, the stakes were high. But by fuck he was going to win.

Into the bookshop they went, a man, a wisp, and a demon. And for some reason, Brandon felt that this was exactly the team he wanted to get this job done. He wouldn't change a thing. The bookshop felt different. It felt colder, older. He saw no cats, either. They could have been watching from somewhere, he supposed, but he did not feel their presence. Magali walked behind him, El tucked safely in his arm. Why was it when he had to fight for the world, fight for lives, that he ended up with lives he cared for? He shook his head, clearing his mind. He needed to focus.

He stepped up to Meredith, who was standing in the middle of the bookshop as if she was about to referee a fight. Perhaps she was, really. It didn't matter the what the method was, or the delivery. It was still a battle of wits, a dance of souls.

"Hello, Meredith," he said. Nice and simple.

She smiled back unexpectedly. "Hello, Brandon. I wish you luck today." Her words resonated on, vibrating, even after she had finished speaking. She wished it to be so. He saw the hope that stretched out as if it were a page, a part of the future. He hoped that El had spotted that, who was probably deep in the expression of pissed right now.

She stepped aside, giving him centre stage. He looked up to the Bookshop, the entity that was in effect trapped in the bookshop, and he looked at it. Man to creature, man to memory.

"Hello," he said. He took a deep breath. He could see the smoke more clearly now, but more, he could see the smoke, the pain, the grief. Each rose as clouds, distinct, rising as if they were cases that needed to be heard, grievances. The Bookshop was wounded. And caging it did not help.

He saw the smoke swirl in such a similar fashion to El, and he had to smile, his tears rising as the emotion took hold. "You remind me of El," he said. He shot the words out like arrows, watching them strike home. "I have a proposal for you, Book-shop. I bid that you listen."

The smoke detached itself from the ceiling, slowly sinking until it arrived at the floor, stretching out into a wide dark mass.

"I wish to negotiate my terms. Will you hear them?"

Yes, Brandon, yes. It spoke into his mind, letting the words flow so he could read them easily.

"I took a book from you and gained knowledge that I need to pay for. Is that correct?"

Yes.....

So, this was going to be an interesting conversation. Brandon resisted the urge to roll his eyes. Being a smartass was not on the list of things to do today. He focused, letting his sight expand to see the colours and shifts in the pattern. Within the smoke, there was an oil slick smudge of black with a hint of petrol green, just as if it shone in the dusk. He suspected that was the key part of the entity, and the swirl outside was separate, the projection of the emotion, or something.

Whatever it was, he needed to get it to speak more than one word. But first, the proposal.

"I want to pay you with my experiences, with my story. A story of someone's life, especially one that has not been given to anyone else, has value beyond measure. You crave knowledge. You crave emotion. I think I can satisfy that need."

Nobody moved. Brandon wondered if the others were even breathing, they were standing so still. It occurred to him that he was literally the only human being in the room, and that was quite a freaky notion. The smoke shifted, one or two tendrils moving closer towards him. He shifted nervously. Was it going to just grab him and swallow him up?

What knowledge do you have that you think I need?

Oh, well, at least it was using other words now. That was a relief. And it was countering. That had to be a good sign, right? He looked over at Magali, but he showed no sign of having heard the bookshop. This was an unusual reversal of things. He, the one surrounded by silence, was the only one who 'heard' the bookshop. But that also meant nobody could tell him if he was on the right track. He had only himself to rely on. But he had two skills. He was a con man, and he had El.

He took a breath and shifted himself into his old persona, the one he had locked up and put away. It felt like stepping back into an old pair of shoes; it felt good. He had been too disconnected of late. This was who he was. Could he be a conman and still be good? El certainly thought so. They said that the skills are the same, it's just how you choose to use them. Now, he was using it to save three lives. Or to try, anyway.

"You need it because you have never been me. You are multiple, am I correct?" He felt a shift, a shard of light in his inner consciousness. Yes, he was correct. "And maybe you do not understand what it is to be singular, to be alone. Have you ever asked anyone what that is like? I do not hear. My inner world is different to yours. And lastly, I know that we are alike. And I will share that with you, if you agree to take my story as payment."

Magali had reminded him to keep coming back to that: I will do this; this is my payment. Don't let it weasel out and take more. As if he was going to do that. Not before he got the other two out, anyway. After that, he would do whatever it takes to survive. Now he faced death in the face, he knew he wanted to live. It was his number one priority.

The entity was thinking. Brandon wondered idly what it was thinking, what it called itself. He needed a name, really. It was a hook, a way to show someone that they were heard. He needed the bookshop to be in on the conversation, the deal, invested. It couldn't be that if he didn't have a name.

Yes. You may give me your story as payment.

Brandon blinked. That was easy. Although they still needed to thrash out what exactly a story meant. He didn't want the bookshop playing guitar with his entrails in accompaniment as he screamed out his life history. And he really didn't want that image in his mind because it was both horrifying and hilarious. Would it say, give me an A, and then, *twang?* Pull yourself together, for fucks sake, Brandon. You idiot.

"Very good. I will tell you a story, and then you will let me go free. Correct?"

No. You will tell me a story that I need to hear, and then I will let you go free.

"Will you hurt me to get that story?"

There was a pause. The shadow deepened, taking on a deep purple hue. It was quite pretty. *If you do not give me the right story, yes. I will.*

Brandon gulped. That was not unexpected, but still unwelcome.

"Agreed. But I want to offer two additional stories."

The atmosphere shifted around him, and quickly. Meredith certainly heard him, and she was watching him intently. Did she know of whom he was buying out? Magali merely nodded. But El, El was lighting up like a police car on its way to get doughnuts, or whatever the American cops did on those shows. He ignored them. It didn't matter if El wanted to stay as a book or become a wisp. What mattered was that now, they would have the choice. He had to give them that. And he would.

What do you want in exchange for these two stories? And what will be in these stories?

Old Booky was interested. He had them on the hook. Now, he just needed to haul them out.

"I will tell you two additional stories. The first will be about friendship. And I want you to release the wisp in the book." He winced inwardly at not naming El, but he did not want the bookshop to have El's name. He suspected it would give them more power if they knew that.

The smoke moved, rolling across the floor towards El, who stared implacably back with the look of indifference. Brandon found his mouth twitching despite the gravity of his situation. That book had more balls than he did.

You want to free this book?

Its tone was as clear as day. They had not expected it. Good. Keep them off-kilter, keep them guessing. He shrugged. "Sure. Why not?"

The entity paused. Brandon held his breath. His heart was pounding, but hopefully not loud enough that the bookshop knew or didn't notice the difference. It was probably pounding before, anyway.

And the other?

"I want to retrieve Magali's friend, Matthew, who gave himself up to you."

That one is mine. I will not give him up.

He narrowed his eyes. Now they were negotiating!

"And what does he do for you? Is he keeping you happy? Is he entertaining?"

The smoke moved closer, changing into a shape that almost looked human. When Brandon looked closely, he could almost see a galaxy of stars where the brain should be. He wondered how many people it had in there. He wondered if he could yell for Matthew and see if he responded. But he kept his expression slightly bored, implacable. He had an excellent game face, and he knew how to use it. The smoke looked deep into his eyes.

"He's a Guardian, right? Yeah, I know about those. Now, it seems to me, that this Matthew that you snagged is a dud. No offence to him, I'm sure he's a lovely fella, but he's got no blood lust. He's not going to sell anyone out to the bookshop. If your Guardians start voting on your next dessert, he's going to be the nay to your other ayes. I think you should just cut him loose, frankly. Tell him he failed his probation period or something. You've got plenty of others in there, haven't you?"

He knew he was just throwing shit at the wall and seeing what stuck. But this was how he played his best cons, just winging it within a vague plan. So he eyeballed Old Smoke Face and waited it out.

What would the second story be about?

Brandon resisted the urge to shout out in celebration. He was almost there. But he just yawned inwardly, knowing it kept his face looking bored. "I'll tell you a story about how we do anything to survive, unless it makes us something that is not what we are. Just like your Matthew. He gave himself up because he could not become a survivor."

Smoke-Face, Old Booky, breathed into his face, so close it could almost touch him. The breath was cold.

And when you have told me all these stories, what do you have left to tell me to get yourself out, Brandon?

Now he had him. Her? It? What even was it? A they? A conglomerate of hate, of death? He eyed the smoke face, looked for the eyes, and smiled. "I'm saving the best for last, Bookshop. I'll give you pain, and grief, and how it makes you human."

The smoke cloud figure retreated, eyes not leaving Brandon's face. He did not move, watching the smoke, staying exactly where he was, not antagonising the creature. His next steps were to build rapport with it, but he couldn't do that till they were alone in its lair. He waited.

Meredith stirred first, taking a breath, and then Magali. Meredith flicked a glance at him and then spoke quietly. "The bookshop accepts your terms. Magali, do you think the terms are fair? Should Brandon accept them?"

Magali stared at Brandon, his eyes serious. "He doesn't have a choice, Meredith. He will just have to hope that they remain fair, because he's on his own."

He walked forward and touched Brandon gently on the arm. "I think that you will get a break after each story. I will not leave this space, where we are, until you return. I promise that." His promise settled between them, edged in gold. Brandon knew that he meant it, that a promise from a demon was rare, hard-given. He also knew that Magali was telling the truth. He smiled, wishing he could say out loud how much he appreciated that the demon would stay. But he swallowed the lump in his throat and just nodded. "Take care of El."

Magali nodded and stepped back. Brandon looked over to El, who was resolutely blank, with no lights flashing at all. "I know you're mad at me. I want to give you a chance to choose what you want to be, El, and I will not be sorry for that. Take it or leave it. And don't watch any more Terminator without me, not till I get back out. If you do, I'll know, and I'll spoiler you." He took a deep breath.

"I guess now's the time to say, I'll be back."

Yeah, that was nicely done. He squared his shoulders and walked resolutely towards Old Smokey McBookface. Something told him that it would do the rest. It did.

A TALE
OF FRIENDSHIP
AND FIRE

As Brandon got near, it shifted, arms coming up, and it caught him in its embrace. They swirled together, or the bookshop itself started to swirl, and the figures that stood there were indistinct. He could see others, other figures, as they left, some shouting, some screaming, some entirely still like statues. The Guardians, maybe? He wasn't going to end up being one of those. That was for sure.

They slowed, at last, and then finally stopped. Brandon staggered and lurched, trying not to vomit. His eyes couldn't catch up with himself as his head spun, so he shut his eyes and got to his knees. The ground beneath him was smooth, but warm.

When his brain slowed, he opened one eye, gingerly, then two. The room was pitch black and seemed to stretch on forever. There was no sign of the bookshop. Or the entity, Brandon supposed, as they were out of the bookshop. Or in? He didn't know. In or out, he was here, and they were there, and he had to get down to business.

"Well, what about that story then?"

His words echoed, rolling around the space. He could feel the vibrations in his skull, making his head pound. He was glad he was still on his knees. He couldn't fall down from the floor.

A light appeared on the floor, moving closer. It was a lot like a spotlight, a shard of light in the dark, but it seemed to have no source. He watched it come nearer and wondered what on earth to do next.

The light stopped a few metres away from him, making the darkness around feel even deeper. And the bookshop entity spoke into his mind.

I want your stories, Brandon.

This time the voice felt different, more dangerous, and some-how, more female. He wondered if it were reconnecting with the memories that Magali said it was born from. If it were reconnecting with its human side it might not be a bad thing, unless it reconnected with all the anger, he supposed. But feelings were feelings. And empathy brings out feelings. He'd deal with whatever he got.

"Yes, yes, I know. That's why I'm here. Don't you want to do this more comfortably, though? Around a campfire or over a nice beer?"

The silence was heavy, malevolent. That wasn't the best move then. Less negotiating, more telling.

"My first story is about friendship. I've not been all that familiar with it myself, not until recently, but I've seen films and seen people who had friends that would go to hell and back for them. I know that the songs all say that a soulmate is the thing, but I think a friend is a true soulmate.

I've been alone my whole life. I always convinced myself that I didn't need a friend, that I didn't need someone to have my back, but I did. I knew it. I tasted the jealousy so often when it rose in my mouth. When I heard about friendships.

My father told me once about a friendship he had, years ago, when he was growing up. He grew up in a city that was at war, where neighbours tried to kill each other because their version of God was slightly different. It was that bad there that you couldn't even go into certain pubs or shops if you were the wrong side."

Brandon paused and coughed. "This is going to be thirsty work. Can I get a beer? Is the bar open?"

Tell your story.

He rolled his eyes. "Slave-driver. So, my dad, he decided at 17, in his infinite wisdom, that he wanted to join the Army and be a soldier. The Army was moving into the city to protect the people, and he wanted to be part of that. But the other side, they saw that as treachery. They decided they were going to kill him. Now my dad didn't know that, but his friend, who was on the other side, and was training to be a priest, heard about it. He warned my father, who left the city, and the friend died in his place. My father carried the weight of that all his life. It ate him up with guilt. But his friend believed in him. He had to believe, too."

Would you have done that, Brandon?

Brandon paused, thinking. "I don't know. I really don't know. I think to believe in someone that much, you have to believe in yourself, or in God, maybe. You need to believe that your sacrifice will mean something. I don't think mine would."

And yet you are here.

He laughed. "Yes, I am. I am here because I owe you for the knowledge that I took, but I have made friends along the way. I walked into the bookshop that first time, alone, even though I was meeting a friend. He is a person who isn't as close as he should be because I have never opened up to him. I've never let him in. I've always been too scared to let him in. To let him see what I am on the inside. But he stayed friends with me anyway. I just kept him around as it was nice to have him around. I've always been alone. But learning about empathy, and seeing how people look on the inside,

I've changed. I know that who I am, is worthy of friendship. I'm going to be grateful for those connections."

And what if he hurts you? What if he doesn't like what you are underneath?

"It doesn't matter. Because he hasn't ever been given the chance to know me. I've been hiding myself from him, keeping him separate. If he doesn't like the real me, that's fair. I'll still be grateful. Because connection is important. It helps us understand and helps us to grow.

I was in prison, once, you know, Bookshop. I spent four years of my life in a cell, and while I was there, I started to read books. I hadn't read before that, not really. I wasn't interested. But then I went to the library a couple of times, and I started to read books. I didn't read much. Do you know that there's an urban myth in prison? That if you don't finish a book before you leave, you'll be back at that prison to finish the damn book. I don't know if it's true, but I know the men got those books finished before they left, just to be sure!"

Brandon laughed at the memory. The light had moved closer and become smaller, gentler. It was like it was sitting next to him.

"Those books became connections for me. They were friends who told me their stories and didn't expect anything back. And then I started hearing stories being told in the prison, when men came in, when men left, when they got news, and I listened to those, too. And I didn't share back, but I witnessed those stories, and I listened to them. And sometimes that's enough. Because that's their story, and they need to share it. It's a two-way thing.

I get it, now. Here I am, sharing with you. Making connections. Life is a story. Sometimes you need to be the teller, sometimes you need to be the listener. And that's what friendship is, too. It's knowing that they're there, that they're listening. Because they know you, and they know you're worth the cost."

And you do this for the wisp? Are you friends?

"I do this for the wisp. Because they have been trapped in a book and they do not know where they come from. I know what it is like to be trapped. I know what it is like to not know who I am. And I think they deserve freedom."

The light had shrunk further, resembling a shape, a figure. It was motionless, looking away from him. Brandon smiled.

"Hello, Bookshop."

Do you know how I came to be?

Brandon sighed. "Magali told me that you came to be after a period of great horror, when many women were hunted and killed because they were deemed to be witches. He said that you were born of smoke and grief and pain."

The floor beneath him warmed, and he could smell woodsmoke in his nostrils. The light had changed, adding tendrils of grey smoke that looked like veins.

Our story is a dark one. It does not have a happy ending.

He waited in silence, wondering if it would continue. It did not. "Yes, your story is dark. It holds much pain. You were a community, once, and perhaps still are. Did you not find friendships and shared understanding? Did you teach each other of knowledge and lore?"

Once, yes, we did. But it only brought us sorrow. Our wisdom was what brought the hunters. We were grown too strong. They feared us. But in killing us, they made us what we are now. Hate. Death. Rage.

The ground was getting hotter, with cracks beginning to appear, running across the surface like flames. He touched the ground carefully, feeling soot on his fingertips. The ground was burning. The flames of the trials.

"And now, you listen to stories and do not show your pain. You hunger for them. Perhaps you need friendship still. Perhaps it is not too late for any of us. We just need to reach out and tell our stories. To trust."

The figure was covered in soot now, a shape of ash and rage. It turned its head towards him, eyes that were pools of night, pinning his gaze. He could not move. Fire blazed into light around them, trapping them in a circle, a fire that roared red hot, hungry. Shapes appeared in it, women burning, screaming, dying. He saw faces with hot grins, greedy eyes, and blood lust, as they watched the women die. He saw the smoke rise from a rose-tipped sky, curling into shapes of grief.

Tears ran down his face. He let them. He listened. The smoke shifted, and the fires died down. At last, the ground cooled, and the figure stood, walking away.

Brandon came to on the wooden floorboards of the bookshop. He was face down, and he was chilled to the bone. It was night. He pushed himself up, carefully, feeling aches in his bones. He tried to lick his lips, but his tongue was dry.

Faces danced in front of him, their mouths moving, but he could not work out what was being said. He waved them away, feeling crowded. Just give me a minute, he wanted to say. Someone put a bottle into his hand, and he accepted it gratefully. The water was cold on his tongue, and he drank deeply. It wasn't beer, but it would do.

The faces came back into focus, and this time, he recognised them. Magali was nearest to him, his face concerned, and Meredith was there too.

"Where's El?" he forced out, his throat feeling raw. He felt like he had been running through a burning building or something. The faces in the fire loomed up in front of his eyes, and he bit back a sob. If it had sent him back, it had to have accepted the story. Otherwise, it would be burning him up or something. Wait, it already did that.

Magali leaned closer, eyes searching his face. "El is here. Meredith has told us that the Bookshop has accepted your first story. She thinks you did well. Are you alright? Are you hurt?"

"No, I don't think so. I'm going to need therapy after this but I'll deal with that afterwards. Where is El?"

Magali turned and pointed. The book lay on the table, pages open, but there were no lights, no sign of life. Brandon frowned. "I don't understand. What's happened?"

"Well, El was freed. There was a weird earthquake and a lot of smoke, and then El was just ejected from the book, I suppose. They flew out so hard, I thought that the book was going to suck something else back in. There was energy unlike anything I have ever seen before. And then the book became just a book."

"And El? Are they alright?"

Magali smiled. "See for yourself."

Brandon turned, looking around the room. The book was lying there, absolutely looking like just a book. And then he saw the light, a green-blue spiral of light that kept winking in and out in a pattern that was absolutely and unmistakably El. He sagged with relief. "You're alright!"

El danced again, lights blazing.

Meredith stepped forward then, her eyes serious. "Well done, Brandon. Take a moment and gather yourself. The bookshop will be claiming their next story very soon."

He took another swig of the water. "Next time, bring me something stronger. Please."

The faces moved, scattered, and danced, as the bookshop sucked him back in again.

A Tale of Survival and Sacrifice

He was back in the place. It was empty, but this time there was one huge stained glass window that stretched from the floor upwards and a single red armchair. The window seemed to keep going forever. His brain started to hurt as he thought about that so he let it go. He walked over to the armchair, hoping it wasn't going to eat him or something if he sat down. It looked like an armchair, certainly. He pressed it carefully, checking for hidden teeth or claws. It felt exactly like a nice chair that you saw in a bar.

"Alright, I'm sitting down. Thanks for the chair!"

The window cast strange light that seemed to change colour and move in ways that should be impossible. But then, as the window was a window to nowhere, he supposed the light and shadow could do whatever it wanted. It was nicer than the dark and the flame. He would take it.

Tell your story, Brandon.

Well they were right back to that, then. At least it wasn't scaring him to death, he supposed.

"Alright, Bookshop. Survival. When I was in prison, I read a few books, as I told you. I started with memoirs because I did not want to read a story that was not real. I did not trust in my own mind, in my own imagination. Eventually, the librarian convinced me to try some fiction, but I think I always preferred something real. When it comes to movies, I can go to other worlds, but my own mind is too small to conjure it. I am not a creator.

But I read a story when I was there, which I often think about. It was about a man who lived through a war, and horrors that I cannot even understand. He was in a world where people were hunted and caged because of their religion, because a madman wanted to wipe them out. And this man got caught up in it and was caged for a long time in a prison camp in France. His story was brutal. He withered in there, because they took everything from him, even his hope. He could do no more than get up, work, walk around, and sleep. He was an animal, little more than an animal, who had no more space in his mind to dare to escape it. He could not set himself free.

But then something changed. Two events changed him, really. The first was when he saw a fellow prisoner start to inform on others, and ingratiate themselves with the guards for more rations, or less work. They indulged him, I suppose, and let him be a mini guard, a man without power. He was hated, of course, but he was feared.

And the man loved his work, spying on people, getting people killed, and enjoying his extra rations. He was still a prisoner, of course. He sold his soul for extra bread. And slowly, he rotted from the inside, becoming as hated, even more hated, than the men who caged them all. The author loathed him. But the author was also afraid that one day, he would become like him, and fawn over his captors for a little approval, an extra piece of bread. And when the hunger hit hard, or he was alone in the night, wondering why he was still alive, he would think about it. Should he do that?

But he never could. For him, that way of survival was not survival at all. It was changing into something that he was not. He had to find another way.

He met a visionary, a man who spoke of the resistance, of plans and escapes and ways out, of brave heroes who were nameless, living in plain sight, saving their fellow humans. This man said that sometimes, even surviving, just the act of not letting your spirit be cowed, was a form of resistance. That if people want to destroy you, continuing to breathe is in itself an act of resistance.

And this man listened and understood, and at last began to put himself back together. He escaped the prison camp somehow and joined the Resistance. He survived the war and became famous in his own right, as a great teacher and speaker for freedom. But it was that, that stuck with me. Sometimes, just breathing is resistance.

When I was in prison, I saw many men like that. I saw some who fawned, diving into this new world of tooth and claw, trying to find their own place, giving up who they were in order to survive. They ended up selling their souls to bad men, both prisoners and guards, and they became dead inside. I saw men who resisted, quietly, loudly, and everything in between. I saw men who refused so hard that they died for it. And it made me realise. We all fight to survive. We all do. I want to live. The more I stare death in the face, the more I want to live.

I want to breathe, Bookshop. I want to touch grass and feel the wind on my face. I want to pick up a book, and watch TV. I want to talk to people and see the light in their eyes. But I won't sell my soul to get that. Just like Matthew did not. Magali told me that he gave himself up to you as he refused to be responsible for other people's lives. I get that. I also get that you're hungry, that you need to eat. I understand that. But I know why he wouldn't bring you the sacrifices, your food. He wanted to survive, until he was faced with a choice that he could not make."

Brandon paused, wondering where the Bookshop was this time. He suspected it was the window, as it seemed to be breathing, the lights moving gently across the floor.

"You had to survive, Bookshop. You survive now, the only way you know how. But what if there's another way? What if there's a better way than keeping yourself caged, letting yourself die inside? What if you can sustain yourself on something else? What about trying a different emotion to feed from? Have you tried that?"

The colours swirled on the ground. He waited.

Would you give someone else up to survive, Brandon?

That was a tough question. Brandon thought, hard. "I don't know. I don't know if I would give someone else up to save myself, but I would probably give someone else up to save someone close to me, if they were that close. I couldn't live with it if I couldn't save them. Is that as bad?"

Good and bad does not exist. Or dark and light. It is intention and feeling. Some of us were betrayed. They gave us up to save themselves, and mourned as they lived and we died. People that we knew as neighbours, as friends. Their fear was such that they delivered us into pain and smoke. More people will sacrifice others to survive than sacrifice themselves.

He watched the lights darken and thicken into jagged shapes edged with slick black. Oily marks appeared on the ground, stretching out into lakes of jet-black sheen, gobbling up the lights. That was the rage, the strong emotion, that clung to the edges of the entity. He was peeling it back, layer by layer. He knew that he could reach it, help it see, if he just said the right words. But he did not know what to say.

"Perhaps none of us know how we will be until the time comes. We all wish we were heroes, but few of us are. They are the lights that we must look up to."

Us?

Brandon smiled. "Us. We are more alike than you know, Bookshop. We'll talk more about that in my third story."

With a flash, the window disappeared and the floor vanished into smoke. He found himself on the floor, again. It was cold, and a wintry light streamed in through the windows of the bookshop. He blinked, shut his eyes and opened them again. Scratch that. The light wasn't streaming in through the windows. Half the bookshop was gone, as if someone had cut it in two. The wall just wasn't there, so the bookshelves stood next to the outside, and the alleyway that ran to the right of the shop. He pushed himself to his feet, swaying. He was exhausted. He could murder a pizza. At least he wasn't scorched and parched this time. The bookshop let him off lightly. He turned, looking around. Magali was dozing in a chair, his face lined with exhaustion. Brandon smiled. He had stayed. He stepped over and touched his arm gently. Magali stirred and sat up, rubbing his eyes.

"Brandon! You look better than you did last time. Are you alright?"

"I've been better. But I'm alive. Let's just be glad of that. Where's Matthew? Has he come out yet? And El?"

Magali shook his head. "Not that I have seen. But you are back, therefore he must be freed. Surely. El has been back and forth. I think they're adjusting." His tone was edged with doubt and worry. He pressed his lips together in a thin line. "Perhaps we have to wait for them both."

He stood, offering Brandon the chair, but he waved him away. He needed to stand for a moment and prepare for the final story. He suspected that would be the hardest one.

A cat walked carefully from the shadows, tail high, with a slight curl to the end. It did not look at either of them as it walked past, giving them a wide berth. Magali held his breath. Brandon watched, feeling his heart almost in his mouth. He did not dare to interfere. Slowly the cat reached the edge of the bookshop, and put its paw into the snow. It stepped once, and then again, and then again, leaving the bookshop entirely. He watched in awe as the cat shivered and stretched, then walked away, obscured for a moment by a bookcase.

He leaned forward, trying to catch sight of it on the other side. But no cat emerged. Instead, a dark-haired middle-aged man stepped past the bookshelf and walked up the alley. He did not look back.

Brandon closed his mouth, which was hanging open. He turned to Magali who was still watching the alley with an expression that he could not interpret. "Was that-"

Magali nodded. "That was Matthew. You have freed him. I am in your debt."

"Well, he could have stopped to say goodbye. Or something!"

Magali shook his head briefly. "He probably is still enchanted. He will not remember this episode, perhaps, and merely wake up in his house. I do not think that the bookshop would let him take those secrets. The bookshop will keep the knowledge. The memories."

There was something deeply sad in those words. Brandon wondered what memories Magali meant. But that was his story, and he would not ask.

Magali stirred and smiled. "Oh, I nearly forgot. You ordered beer." He leaned down, lifting up a bottle and an opener. "Will this do?"

Brandon grinned and reached for it. "You could have gotten me alcoholic rice water and I would have thanked you, Magali. I need this!" He opened it deftly and lifted it in salute to Magali who smiled back, his eyes still sad.

He turned back to watch the snow falling gently, covering the tracks of the cat that became a man. Soon, he would face his last story. And this one was the hardest.

A TALE OF BEING HUMAN

He was back in the dark at last, but this time the transition felt easier, as if it had grown used to him, this space. Brandon landed, worrying about telling his story, worrying about El's adjustment, worrying about Matthew, worrying about the sadness in Magali's eyes. He worried about the bookshop, too. The more they talked, the more he could understand it, the rage, the grief.

Dark was not bad. Dark was dark. Just as humans were not bad, or good. They were just human. Brandon knew that. But it was still chilling to see the humanity in the worst kinds of people and to see the corruption in the best kinds. The world had no sense to it anymore. If it ever did.

He would need some props for this last one, he knew. This story was his last, and it would take every bit from him. Brandon shut his eyes, building his stage in his head. When the man had come to the prison to deliver his words, he had a chair, a microphone, and a stand for his papers a bit like the ones that the priests had in church. But Brandon didn't need the microphone or the stand. The bookshop could hear him just fine, and his words came from his head.

What did the man call his work? Slam. It was slam poetry, he called it. He was a local poet, one who did a lot of work in the prisons. The man had turned up in trousers and a jacket, a loosely buttoned shirt and glasses. He looked like any other academic, like any of the other teachers in that place. But he had smiled a genuine smile, and he hadn't flinched from shaking their hand. Some wouldn't touch them at all, sending a ring of invisible space up as if the prisoners were vampires, or infectious, or both. He didn't do that. The poet guy talked with them like they were people. It was nice.

And then he got on stage and started talking, bouncing, raging, crying, talking so hard that Brandon wondered if the man was entirely sane. Why would someone spill their secrets like that? It made no sense. But it worked on some of the men. Some listened with hard-set faces, some cried. Some nodded, some smiled. A fair few stayed behind to work on writing their own slam poetry. It was a good break from the routine, something different to do. A lot carried on writing, taking their notebooks everywhere with them. Brandon didn't stay, of course. But the memory stayed with him, curled up in his mind, waiting, dormant, for this moment. Perhaps it was meant that way.

This was how Brandon would do his story. He would slam that story right into the bookshop and make it see itself, its own humanity. It was his last shot. And it was all he had.

"I'm going to need a stage, a chair, and a light, Bookshop," he called out quietly. His bravado was spent, now. It was just him and the Bookshop. It was time for the truth.

The light appeared first, one, two, and then three lights, crossing each other, making three circles of light on a white wooden stage.

A chair appeared, one of those exactly like the poet used. Brandon looked down at his clothes critically. He hadn't bothered to dress up for the occasion, unless you counted black jeans and a t-shirt to be dressed up. But this was who he was. It would do.

His palms were sweaty. He walked towards the stage, calming his breathing, which came out in gusts of nerves. It was just a stage. Just a poem. Anyone could do it. It was just words.

He climbed the stage and stepped towards the chair, pausing for a moment. Through the lights he could see thousands of souls, clustered together, waiting for him to tell his story. The bookshop really was a we. There was a great deal of collective memory here; too much, perhaps.

He couldn't bring them all to one resolution, that was impossible. The panic rose up in waves and he rubbed his hands again on his jeans. He had to just do enough. Brandon nodded towards them all. "Thanks for coming," he said, rather unnecessarily. But this was his show. He would play it.

He looked out and took one deep, long breath.

"This story is called Human, That's Me."

He opened his mouth and paused. There were thousands of faces, indistinct, flowing within the mass. All looking at him.

"I am a man, yet I do not know who I am.
I am a son to a man who did not know who he was
Who had no roadmap, no way to silence his rage
As he brought blows down on my head
All for my own good he said
I am a brother to no one
I am the silence
Trapped in an empty bubble of quiet
When others move around in sound
I am other
The silence of shame
Knowing that I am not one of them
I am a brain, a nimble finger

I am a running shoe, always on one foot
I am two eyes, always open, alert
I am a victim, dragged into shame
By those who told me that I tempted them
That I was their way to redemption
My silence my price
For their sin
I am the child who found locked doors
And a mattress on the floor
Children with hard faces
Who roamed with me, fearless
From prison to street to home
Yet we had no home
I was the man who lied and never cried
Weaving words
Battles
The long con, the short con, the brave con
But never the last con
That was my rainbow, the gold, the fire that waited
That I never found
And then I was the con, locked away again
Listening and waiting and never living
To hang my hat up, and put that away
A half-life, existing in halfway houses and probation
Faces that did not trust or care
Hard faces
I was the man without a book
Without a song -"

Brandon faltered, the silence wrapping itself around him. He could not do this. It would be better for the bookshop to just take him. But the audience waited, closer this time, gathered around closer, their faces fixed on his. He felt wet spots on his face. Tears. When had he begun to cry?

"I am the anger and the rage
Because nobody saved me
I am the watcher in the night
The one who never sleeps
Watching the green light
Blink the time away
I am the one with clever words
To hide my frightened heart
The man with all the exits covered
The shoe on one foot
I am the man who wishes for
Impossible things
For that boy, for that man, for me
I am the one con, the long con
I am the demon wearing human skin
I am what they made me
Yet I am not just my words
I am the man who lives
I am the man who wants to hope
I am the man who wants to dare
To dream
I am a man. And sometimes that is enough."

It was all he had. Emptied, Brandon fell to his knees, wondering if this was how the other men had felt, when they came out quietly from their class, notebooks clutched tight, eyes peaceful. They had found something there. He wondered if that was what he found too. He looked up, his head heavy, and looked out at his audience. The faces were still there, floating in the dark. One by one they disappeared, bubbles popping in a sea of black, and he waited in the lights, head bowed.

It was all he had. Sometimes that was enough. He was the silence. He was the silence. He was alone.

At last, Brandon stood, wondering what was next. The bookshop had not sent him back, and he didn't see any change in the place.

What did he need to do next? Was it off to get something to counter his story with? The last two times it interacted after the story. Had he bored it to sleep this time?

Brandon stepped from the stage, and it disappeared quietly behind him. Two of the lights went out, but one followed him, keeping one ray of light, one circle, lighting the darkness. He walked for a few minutes, feeling the gentle rhythm of his feet hitting the ground. And then he stopped. "I gave you my story, Bookshop. Now you need to decide whether to let me go or not."

The light moved and then split in two as a fragment broke off, moving and shifting into a shape, an almost white shadow, a silhouette. It moved closer, looking at him.

You gave me the story. I will let you go.

Relief rose up, and tears fell from his eyes. His chin crumpled as his eyes burned. It would let him go. He had done it. Yet, it had not let him go. What more could it need?

You speak of being human, of caring for others, of saving others. You have a secret wish that I will be satisfied with these stories, that I will stop my destruction, that I will be sated by your words, and not kill.

You know what I am, Brandon.

Brandon felt the words sink into his skin, marking him. He knew what it was. Yes, he did. He felt the truth of it.

"You are me. You are all of us."

Yesssssssss... The word was drawn out, a slow flowing of acceptance. It was him. Each and every scream and tear and lost hope, each of those were him, and the Bookshop. He was a part of it as much as every soul trapped there. Every life shattered, every lost child. It was legion.

I will not stop consuming. I will not stop killing. And you are free to go, Brandon. I keep my word. But now you know that when you leave, I will continue. Because this is what I am. It is what you are. It is inevitable.

The tears ran hot down his face. "You can't put that on me, Bookshop. I did not make you what you are. You can choose to not hurt people. You can always choose. What is this, anyway? Are you going to keep me here now, as your pet? Are all your other ones not good enough?"

No. You paid your price. I will not keep you.

The figure slithered closer, form shifting, growing, until it looked like a woman made of smoke. The face was indistinct, moving, but Brandon could feel something looking out at him. He looked up at it, holding its gaze.

"If you are not going to keep me, and you say that you will still consume, what do you want from me?"

The figure smiled a horrible smile that made Brandon quail. It might come from him, from others, but it was not human. He should have remembered that.

I want your stories, Brandon. I want you to come back to this place, every year, and tell me stories of the people you have met, of their lives. If you do that, I will cease my consumption of innocent souls.

"That's it? I come back every year with another story? And you won't kill?"

The figure stared back at him. "Oh, you won't kill innocent souls. Right."

Well, that was a whole different ball-game. Could he live with that? Was it enough? Perhaps he could convince it to abstain entirely, after a few years. Coming back here, every year, for the rest of his life. How long could that be? He was only thirty now. Could he do that? The figure waited for his answer. Brandon sighed. What else could he say?

"I will come back every year to tell you a story, Bookshop, and you will not harm the innocents. I accept these terms."

Again the figure smiled, before slowly fading away.

Yessss.... the words caressed his ear and imprinted themselves on his skin before fading. The light faded too, gently, and Brandon opened his eyes. He was back in the bookshop. In his world. He was alive.

A FAUSTIAN DEAL

Five Years Later

He pushed his way into the busy bar, looking from left to right for the familiar face of his friend. It wasn't hard to spot him. Magali was at the table, jacket over the chair, rocking his flamboyant shirt. He got up and hugged Brandon warmly, his smile wide. "It's good to see you!" He drew back, inspecting him. "You look great, my friend. Bali suits you." Magali gestured for Brandon to sit and then signalled to the waiter. "The food is good, if you are happy to eat here? We can go somewhere else?"

"No, this looks fine. I'm hungry."

He flicked open the menu, raising his eyebrow at the prices, marked discreetly in the corner. Magali was such a snob. "What's wrong with Pizza Hut, Magali? Why do you have to waste your money here?"

Magali narrowed his eyes in mock outrage. "Don't bite the hand that feeds you, Brandon! Let me spoil you. I only see you once a year."

The waiter arrived with a tray, setting down water, glasses, a bottle of wine, and Brandon's beer at his elbow. Brandon waited till he was out of earshot before he spoke. "Has everything been quiet with the Bookshop?"

The demon nodded. "It has been remarkably well-behaved. I think your story last year was particularly good. What do you have on the playlist this year?"

He smiled. "I met a fascinating guru when I was visiting Cambodia, and I spoke with an old woman for many hours about the nature of grief and how it makes us write. I think I will use those. How's business?"

"Yours, or mine? I took the liberty of checking your stocks, and everything is in hand. You will have enough to travel wherever you need to next year. And I have hired you a new agent who is keen to discuss your poetry collection, if you are prepared to publish it."

Brandon was impressed. "You've been busy! Yes, send me the details. I'll look at it all. I'm not going to linger after the Bookshop, I have a flight tomorrow. But I will get back to you. I appreciate your help." He paused and took a drink from his beer, wondering if he should ask. Magali looked sad behind the smile. He always did.

"And how is Matthew?"

Magali blinked, just a moment, before he guarded his expression. "Matthew is doing very nicely. He has not regained his memory, of course, but has discovered a love of painting. I believe he has found some modest success with a small art enthusiast who is encouraging him to do an exhibition."

Brandon smiled to himself. "You're still meddling, Magali. I thought you weren't doing that anymore."

"I like to meddle sometimes. It's nice to know he is happy."

"Did he, find anyone, yet?" Brandon spoke carefully, remembering their previous chats. Magali had cared for Matthew deeply. Not that Matthew would ever know. Magali shook his head. "Sadly, no. And that's a meddle too far for me. But I am hopeful. I am going to see if I can get him to travel this next summer. I think it would be good for him."

Brandon laughed out loud, exuberantly. "How are you going to do that? Are you going to pretend that he's won a holiday or something?"

The demon actually blushed. He actually blushed! What an old woman. Brandon laughed again. "And how is El? I haven't seen them since they went off to find their relatives in the north somewhere. I'm hoping they check back in soon – but the weather in Bali doesn't suit them. They said they'd stop by to see you."

Magali smiled. "El visited. They made me watch the entire box-set of Pirates of the Caribbean."

That did it. Brandon roared with laughter, nearly spilling his beer. He did not know how this day could have become such a blessing, even with his obligation to keep. It was probably his favourite day of the year.

Ten years later

The floor was hard as he came to, gasping, wanting to retch, right there on the floor. Magali rushed over from his customary spot, and bent down, his eyes filled with compassion. "Are you alright, Brandon? Was it a difficult storytelling?"

He helped him up, offering him water and then a freshly wrapped sandwich. Brandon took the water and waved the sandwich away. He couldn't eat that. He would be sick for sure.

"Thank you, Magali. It was, there were new souls in there, dark ones, with so much pain. I wonder if it was the right decision, sometimes, letting the Bookshop consume only non-innocents. Not that I think it should consume anyone, but it gets darker by the year. More cruel, more brooding. It is harder to contain, harder to soothe. And I fear more now than I did. I have more to lose."

Magali listened, his eyes intent. "I would not let anyone hurt your spouse and children, Brandon. That is not allowed."

"No, I don't mean that. I mean that I am more afraid than I was. I am afraid of them dying, or of something happening to them, or me being a bad parent. There is always much at risk. I just want to get it right. And it is harder to find the stories, now. I can still travel, Val doesn't mind, but I have to take shorter trips, and find the stories, rather than let them happen. It's a difficult balance. I am a different man, now."

The bookshop creaked and rumbled, quietly. The smoke had faded and curled up gently into the edges. He looked around. "Well, it may have cost me in life expectancy but it is calm. I'll take it."

He stepped forward and shook Magali's hand. "Until next year, then?"

Magali nodded. "Until next year. I'll be here."

Brandon knew he would. He always had.

Twenty years later

Magali had booked his favourite restaurant again. Brandon smiled as he climbed out of the taxi, already weary. It would be good to see him, his dear friend. Magali opened the door of the restaurant, his face wreathed in smiles, and a familiar blue light popped up out of his shoulder, doing the party dance.

"Magali! El! What a surprise, I didn't know you were coming!"

El did the lights, up, down and all over, like they were directing aircraft into traffic or something. Brandon smiled again, feeling lighter for the first time in a long time. "It's good to see you, El! Where have you been?"

El projected a picture of something that looked like a desert. "Did you go looking for Han Solo, you thirsty wretch?" Magali crinkled his brow in confusion, El did the line of indifference and then a laugh, and Brandon grinned.

"It's good to see you both. It makes my heart glad." Magali agreed, showing them their table. The place was empty, which was unusual for it being nearly the weekend. He looked around quizzically and then back to Magali. "Oh, I bought the place out for the night. It seemed like last time, the hubbub was too much for you. I wanted you to enjoy yourself. Is that alright?"

Tears came too easily to Brandon's eyes now, but he did not blink them away. Tears were part of who he was, and he was at peace with that. "I love it. It's very alright."

Magali studied him closely. "You look... healthy. How are you?"

His tone was light but Brandon noticed Magali's hand at his elbow, making sure he did not stumble. He was as observant as ever. Gratefully, he subsided into his seat, as Magali took the spot opposite and El zipped around the wine glasses in a fig-ure-of-eight shape.

Brandon took a deep breath. It was time to just say it. "I'm dying, Magali."

The air stilled as Magali watched him, his eyes dark. "How long?"

"I won't be here next year to tell a story to the Bookshop, put it that way."

Magali blinked, just once, as he processed the information. "Does it know?"

"If you mean the Bookshop, no, I have not told it. It would probably have found a way to extend my life, to make me keep coming back. No, only you know, and, my family, of course. The important people."

"Do you want a way to extend your life?" Brandon went to laugh, then paused. Magali was being serious.

"Are you asking me if I want a deal for more years, Magali?" El had stilled, resting against the menu, listening.

Magali shrugged. "It is possible. And doctors find miracle cures for everything nowadays. It wouldn't be difficult to find you a specialist in the US or something that could offer experimental treatment. You could take a couple of weeks as a cover for your wife, or even stay in a hospital if she were likely to suspect, but she would be glad to have you for longer. It wouldn't be difficult."

He put his hands up, helplessly. "I can't afford that kind of deal, Magali. I'm sorry."

Magali's eyes narrowed, and for a moment Brandon could see the demon under his skin. "We haven't talked terms yet, Brandon."

Brandon smiled, sadly. "It doesn't matter. I don't want to sell my soul, now. Not even for a few more years. I've known for a long time that each visit ages me prematurely. I do not feel fifty. I feel sixty, or even sixty-five. I have experienced life and been happy, this last twenty years. I found friends. I discovered books, and travel, and my wife, and then we had the twins. I do not regret it. For me, taking a deal would mean I did not believe that I was human, that this was not enough. It's been more than enough. I've been given more than I could have hoped for.

So, I'm going to eat with you two, my excellent friends, and I am going to go to the bookshop one last time and tell it a tale of how dreams aren't actually as good as the real thing. And then, I am going to go home and say goodbye to my family. OK?"

Magali sat motionless, then nodded. "I understand."

Brandon turned to El. "Will you be alright out there, on your own? I worry."

El did the lines up and down dance, then flew closer, closer than they had ever flown, and touched his cheek. He felt the tears again. "I'll miss you too, El. But this is how it works."

Brandon took another deep breath. He had a difficult question to ask. "Do you know how long it will be before the Bookshop starts again?"

"You mean, when it starts to revert? I think not right away. There will be a slow awakening. But it will, eventually. That is its nature. It knows, it understands, and it grieves. It was never going to be permanent. But you saved some souls along the way. You saved El. You saved Matthew. Perhaps you even saved me. I think that's enough for one person."

The waiter arrived with water, eyes flicking back and forth to the blue light that now appeared to be doing a dance on the rim of the water glass. He deposited the drinks and excused himself, fear and doubt enveloping him like a cloud. Brandon smiled.

He knew better. They had saved him. Every single year, after every single story, they had saved him. He raised his beer bottle in salute to his friends.

"I want to make a toast."

They leaned in to listen, Magali with his glass at the ready. "Death smiles at us all," Brandon said, with a catch in his voice. His excellent, excellent friends. "All we can do is smile back."

Magali smiled through his tears. "You'll be a plagiarist to the last, Brandon. I know that quote. I heard Marcus say it the first time!" He thought for a moment, a mischievous glint in his eye. "He may have stolen it too."

Brandon did not hear the chink of glasses or the rich tone of his friend's laugh, but he felt them in his heart. And so too, did the bookshop, from not that far away, as it stirred from its slumber.

Yesss, it said.

AUTHOR'S NOTE

This book felt like a long time in the making. I knew all along that there would be four main protagonists, and that they would each experience the bookshop differently. I didn't know how different they would be. Having at last finished this story, I would like to let you know what they all did next.

Rachel, of course, didn't end up anywhere. She was lost in her own world, her mind swallowed by the bookshop.

Matthew moved to Italy and lived in a small cottage on the edge of a vineyard in Piedmont, painting. He never knew why he was drawn to that spot in particular, but he loved the wine, and he lived out his days with paint spots on his hands, fat and happy.

Lucy was a recluse in Colombia. She always kept her face covered, and the locals often referred to her as the Widow. She kept the book with her screaming face in very close, but never opened it again.

Brandon died with his family around him and was buried in the local graveyard. On his instructions, they wrote the following on his gravestone: I was the silence. Now I am the song. He was not forgotten by all that loved him.

El continued their travels. Whether they were in fact trying to find the film characters of favourite films is a mystery as El will not acknowledge or deny. But every year they kept up the tradition of meeting Magali and they regaled him with their stories of far flung countries and interesting people.

Magali left the art world – he still had a passion for it but decided he needed a change. He stepped into contract law with a few other demon partners and set up a bustling law practice somewhere in London.

Meredith is still with the bookshop, which did eventually awaken after Brandon's death. But that is another story that does not continue here.

E.M. Nov 2023

NEXT RELEASE:

A curse that is uttered will never die. Two women's lives are separated by time, but tangled together by chance and blood.
London, 1940.
Britain was at war.
Emily was thrust into a different and dangerous world, of munitions factories, rationing and fear. Her husband was far away at war and she was alone with their children. But evil walks the streets when it is dark.
London, present day.
Gemma's life was perfect. She had just moved into a new apartment and life was looking up at last. But the building harboured dangerous secrets and the Woman in White stalked, looking for revenge.

Release date: 21st April 2024.

About the
Author

Eryn was born and raised in Oxford, UK but nowadays lives in South Germany with their young family. They want to travel the world and visit all the mountains, lakes and of course, vineyards. When they are not dreaming of travel or writing poetry, they work as a freelance English teacher.

Eryn has written one other novel, which is a cosy dystopian dragon fantasy called The Sunset Sovereign, and is currently working on Book 2, which will be called The Sunrise Sovereign.

They have written a series of dark dystopian sci-fi novellas set in Woestynn, and a horror novella based in an asylum called 72 Hours.

They have plans to work on a cosy librarian sci-fi series called Space Dowagers, a series of steampunk/post apocalyptic fantasy fairy-tale retellings and of course, lots more horror.

Their current obsessions are EMDR music, new pens and jigsaws. But their first loves will always be the Gothic, dragons and cloud watching.

www.ingramcontent.com/pod-product-compliance
Lightning Source LLC
LaVergne TN
LVHW041454170726
843492LV00005B/1232